THE

PRIEST

A Confession of Crows

By

Jayne Stennett

A MURDER OF CROWS

One crow for malice

Two for mirth

Three for a funeral

Four for a birth

Five for a secret

Six for a thief

Seven for a tale never to tell

Eight for Heaven

Nine for Hell

Ten for the Devil

Wherever, he may dwell.

© Jayne Stennett

CONTENTS

ACKNOWLEDGEMENTS

To all of my dear family and friends who encourage me to continue on my journey as a writer, I hope that I have made you just a tiny bit proud of me.

To Edgar Allen Poe for his works and inspiration without which the dark and macabre aspects of my writing would still be in my head.

To Ireland and my ancestors – such a rich heritage, culture and mixture of religion, folklore and tales of the Sidhe, from which I have borrowed for my books. The pleasure I have had in bringing to life my characters outweighs the hours spent in the darkness of night and the light of day, spilling my thoughts onto the page for you to enjoy – I hope.

PROLOGUE

"There is no more beautiful a sight than a young woman who glows with the light of the spirit, who is confident and courageous because she is virtuous."

Elaine Dalton

Rural Ireland – 1969

Dora O'Riordan pinched her cheeks and bit her lips to add colour to their paleness. Her freckled face stared back at her from the mirror that sat atop the old wooden chest she had inherited from her grandma. The mirror sat precariously balanced amongst the bone-handled brush and comb set which her brother had carved for her last Christmas, a statue of our lady, her best Sunday gloves and her rosary. The latter she had received at her holy communion and now hung across one corner of the mirror.

She had one ear tuned to her father's snoring and one waiting for the slight rattle of the sharp little pebble thrown by her best friend Bridget which would soon hit the bedroom window. The summer of love had almost passed this sleepy Irish community by but the music telling of free love and sunshine in San Francisco had wooed the younger generation into leaving behind their inhibitions, morals and the virtues that were so deeply ingrained in Catholic society. She had decided to rebel tonight and things were going to change for her. Her excitement was palpable; she had never disobeyed her parents before. 'The Devil's tunes' were played at these crossroads dances according to her daddy. 'Teens have no moral fortitude nowadays' he'd say, but she was determined to go nonetheless. After all, nothing had happened to Bridget and she had even met a lad there. Dora was determined to have a better life than her parents.

1

She turned and looked across the room; her younger sisters, Mary and Siobhan, were asleep in the large double bed where they all slept together. Her two younger brothers, John and Francis, only four and two years old, were across the room in another large wooden bed, fast asleep, with yet another baby girl asleep in her parents' room next door. She looked at the youngest boy Francis's face, his little thumb resting on his lip as it had fallen from his mouth. She tenderly covered him with the only rough woollen blanket that they possessed just as she heard the familiar rattle of the stone on the glass.

It was a cold night and she was unable to get her outer garments and boots from downstairs or her parents would notice. So, dressed in a woollen shawl over the top of her best Sunday dress she slid the window up. The cold breeze blew into the room and caused her sister to stir and open her eyes just in time to see her sister Dora's leg pass over the window sill. Dora climbed out onto the branch of the tall oak that resided by the side of the house.

Many a time, its leafy branches had hidden her from her mother's or father's view as they had sought her out, calling her name to come and help with some chores. From her hiding place she could hear their curses as their calls went unanswered. Now, she slipped quickly down the tree agilely, from branch to branch, until her feet felt solid ground. She saw her friend waiting by the side of the barn and she tried to stifle a giggle as she ran into her arms. Excitedly, she looked up and whispered:

'Oh, Mary mother and Joseph Bridget! Me da will kill me if he finds out. Now are you sure it is tonight that they are meeting at the crossroads?'

'Yes, Billy said he would meet us both there and he is bringing a friend to meet you. Now come on, we have a long way to go before we get there and we don't want to be late. Billy said he is going to ask me da for me hand on Sunday at church. I don't hold out much hope as his elder brother gets the entire farm when his da has passed and he hasn't any prospects except to work on the farm for him. Plus, my da hates his da, he thinks they're a bad lot.'

'But you are too young to marry yet, Bridget! You're only fifteen!'

'Have ye never heard of long engagements?'

The two girls linked arms and giggled their way along the lane in the dark, holding on tightly to each other as they slipped and stumbled in the mud. Before too long they could hear music in the distance. This was the first time that Dora had been to a crossroads dance. Bridget being a little older had been going now for a year and had regularly sneaked out, often just to come and visit Dora on the neighbouring farm. She often brought with her tobacco and beer that she had sneaked from her father's stash and she would laugh and pat Dora on the back as she choked on the pungent smoke as they practised being sophisticated, holding the cigarette in between their fingers, drawing the smoke into their lungs, and ending in a cough. Dora had so far refused the drink as she could see the effects on her father when he came rolling home from the pub. She hated him then as she held the little ones tightly, singing to them to cover up the noise from their mammy's brutalisation. How many times had she listened to her plead with him to stop as the baby cried in the cot beside the bed. *'Please, Patrick the weans are frightened … please.'*

 Bridget was an only child, her mother having had such a terrible birth with her that they both had nearly died. An operation performed on her ma at the time meant that she could no longer bear any more children and was unable to perform her wifely duties. What Dora didn't know, which her friend had not told her, was that her father had now turned to her whenever he felt the need, instead of her mother … so far, she had been lucky to not get pregnant.

Dora thought how lucky Bridget was as she herself had to help her mammy all of the time with her younger siblings. She also knew that it wouldn't be long till more babies appeared when she heard her father's grunting and her mother's suppressed sighs coming through the wall on a regular basis. She had only ever heard her mother refuse her da once; it was only a couple of weeks since the arrival of her younger brother Francis and she was still recovering from a very difficult birth. She had heard the doctor tell her father to wait a few weeks before he enforced his conjugal rights on his wife. Any advice given was completely ignored; her da had gone to the market and spent the money that was meant for food in the pub. The next morning, the evidence was clear on her mammy's face that you never said no to a man.

For Dora, being hungry was a regular occurrence and she would often be sent to pick nettle tops for a stew to fill their hungry bellies, which it never did. The grinding poverty that they both experienced drew the two girls together, a shared life of hardship and the fact that being a woman meant that they were worth very little to the men in their lives. They both swore that they would have a better life and that they would marry someone who respected and loved them and that they would only have two children, a boy and a girl. One thing that they both knew was that life was hard and love was something that pop stars sang about.

The idealism of youth carried Dora through her daily tasks. She had noticed her father looking at her oddly lately. Did he suspect she was sneaking out? She knew that if he caught her, he would kill her and any boy that she may have been out with. She smoothed her pinny down over her dress and felt the small bud-like breasts that were forming there. She wanted them to grow as big as her friend Bridget's which strained at the thin material of her dress. Bridget was very proud of her breasts, strutting around the playground and pushing them at all of the boys precociously so that they blushed and the girls giggled at their reddened cheeks. But Bridget was a whole two years older than Dora who still had a lot of growing to do before womanhood settled lightly on her body.

She had started the curse two months ago and when her mother explained how her body could now produce children, Dora was horrified and declared that she was never having any anyway. Her mother just smiled as she taught her daughter how to roll the strips of rags and how to fit them into her undergarments and where to place the dirty ones in a bucket with a lid in the jacks – the outside shed that housed the toilet.

She shivered at the thought of her da finding out but by now the girls were nearing a large bonfire that had been built in the middle of the Kilkerny crossroads. Music was being played by a boy on a fiddle, loud and jaunty. It made Dora want to dance and tap her feet. The sound reverberated through her body in a delicious way. Her face glowed with excitement and she hastened along, pulling Bridget in her wake, their freedom intoxicating.

'Come on, I want to dance … I can feel the music in my feet.'

'No wait,' cautioned her friend. 'I don't see Billy and look there are no other girls here, only boys …Where can he be? He promised he would be here for the ceilidh.'

Dora was past listening to her friend and she ran nearer to the fire. She stood there and started to sway to the music. She closed her eyes and thought how exciting it was; she had never been to a dance and longed to feel the arms of a boy around her waist as he swept her around in a circle. Suddenly she felt her arm roughly grasped and someone spinning her round. She found herself held tightly in a pair of strong arms.

'Well, what do we have here, boys? A present from heaven itself! Howsabout a wee kiss now, girly?'

She found herself spun around and passed from one boy to another until she began to feel sick and dizzy; her friend's pleas fell on deaf ears and the raucous laughter and groping of her body continued.

'She only came for one thing, ain't that right?'

The boy started to kiss her on the mouth as she struggled to escape. Fighting for air and breath, she broke away but screamed as she was grabbed again by another pair of arms. She heard a whisper in her ear.

'It's OK, now come with me; I'm Billy's friend – come on now, what were ye thinking, going into the circle? Only girls who are little more than whores step into the circle and then they are free for anyone to take.'

'I didn't know,' she sobbed. 'I wanted to dance. It was the music.'

'Ye don't know a lot do ye? What in the name of our lady did Bridget think she was doing bringing a bairn to the crossroads?'

Dora shook his hand away from her arm and, wiping the tears on her sleeve, she pulled herself upright and glared at the boy, who now stood with a smile on his face, looking down at her. His blue eyes twinkled and his blond hair long at the front flopped over his face.

'I am not a bairn. I am nearly fourteen and I don't need yer help, thanks all the same.'

She brushed her clothing down and, pulling her shawl straight across her shoulders, she looked around desperately for her friend.

'I think Bridget has abandoned ye; she disappeared with Billy ages ago. I will walk ye home so that ye get home safe.'

Dora looked around in desperation – what was she to do? Where was Bridget and could she trust this boy? She looked up at him; her eyes roamed his body and he could see her fear and desperation in them.

'Please come with me. I promise that I will get ye home safe; if ye stay here much longer the others will come back and there are too many of them for me to fight,' he said wryly.

'Ye would fight for me?' Dora said coyly, looking at her hero with new eyes. He seemed rather cute and his eyes were so blue.

'Well, I couldn't see ye hurt now, could I? Ye are like me wee sister; she is your age too and I wouldn't want her out here with that pack of wolves.' He nodded his head towards the group. Looking at her shoes, Dora was disappointed that he thought she was like his little sister and that he couldn't see her womanhood developing; but she thanked him and they started for home. They spent the night talking and laughing until suddenly she found herself at the gate to her farm. Looking up, she asked, 'How did ye know where I lived?'

'Oh, I know much more than ye think, Dora O'Riordan.'

She gasped; she had been careful not to tell him too much detail about herself and she was intrigued when she looked up into the amused blue eyes. He kissed her cheek gently and, turning her towards home, he said 'Ye better get in before yer da finds yer gone.'

He walked away and suddenly she called out after him.

'Wait … I don't know your name?'

'It's Brendan … Brendan Doyle. I live on the farm further down the track.'

'Will I see ye again?' she asked.

'Oh ye can be sure of that,' he replied.

1971

Three years on and sixteen-year-old Dora O'Riordan sat at her dressing table, pinching her cheeks again to bring colour to their paleness. Adding a smear of lipstick, she moved her hand to rub her belly, the movement of the child inside of her causing her to wince.

'Oh, you stop that now! Yer daddy and I are getting married today so ye better be quiet while I say me vows, or Father Peter will take even longer getting through the ceremony and I will have ye in the aisle.'

She smiled to herself as if in response the child kicked her even harder.

'Too much like yer daddy, 'tis impatient, ye are; well, ye just have to wait till tomorrow at least.'

But baby Doyle came into the world at 11:59pm on the day of his parents' wedding. The labour had begun in earnest as Father Peter doddered his way through the wedding vows, as slowly as his rheumy eyes would allow. Dora wished that Father Benedict had been allowed to take the ceremony as she felt the pains increasing, but she managed to hold on for a few more hours. Whether it was the shock of Dora practically giving birth in the church aisle during the wedding or whether it was just his time, Father Peter departed the world an hour before the child decided to make an appearance. The congregation speculated for several Sundays leading up to the christening, murmuring that one soul came into the world as one soul departed, so surely the boy would be called Peter after the priest. And were not his parents lucky that he didn't arrive twenty-four hours sooner?

After all, nobody wants to be born a bastard.

CHAPTER 1

'A person's rightful due is to be treated as an object of love, not as an object for use.'

Pope John Paul II

The child felt the rain trickle down his back; it soaked into his hair and a shiver ran over his shoulders and settled on the ends of his arms. His woollen jumper cuffs were now soggy with a mixture of rain, tears and snot from where he had scrubbed at his nose, his face streaked with mud and tears. He pulled himself further under the bracken next to the faerie thorn and tried to tuck himself under the lowest branches until he hoped that he had become invisible to passers-by. He so often wished that he had the ability to become invisible like the little people and as he started to cover his legs in grass and leaves to form a makeshift blanket, he wished that the Sidhe would come and take him away as he slept. He laid his head on a mossy mound beneath him and found that he could no longer feel anything much.

The pain in his legs and back had become less agonising and his headache, although still pounding from the run, was beginning to abate. His heart began to settle from the hammering it was making in his chest, and the pain in his lungs as he drew in each breath was fast receding. He breathed in and out to the sound of the caw of the crows roosting up in the branches he had disturbed from their rest when he hid himself. They were just beginning to settle again and their cawing and murmurings were a salve to his ears, giving him something else to concentrate on other than his own heartbeat.

He felt cocooned as if he was in the nest, too, nestled in the soft downy black feathers that lined its moss- and mud-covered branches and twigs. He had climbed high up into the branches to see the nest earlier in the day and had counted five beautiful eggs of a greeny-blue hue, speckled brown towards the ends. The crows never minded his interest in them and he brought them treats of bread crusts and the odd piece of barmbrack cake still warm from his mammy's griddle. Their beaks had been gentle and tickled his hand and fingers as he held the food. He gently held one of the eggs in his hand and he could swear that he could feel the chick's heartbeat pulsing through the shell into his own palm. He felt it mix with his own heartbeat in synchronicity, in a symbiotic way.

He would pay later for his misdeeds but in the meantime, he needed to rest. He closed his eyes and felt the pull of sleep sweep over him, his body relaxing with every shuddered breath in and out. No one would find him here; he was safe at last. The Sidhe and the crows would protect him whilst he slept. After all, it wasn't the first time that he had run away. He knew that if he had stayed in the house that he might never see another day break. Whereas from his hiding place, on many occasions he had watched the warm orange glow of a new day creep over the far horizon, its beauty always a balm to the boy's soul.

His small body shook in fitful sleep as the last few hours were re-lived over and over in his dreams. The darkness of night held no fear for him, he was safer in his haven than in the cottage, which he could see in the distance. The lights were now blazing in the windows. He knew that even hidden as well as he was, the diabhal would find him … there was no escape from him. He watched, suddenly alert, all vestiges of sleep gone, as the door of the cottage swung open and light flooded out into the darkness.

He saw a figure standing in the doorway and listened as he heard his name called. His da stepped outside and held the lantern high in the air. He watched from his hiding place as his mother stepped out behind him, only to be knocked back inside by the diabhal's fist. She cried out his name, begging her husband.

'Please, Brendan, leave him be, he didn't mean it, he's only a child!'

But the man was no longer listening.

'I will knock the sin from his bones! The diabhal has a hold on him! Why else would he neglect his schooling and his duties at home? He spends all day with the crows; it's got to stop, even if I have to knock sense into him.'

Brendan Doyle swept through the doorway into the darkness; he knew where the boy liked to hide, it was just a matter of finding him.

The child held his hands tightly over his ears and his lips moved in prayer.

'Our lady, please don't let him find me, blessed mother keep me safe.'

His prayers remained unanswered as an arm appeared through the bushes and he was grabbed by a strong hand. An diabhal had found him …

'Blessed mother let me see another day. If not, may you take my soul.'

He felt himself being dragged from his hiding place, the crows disturbed once again taking to the air in a cacophony of sound, swooping and crying out at the figure below as if in protection of the child, but also of their nests. The sound of his boots bumping the ground as the heels hit the ruts of hardened earth were all that the boy could hear, beating in rhythm like a drum as he was pulled across the field towards the lighted doorway. He focused on the sound and in his head he flew high above as the wind lifted him, his wings feeling the beat and falling into a rhythm with his own heartbeat. He started to caw, calling to his crow family as he looked up into the angry face of his father …

He shot into a sitting position and wiped the sweat from his eyes. The images in his head receding, dissipating like mist, evaporating from his mind's eye, as he woke up. He lifted the blind on the window; it was still dark and his eyes drifted to the clock by the bed, its luminous hands pointing to three am. He laid his head back on the pillow – too early to rise just yet. His devotions were still a couple of hours away. He placed his hand on his chest and he could feel his heart beating rapidly. His thoughts turned to the dream. It had been recurring a lot of late. He counted his heartbeats and it matched with the drumming of the boy's heels over the ruts in the field in his dream. Closing his eyes, he was almost back there, smelling the earth as his boots ploughed troughs through the soil. The sound of the cawing birds dissipated as he opened his eyes and his heartbeat returned to normal. He had a few years of peace from the dream in the intervening years: it had been at its peak when he was still a child. Age had led to acceptance, but since reading about the graves found in Bally-Bay, his thoughts had turned more often to his childhood and his home.

Giving up on sleep, he climbed out of bed, pulling on his clothes before putting his outer coat over the top. It had been getting colder in the mornings now that summer was drawing to a close and the older he got, the more his childhood injuries ached. His back and legs played up in colder weather, and he had been struggling of late with performing his priestly duties in both senses: physically, and with his own beliefs in question. Rubbing the back of his leg, he felt the lump at the side of his knee where the bone had been set badly; it made him limp and he walked with an awkward gait. Still, he thought, 'I'm lucky I didn't lose it.' His thoughts turned back to the dream, and the memory of that night returned with such a force that he stumbled towards the bed. He had been told that the amnesia, after his father had nearly killed him, would probably be temporary, and that he may gain his memory back but it had never happened … up until now, almost forty years later, that is …

He was already up and about so he might as well go to the chapel; perhaps a penance and prayer would bring clarity to the memories and hopefully an understanding of God's mission for him. He slid his soutane over his head, adjusting the collar and checking in the small mirror before he left his room, he made his way to the chapel. Slipping silently through the door, he lit a candle and genuflected at the statue of the Virgin Mary and made a sign of the cross. He slipped inside the confessional box. He knew that only God could hear him and he wanted to try and make some sense of the images inside his head; he also knew that he had been struggling with his faith. Like a lost soul, he opened his heart and poured everything out to his imaginary idyllic presence that had been festering in his heart. All of the pictures that plagued him like a video whenever he closed his eyes, and as he lifted his hands in prayer, an understanding grew inside him.

It had been the names of the two detectives on the Bally-Bay case that had started the memories returning and now they were coming in thick and fast. Each day brought a new onslaught of memories of abuse, depravation and humiliation at the hands of his parents. Not just his parents but also from the Jesuit brothers at the college where he was sent aged eleven after his injuries had healed.

The priests were sometimes worse. He remembered now the feeling he had as he had turned his father's shotgun on both of his parents. The image in his mind of their heads exploding over the pillows as he finished the job once and for all. He closed his eyes as the scene played like a movie in slow motion. He could feel the warm blood and brain matter spray onto his face and arms and moved to wipe it away as if it had happened just a moment ago. Of course, his hand came away clean. He had felt elated at the knowledge that he would no longer be used as a punch-bag or an outlet for sexual frustration. He had dealt with his father first; his mother had barely time to open her eyes and focus on her son before she too met her maker. He had passed out from his injuries long before he was able to reload and finish the job of including himself in the slaughter. He was blissfully unaware of the extent of his own injuries until he awoke a week later in the hospital with no memory of what had happened.

This was how Father Benedict had told him to play it with the gardaí, to say he remembered nothing. So, they had decided that an intruder had beaten the child as he had tried to stop them from killing his parents. For the boy, it wasn't so far from the truth as he had no recollection of events from that night ... that is until now.

Each day, a new memory resurfaced, he remembered more and more as he followed the story in the newspaper of all of the girls that never left St Theresa's but lay buried with their babies in the grounds. He even began to remember the children at the school in Bally-Bay where he grew up. He remembered *now* ... especially after reading the names of DCI Sean O'Dowd and DCI Steven Ryan, who as boys long ago had been the source of much of his unhappiness. Back then, the two boys had delighted in his hurt and humiliation. They had teased and bullied him every day in the tiny village school attached to St Theresa's. He remembered them so well, their names burned into his soul. He closed his eyes and pictured them all as children, and allowed himself a few moments to wallow in the self-pity that accompanied each memory, then afterwards scanned the pictures of them both in the newspaper. The hatred he felt for them settled comfortably on him as if he had been awaiting its arrival. Remembering it all, he looked at every facial feature, every nuance. They had no idea what he went through every day and they didn't care. They went home at night to a warm home, a loving family, a hot meal, in the knowledge that they were safe. He went home to hell.

He flung open the confessional door, almost staggering with the weight of the knowledge that had been thrust upon him. Then with a purpose he returned to his room, packed a few essential items and, grabbing his white crow, he left his life, the only one that he had known since childhood.

CHAPTER 2

'But I have been watching the crows since childhood. I loved the colour on its face.'

RK Laxman

His fingers stroked the white head as it nuzzled his hand with its beak; he stroked down its back, the feathers now turning darker until they were mostly black. Small patches of white speckles ran around the front of the crow's breast and up its neck. He had saved the crow when it was only a baby from its own brothers and sisters. They would surely have been compelled to kill this oddity, this bird that didn't fit in, a bird that was different from the others. He had researched the causes of the white feathers and had established the cause as leucism, often caused by a diet low in protein, or sometimes by genetics, which didn't affect its health. It didn't suffer from albinism as its eyes were still black as coal, not red, and its feathers were not completely white. It turned one eye towards him now, waiting for a morsel of food from its protector.

He himself knew what it was like to feel different. To be ostracised for the way you look, to be beaten by others who had no understanding of your life and why it was different from their own. He also had known hunger and now that food was plentiful for him, he found that he needed to control his urge to feast at every meal, the same way that the crow would too if he let it.

He gathered the bird into his arms and it nestled into the crook, content to sit and be stroked. As his hand ran gently down the feathers, he told the bird his confession, and knew that it would be safe with his secret keeper, his sin-eater. He returned the bird to a large aviary that he had built up on the flat roof, along the back wall of the building. He shut the cage door and, turning towards the roof edge, he climbed up to the highest point, stretching his arms wide as he felt the air beneath them rise, lifting him to the tip of his toes. He felt no fear of falling, only freedom, and sometimes he wished that he would fall just to see if he could fly. His confession had been given to the secret keeper and he felt cleansed, purified, and ready to take the next step. All he needed now were for the crows to reveal to him the next name and the sins that they had committed. He would take their confession, so that he could re-tell it to the sin-eater. The sun was just starting to go down and the birds were returning to their nests.

He watched as the black forms swooped and dived towards him, the air lifting their wings. The sound grew with the numbers and the crows cawed out their song to him as he stood patiently to hear it. The sound rumbled deep in his throat as he joined in with the cacophony, seeking the comfort of a brotherhood, a symbiotic understanding and a beating of hearts and wings in unison. The numbers grew until he could barely be seen beneath the black-feathered forms that brushed past his face, taking his words and his tears with them. He remained silent now, until the last word was spoken and the last bird had gone. All that remained was a pile of ebony plumage, their greeny iridescence tinged with purple hues.

He let his heels fall back down and sure footedly stepped down from the top of the air conditioning unit that he had been standing on. The rusted outer casing caught his calf and he swore as the blood from the wound dripped onto the feathers. He swiftly gathered them up and went to dress his wound. His thoughts turned to the next confessor that the crows had told him about and he began formulating a plan in his mind.

The cut stung as he poured the antiseptic over it and, dabbing it dry, he placed a dressing over the wound. Time now to eat and rest, he thought, pouring himself a glass of wine, but perhaps a little celebration first, before he saw Father Murphy on his way to hell. He giggled like a child then, as he thought that he certainly wouldn't be seeing much of anything, let alone heaven.

'Rest in agony,' he toasted. 'May you rot slowly. You won't be lonely for long, not once the others arrive.'

He swallowed down the wine and set about making himself a meal. He opened the fridge door and, picking up a bloody paper-wrapped parcel, he walked outside to the aviary. Opening it, he placed the eyes that were inside the parcel in the feeding tray.

'A veritable feast for us all tonight; enjoy my beauty, it's only fair that we share the feast.'

He stepped out and, closing the door, he smiled at the squelch of the bird's beak as it entered the gelatinous ball.

Father Murphy's death had come slowly. After all, it took time to remind him of the times that the child had come to him for help. How the priest had pleaded for his life, as once the child had pleaded with Father Murphy to save him from his father, afraid that he would not see tomorrow. It had taken a long time as the child had suffered for so long. His pleas had fallen on deaf ears. Instead, Father Murphy had beaten the boy for lying in his confessional about his hardworking parents. After all, everyone knew that the boy wasn't all there, that he was touched by an diabhal, a troublemaker and a liar. He had even been caught thieving from the other children's lunch bags.

Years later when the priest was made to see the truth, he had begged for his life with as much vigour as the child had once begged for his. This time it was Father Murphy's pleas that fell on deaf ears. He had felt a great satisfaction as he had removed Father Murphy's eyes – after all, what use were they to him? He never could see the wrong-doing of others, and wasn't that the job of a priest, to offer direction to lost souls? To help those who were not following a righteous path … to steer them in the right direction? No wonder he couldn't help the boy: he had been blind all along to the sin of the fathers.

He had simply released Father Murphy from that burden of failure. The confession had come slowly at first; he didn't want to admit that he had sinned himself, as a priest. After all, does it not state in the bible *'suffer little children to come unto me'*? Oh, and he had suffered alright! Now it was the priest's turn. He drove the point of the dagger into the eye-socket and, lifting the eyeball from its resting place, he cut the nerves and muscles holding it in place; then he repeated the procedure with the other eye. The priest's sobbing, asking him for mercy, gradually faded to be replaced by groans and then nothing as he propped his body up in the confessional box.

'There now, Father – all ready to make your confession? I think your eyes will make a good penance and I do believe that you are heartily sorry. I'm afraid our God of mercies has left the building, so *I* will have to do.'

Making the sign of the cross, he continued.

'May God give you pardon as I absolve you of your sins.'

Tucking a piece of paper with the words *'One for malice'* into the front of the priest's soutane and placing a black feather into one of the bloody eye sockets, he left the church.

He ate a simple meal that evening, enough to sustain his body and energy levels. He was tired now after his exciting day, so he lay down on the cot in the corner of the room. Pulling the blanket up to his chest, he sighed deeply in satisfaction, happy with his day's work. He re-lived the best parts in his head and smiled to himself. His hand crept below the blanket to his crotch to find a growing erection there.

CHAPTER 3

'When a dove begins to associate with crows, its feathers remain white, but its heart grows black.'

Unknown

The whispers started almost immediately that he succumbed to sleep. The sound of many voices was pounding in his head, the words indistinct. Suddenly an image of his mother popped into his head, her face contorted in anger, screaming at him. Then the pain started in his groin, the heat spreading over his genitals; he dropped his flaccid penis which had lain in his hand since he had pleasured himself earlier. Now the images came thick and fast: the nearly boiling water being thrown over him, his screams as his mother scrubbed at his crotch area … but worst of all the words that she spat into his face now clear to his ears.

'Filthy animal, disgusting behaviour!'

Sex was filthy and only an diabhal's creatures touched themselves.

He remembered how he had been found by her in the top meadow. He had been lying in the grass watching the crows circle and call to each other. He had felt happy for once, and peaceful. The sun had lulled him into a false sense of security, making him relax and his hand had just gravitated naturally to his trousers. He had fumbled with the buttons on the grey woollen shorts but had felt excited and exhilarated as the air had touched his skin upon release. For the boy, the experience had been a sensory rather than a sexual experience … a comfort.

He gasped as he remembered the pain of his rough clothing

sticking to the burns on his skin for weeks, the rawness and pain making him unable to walk properly. Then he remembered the jeers of the other children, the humiliation.

'Ha ha! Look at that eejit Doyle! Have ye shit yerself like a baby? His mammy should have put a nappy on him. You stink! You stink! You stink! Doyle has shit hisself, Doyle has shite hisself.'

Their cries still echoed in his ears as he awoke, no longer re-living the agony, the pain in his groin abated as he came to. He smiled; yes, he knew that the crows had told him who was next, and he had plans to make. Leaping from the bed with excitement, still naked, he picked up a pen and paper and began writing down the next victim's name and thinking about how he would get him to confess his sins.

The plan was a good one; always eager to offer his services when it came to young boys, Father Feelan was easily enticed with the promise of the opportunity to be left alone with them. He was well known for his acts of charity and was always the first to dress as Santa at the children's Christmas parties. It gave him lots of chances to sit the boys on his knee, or to be the clown that entertained them at the summer picnic: lots of places to jump out and chase them to secluded tented areas to indulge his little pleasures. Oh, he had a lot to confess and he would be given the opportunity very soon. He felt more comfortable taking a life now after Father Murphy's demise. It would be easier second time around. Either way, his confession would be taken and Father Feelan absolved of his sins. The sin-eater would feast well again tonight as Father Feelan's sins had been plentiful and the penance would be mighty.

*

DCI Sean O'Dowd leant over the body of Father Murphy and stared at the bloody mess where his eyes used to be. Looking up at the young forensic officer James Connolly, he said, 'I knew him, yer know. I only spoke to him a few months back when I was working on the St Theresa's case. I never liked the man but I wouldn't wish such a death on me worst enemy. Was there anything recovered from the body?'

The forensic officer handed Sean two plastic see-through bags, the first containing a black feather and the second a note.

'The feather was recovered from one of the eye sockets and the note was tucked into his clothing. We are still looking for the murder weapon, but no luck so far and no sign of his eyes either. We can work out the time of death later when we get him back to the morgue, but looking at the lividity in the legs I would say that he has been sat here a while.'

Sean shuddered and glancing at the note he read out loud: '*One crow for malice.*' What do ye think that means?'

'I don't know about crows but isn't there a kid's rhyme about magpies?'

'Yes, you are right. It's a start, anyway. Time to find out if Father Murphy had any enemies. Can ye get me a copy of the note on my desk later today, please? I'll leave ye to it then.'

Heading out of the church, Sean made his way to the manse next door. Knocking on the door, he waited for it to be opened by young garda Connor O'Brian. He had been on Sean's team since he proved his worth on their last case. Siobhan Connelly, the young garda who had worked closely with him, had moved on to be a DC after Sean had encouraged and supported her through her detective exams. He knew that he wouldn't have Connor for much longer, either. He had been very impressed with the young pair and their commitment to the job, also their loyalty to himself and DCI Steve Ryan, his best friend and colleague. Steve had run into some trouble with a stalker, a colleague, in fact, who had tried to disgrace him and ruin his career – and his life. Sean had no hesitation in putting them both forward for promotion as they had behaved impeccably, unlike that eejit DS Josh

Hall who they had sent down from Dublin to help out. Sean smiled to himself as he recalled the hapless DS slipping through the mud on the investigation site and ruining his best shoes: faux crocodile if he remembered rightly. Chuckling to himself at the memory, Sean hadn't told him that there were wellingtons stashed in the cupboard. He deserved to learn a lesson after treating the lower ranks with such contempt. One thing that he insisted upon in his team was that everyone respected everyone else, no matter what their rank or where they were in the team. DS Hall was definitely not a country boy, and he had spent more time chatting up the barmaid in the village pub than actually working.

Thinking now of his friend Steve, who had returned to England, he wondered how he was doing after his meeting with the board of professional standards. He knew that it was just a formality as Steve had done nothing wrong and with Meghan and Steve's twins due imminently, he had more on his plate to worry about than his old friend Sean back in Ireland.

CHAPTER 4

'Then this ebony bird beguiling my sad fancy into smiling.'

Edgar Allen Poe

Back home in England, suspended from duty, Steve found himself standing outside the door of the meeting room where a panel from professional standards was now deciding his fate. He had stood in front of them not half an hour ago, explaining how his DS Sara Dyson had somehow read more into a kiss than he had, and how it had happened at a very low point in his life after a very intense case which had affected him and his family. He told them how she had stalked him, and now … looking back, he realised how wrong he had been not to go to his chief superintendent immediately after she began a crusade of threats and harassment against him, after his rejection of her, even going so far as to follow him to Ireland where she had had an unfortunate accident and died. He hoped that he had shown his guilt and remorse for not doing the right thing but nothing he could have said or done could describe the depths of despair that he had reached, or that he had fallen to, and that he wouldn't have tried to prevent her death even if he could have. He still didn't understand how a confused fumble and kiss between friends and colleagues could have led to such carnage but he felt nothing knowing that she was dead apart from relief. After all, she was the one responsible for his dear mammy's death. The only positive thing to come out of the whole bloody mess was that he hadn't lost the love of his life, Meghan, and that they were soon to become parents, the most exciting thing in the world. He still couldn't understand how she had forgiven him for not confiding in her, or that she had not lost her love for him.

He didn't mind, to be honest, if he was sacked, as he was beginning to lose his love for the job after everything that had happened. He had been through enough the past couple of years and it had shown him what was important in life. He would be sorry to lose his pension, though, and financially with twins on the way he was concerned. So here he was, twiddling his thumbs, waiting for fate to take its course. The door opened and he was called back in to hear their findings.

'We feel that your good conduct as an officer has stood you in good stead and your record, which has up to now been impeccable, shows us that you were doing everything possible to address your own health issues at the time. Your commanding officer has spoken to us with a glowing report on your behalf and, taking the circumstances into consideration, we feel that punishment would not be helpful at this time. The charge of unprofessional conduct has been redacted. However, because you didn't follow procedure by taking your concerns about DS Dyson's behaviour to your superior, we feel that you probably need to have more training and so we have decided to demote you temporarily to Detective Inspector until you have attended the recommended courses. Also, we have recommended that you be moved to a different department where you will be monitored until the course end.'

Steve nodded; he just wanted to get out of there. The room's walls seemed to be closing in on him and he found he was still having moments when his panic attacks were just a blink away. He had been keeping them well under control now, thanks to Dr Evelyn Watson, his psychiatrist, and now that Sara was gone, the pressure was off. This was the last big hurdle for him to overcome and then he could concentrate on becoming a proper partner to Meg and father to their babies.

He quickly thanked the board and exited the room; relief flooded through him as he made his way to the car-park, hearing the lock click as he pushed the button on the fob. He let out a breath that he hadn't realised he had been holding, and suddenly he crumpled. The darkness had almost overwhelmed him again. His sister Bree with her twisted mind had sent Sara over the top; of that he was sure because of the things she had said to him, but he was still puzzling out *how?* She was locked away inside the mental health facility that he had put her in after she had tried to kill him and Meghan and all of her family – she had almost succeeded, too.

An *diabhal* had entered his life. How could he explain to the board the evil and insanity that had touched his life? Sitting in the car, images flooded his mind … Sara Dyson screaming as she fell, the blood pooling below on the rocks that had smashed her skull. Then more screams from Romany, Meg's daughter, as she realised the consequences of her actions. He let the tears flow down his cheeks and he made no attempt whatsoever to wipe them away. When he looked up, he saw Sara Dyson's parents walking towards a taxi at the main entrance to the building. He hadn't realised that they had attended – maybe they had been called to speak to the panel. He sighed; they had obviously come to see their daughter's murderer (as they saw him) punished. He hoped that they were not too disappointed. Even now he could feel no sympathy towards Sara; the pain that she had caused him and his family far outweighed what he had done. She was the one responsible for her own parents' grief, too … not him, no matter how much they believed differently.

Rubbing the heel of his hand across his eyes, he headed home. Just walking into his home and feeling the love from his beloved Meg and Romany filled him with hope, and the thought of becoming a parent for the first time, although very scary, gave him unimaginable joy. After he had told Meghan the outcome, he would ring Sean.

*

Sean had just returned to the station and, coffee cup in hand, was about to seat his backside into a chair when Connor approached with a look on his face that Sean had hoped that he would never see again after the last investigation. Holding out a piece of paper towards Sean, he started speaking.

'Sorry, sir, another one came in while we were out; it looks like it might be by the same person. It is another priest, a Jesuit brother called Father Feelan, this time at the seminary – All Hallows. Apparently he also taught at St Patrick's too. He was the philosophy and religion teacher for the youngest students.'

'I thought I heard that place was closing … lack of trainee priests … well, there will be even less of them now.'

Sean took the paper from Connor and, groaning, read the report, sipping his coffee as quickly as he could bear the hot liquid, knowing it would be the last one he had for a while. He scanned the paper in his hand for the necessary details and placed it back on the desk.

Standing up, he signalled to Connor,

'Come on, then, best go take a look. Why do we seem to get all of the nut jobs? Why can't we have a nice normal murder, a stabbing or shooting or something easy?'

Connor laughed as he followed the great bear of a man out of the room.

The car swung into the sweeping driveway of the grey, almost silver, stone building before them. It glinted in the sunlight. Students were still milling around and, climbing out of the car, he scanned the windows then the grounds looking for any sign of Garda. Pointing to a small wooded area in the grounds away from the building, he could just make out a couple of cars and the coroner's van. Heading across a vast expanse of lawn, he watched as a white-suited man ducked under some yellow tape that was enclosing the crime scene. Sean called out a greeting to James Connelly, the forensic scientist, who waited for them to catch him up.

'Well, what have we got then, James?'

He looked at Sean.

'Well, whatever is going on it's similar to the murder of Father Murphy in the confessional as in there has been a note recovered from the robes again and a black feather was left at the scene, but method of death is different – come see for yourself.'

He led Sean through the small wooded area towards the perimeter wall. Propped up against the wall in a sitting position was the body of what clearly had been an elderly priest. The priest's face had a clown's red nose placed on it and a smile had been cut into the face, reaching up each side of the mouth towards the ears.

'As you can see, the smile is not the cause of death.' James lifted the head enough for Sean to see the gaping wound across the neck. Handing the two sealed bags to Sean containing the feather and the note, he said:

'This is Father Feelan. He was found this morning by another priest. Same as before, it looks like a reference to a children's rhyme. That's not all,' he said, pointing to a blood-stained patch on the priest's trousers. 'He seems to have had his genitals mutilated, too.'

Sean read: '*Two for mirth*'.

'Well, he seems to like his rhymes. I'll let you get on and I will expect a report of time of death ASAP. Do you think this is sexually motivated?'

Sean nodded towards the crotch of the priest's trousers.

'Hard to tell at this time, but I will try to get a preliminary report to you later today. However, I have Father Murphy's autopsy scheduled for this afternoon,' James replied.

'Oh well, do your best. Thanks, James. Meantime I need to go speak to a priest urgently … while there are still some left.'

Connor chuckled at his boss's joke and, stepping forward, he scrolled through his notes. As they walked back across the lawned area, he relayed the information to Sean.

'The body was found at nine this morning by err … a Father Paul, who is apparently waiting for you inside the chapel,' Connor said, pointing to the small church at the end of the long stone building. They both headed in that direction.

The gloomy inside of the chapel reminded Sean of the last time that he had been to a church and the body of Father Murphy sitting in the confessional. Once his eyes had adjusted to the gloom, he saw a figure sitting at the front. Making the sign of the cross and genuflecting, he made his way towards him. The priest stood and turned towards Sean, who held out his hand.

'Father Paul? I am DCI Sean O'Dowd. I am sorry about the death of your colleague. I believe that you were the one to find his body. Can you tell me when he was last seen and by whom?'

'Well, that would have been me, last night at supper around seven pm. When Father Feelan didn't show up for breakfast and couldn't be found for his first lesson, I went to look for him. Sometimes he would go for a walk in the grounds, before start of day. So, it was the first place that I looked for him … who would want to do such a terrible thing, Detective? I can't understand why?'

'Well, I was hoping that you might be able to help me with that one, Father. Had Father Feelan mentioned anyone who had threatened him, or seen any strangers around?'

'No, nothing; everything was as normal.'

'Can you give me a sense of the man, Father? What were his interests, etcetera? And have you any explanation for the clown nose found on him?'

'The only thing I can think of is a reference to his good works programme and that he was known for dressing up as Santa at the parties for the orphans and he did the same as a clown at the summer fundraisers. He was getting pretty old and I had been helping him with his lessons and appointments. We have just been informed that All Hallows is closing next year, so he was taking retirement after this semester … sadly, not many young men nowadays want to join the priesthood … numbers have been dropping off for years.'

'So, when you say he played dress-up with the kiddies, were there ever any rumours or allegations of inappropriate behaviour? Being that close to the kids certainly gave him opportunity.'

Father Paul stuttered, and he blushed, not quite meeting Sean's eye; he shook his head.

'Ye see, Father, I am trying to understand if I am dealing with a revenge killing here or just a complete bloody nutter who hates priests … forgive me, Father, but I need to understand the circumstances and the motive. I have priests' bodies piling up left right and centre and I think that they are connected … I will be blunt with ye – was there any reason to think that Father Feelan was anything other than a good man? Whoever it was knew his routine and that it was common practice for him to take a morning walk before lessons.'

The young priest shook his head, not meeting the eye of the detective.

'Well, if ye think of anything or want to talk, here is my card, and if ye don't mind, young Garda O'Brian here will take yer statement while it is fresh in yer mind.'

Nodding to Connor, Sean stepped back outside the chapel and watched as the body of Father Feelan was brought out of the wooded area and placed into the coroner's van and driven off. He had been watching the crowd that had gathered, made up mostly of elderly priests and some younger seminarians. His eye was drawn to a figure further back from the others. The figure moved away inside the building long before the others did. No matter who you were, priest or not, everyone had curiosity, it was human nature, Sean thought to himself. And why had the figure that he had been watching disappeared? Was it because they already knew what was going on behind the tree line?

CHAPTER 5

'A Gathering of Crows'

Unknown

Kissing Meg on the cheek and rubbing her ever-growing belly, Steve reluctantly pulled back the covers.

'Do you have to leave so early, darling? It's only six o'clock,' Meg said, looking towards the small bedside clock then looking across at Steve, face planted into his mobile already. She sighed. She was still getting used to living with a detective. His phone had rung at all hours of the day and night as it was now glued to him. Reluctantly, he had one more day to finish on the course that he had been made to attend as part of his punishment by the professional standards committee. The second part of his punishment, as he saw it, was to move him to a new task force overseen by his old DC, Jason Short, who in Steve's absence had been promoted to DI whilst Steve had been demoted by the panel to DI. There was history between them both concerning Sara Dyson so DI Short was taking every opportunity to tell Steve that he thought that he'd got off lightly and that he should have been arrested for Sara Dyson's murder.

Steve knew that it was some form of punishment and that it was only temporary, but he was struggling not to blow a fuse. To say he was unhappy was an understatement. He wouldn't tell Meg as he didn't want to worry her, but he thought he might talk things over with Sean. He also found himself missing Ireland: the countryside and the fresh air. Just the smell of the sea in each breath and the image of the hawthorn tree on the hill with the twin headstones where his mammy and daddy now lay.

The new house that they had moved into on returning to England was stunning. It had belonged to Meg's parents. She had grown up there, but he missed the cosy family kitchen back at the family farm, the glow from the Rayburn as he warmed his toes, and the smell of something delicious made by his mammy cooking away in the oven for supper.

Of course, his mammy was no longer here to cook delicious things and that was thanks to Sara Dyson. Maybe he was just being romantic and silly, but he would love to bring the twins up back home. As he headed towards the station, he could see himself carrying his own son and daughter on his shoulders as his daddy had once done with him. Maybe not both of them together, he had smiled to himself. Blinking away a tear for his parents, he ran up the stairs ready to face a new onslaught of slights thrown at him by his former DC.

DI Jason Short watched Steve enter the room; he wanted rid of him as soon as possible. Why he had to put up with his old superior, he didn't know. How could he become his own boss, with him in the room? As far as he was concerned, he should be sitting in jail for the murder of Sara, not swanning in here with a satisfied look on his face. After all, everyone had known about him and Sara, that's why she had followed him to Ireland. No one could prove that she had been pushed over the harbour wall to smash against the rocks but Jason had his suspicions.

Steve had felt side-lined from day one and he was so pleased that it was the last day of courses and supervision. He didn't think he would be moved quite so easily but he was longing for his own team again, away from the innuendo and rumours that abounded. Even a nice gritty murder to get his teeth into would be good right now, to save him from death by boredom. When he hadn't been on the course, Jason Short had practically relegated him to answering the phone or dealing with petty break-ins and lost pets. Steve understood

THE PRIEST: A CONFESSION OF CROWS

that being new to his role Jason wanted to gel his team, but Steve had so much experience that it was silly not to use his knowledge, instead of keeping him festering at a desk, feeling frustrated and annoyed after three months.

'He always was a total prick,' he mumbled under his breath as he shuffled yet another pile of papers that had appeared on his desk.

After a morning of paperwork, Steve felt as if he was back at Garda College, thirty years ago, sitting in a classroom, the lecturing officer's voice droning on and on. If he had to listen one more time about his responsibilities as a superior officer, he thought he would scream. Or the five points to running a good cohesive team. Just what did they think he had been bloody doing for the last twenty odd years? He had found the courses patronising and boring.

The reason he had had a problem with Sara Dyson was because it had become personal; she was threatening his family and loved ones, and that was not on. He had been unable to explain the full extent of what had happened as he didn't want to end up in the mental health facility alongside his sister. How the heck could he explain to a board of English officers the cultural history of a very superstitious Ireland, or his own undeniable encounters with the supernatural? They would definitely have thought that he had lost the plot. The fact that he believed that Sara Dyson had been in touch with the devil would definitely seal his fate.

The thing that he needed to forgive himself for now was his reaction to what had happened. Looking back at the past year, he couldn't believe that the same man stood here today. This Steve Ryan and the one before would never have raised a hand to a woman. Always a gentle man, he needed to reconcile himself to the fact that he had acted in a way that he was ashamed of. He wouldn't even try to find an excuse … like, she pushed him too far, or that he wasn't himself at the time. No, he would forever bear that shame of his reaction towards Sara Dyson but one thing that he would never regret was her death.

The day ended and he headed home, grateful that it was all over, hoping that now he would be transferred back to his old department ASAP. He stopped at the deli on the way – he was going to make something tempting and delicious for Meg. Her appetite had been waning the more the twins had grown.

'There is just no room left in there for food,' she had declared only last night whilst pointing at her burgeoning stomach. Maybe something small and tempting was just what she needed. He knew that he had not given her the attention that she deserved over the pregnancy but hopefully now he could relax a little.

Grabbing a bottle of Australian Merlot, he headed for the till. He was going to ring Sean and celebrate his freedom tonight if nothing else.

He found Meg asleep on the sofa and rather than disturb her, he decided to open the bottle of wine and sit out in the evening sunshine and give his friend a call. Dialling the number, he took a sip from his glass. Sean answered on the first ring which took Steve by surprise. He swallowed his mouthful quickly.

'Well, you're on the ball! I nearly choked on me glass of wine!'

'Go on, rub it in that I am still at work! I was going to ring ye, anyway. How did the last day of your course go? Are ye free now on the terms of the panel's decision?'

Steve explained to his friend that today had been his last day and that's why he was drinking wine to celebrate.

'I have some news for ye which ye might find strange. Father Murphy is dead – murdered – and it wasn't very pleasant. I also have another murdered priest which I think is connected and we have just been informed that another is missing. I don't know what is going on yet but that is why I'm still at work. Anyway, how are Meg and Romany? Is Meg doing well with the pregnancy? My Roisin was so sick at the beginning and apparently it's much worse for twins. Ha! But that's nothing! Wait till they are screaming all day! Oh … and the night feeds and nappies.'

'Yeah, yeah, thanks for that! Have ye seen anything of yer kids?'

'I've seen them a few times since I made contact a few months ago. My eldest still doesn't want to see me. As I said before he is an adult himself now and I don't blame him. I was a total shite back then. So, where are ye working now? Are ye going back to where ye were, now ye have finished yer course?'

'I bloody hope so. I hate it here. I'm being side-lined on cases, left to answer the phone, or deal with silly inquiries all because of that fellow I told ye about that used to be my DC. Well, he has now been promoted to DI and I have been sent to work under him; it's total shite. He blames me for Sara's death and has made it quite clear what he thinks should have happened to me. The boss thought that Short could learn from my experience and that I could be an asset to him. Well, I would be if he let me do anything. To be honest with ye, I am thinking of jacking it all in. If it wasn't for the fact that we need the money, what with the twins on the way, I would do it tomorrow.'

He swallowed down the last of his wine and moved to pour himself another glass, tucking the phone under his chin.

'So what's this about Father Murphy?' he said.

Sean explained the horrific circumstances of the deaths of Father Murphy and Father Feelan.

'It wasn't a pretty sight and I am run off of my feet here. I just lost Siobhan – she has been promoted and it's just me and Connor. I hope they don't bloody send me that stupid DS Josh from the Met! He was a bloody eejit, more than useless. I sent him back with a flea in his ear. Hey! Here's a thought – I need a DI! Fancy coming back to Ireland to work with me again? I am actually serious now, I'm not codding ye. Why don't ye think about it? I really need some help with this case … Look, I better go … bloody think about it, please!'

Steve sighed; he would love to get his teeth into a new case but he didn't think that Meg would want to move back to Ireland, especially on a permanent basis. And of course there was Romany who had just settled into Art College. He heard Meg stirring so he went back into the house to get them something to eat. He might just drop it into the conversation over dinner to gauge her reaction. Sean was right – he did need to think about it and the case that Sean had now, he knew, would become complicated which was just the way he liked it!

*

Sean returned to the incident room. Connor had been busy whilst he had been on the phone. He had all of the information that they had gathered already pinned on the board and photographs of the victims in place.

'Well done, Connor. Any news yet from the post mortems? What's this about another bloody priest gone missing? Do we have any information yet? Who and where? Right, let's get cracking.'

Connor handed Sean a report with the name of the latest missing priest and the person who had reported him missing.

'None of the post mortems are finished yet but there is a preliminary findings sheet on your desk. The missing person is Father Kelly. He was the priest of a small parish in Maynside. His house keeper reported him missing this evening after she found his bed had not been slept in and he hadn't eaten his supper that she had left for him last night. Apparently, she had a day off today and had just popped in with some cold cuts for his supper tonight and realised that he hadn't been seen since she left yesterday afternoon, about four. All of this information came from local garda who thought that we might want to take a look because of the other priest killings.'

'So, he has been missing since approximately four pm yesterday. Did anyone check the church? He could have just had a heart attack or a fall, or something simple. You get off home now and we will visit the site in the morning. I'll give the local station a call and see if anyone has checked the church and if not get, someone to call over there and ring me back. I'm knackered, I don't know about you.'

'Yes, sir, thank you. One thing I did discover is that Father Kelly was a resident Jesuit brother at St Patrick's Seminary, like Father Feelan. That is up until a couple of years ago when they cut back on staff because of a shortage of seminary students. He has been in his present parish role for nearly three years.'

'Good work, thank you, Connor.' Sean turned to his office where, picking up the phone, he rang the garda station local to Father Kelly's church and requested a thorough search of the grounds and church the next morning. Leaving the room, he walked across to the board and saw that Connor had pinned Father Kelly's picture on the board. He felt no qualms this time looking at the faces of the priests, not as before with the girls; these faces didn't look innocent. He wondered what they had done and if they deserved their deaths. He also had a horrible feeling that this was only the beginning. Two priests dead and another missing, Sean knew he was going to be extremely busy.

CHAPTER 6

'Nothing is unreal as long as you can imagine like a crow.'

Munia Khan

The sound of cawing intensified as he flung his arms outwards. He always felt free when he was with the crows – his family. His heart raced as he felt their wings touch his hands then his face as they swooped past, testing and tasting the person that stood there. They knew that they had nothing to fear from him. He felt the pleasure ripple through him as each one landed onto his outstretched arms and shoulders, pushing and squabbling over which could get the closest to his head. When finally they had settled, he started to recite to them his contrition prayer:

'O my Crow family, I am heartily sorry if I have offended thee. I detest my sins of allowing these priests to still breathe the same air. I know this has offended thee, you who are the most deserving of my love. I firmly resolve to confess their sins to you and to take their lives as penance.

Amen.'

He listened as their cawing grew and they lifted and circled around his head. He understood the words forming inside his mouth as he muttered Father Feelan's confession. He had hesitated at giving him absolution as he had found his sins so abhorrent, re-living every moment that he and the other boys had suffered at his hands. Too many that Father Feelan couldn't even remember their names … oh, but he had made sure that he remembered his name before he had died; he made sure of *that*. Father Feelan was no longer playing the

38

clown or forcing boys to give him a blow job at the back of some musty smelling tent. That smell had been the first thing that he had remembered after recovering from his amnesia and had stayed with him whenever he recalled the priest. Now he drew in a deep breath and all that he could smell was fresh, bracing air. He breathed so hard, his chest rising, that some of the crows lifted their wings, about to take flight.

'Wait, my beauties, I still have to tell you Father Kelly's confession. Although he confessed to killing my boyhood pet, my beloved one, he will now become food for his brothers. They will be taking revenge on Father Kelly right now. Your brother was a brave crow, trying to protect me from the abuses of evil inflicted on my childish body, and Father Kelly killed him before my eyes. His penance for his sins will be harsh and long. I wonder how long he will endure before he leaves this world.'

He chuckled to himself and felt that human emotion of happiness reverberating around his body. He hadn't felt like this in a long time. It was a release and a pleasure all at once. The euphoria of killing another human being had been an unexpected bonus.

When he had heard God's word and had been tasked with finding the sinners from his childhood, he had wondered if he would be up to the job or whether God had asked too much of him. He was still a little unsure as he hadn't quite recovered all of his memory. Each of the names given to him came in pieces of lost memories and with those came the memory of what had happened to him. He was still unable to remember everything that had happened after he had killed his parents; it was mostly a blur. It was a pity that Father Benedict wasn't still alive as he would have been his first. Father Murphy had made a great alternative, though. The crows lifted from his body, some taking their time to stretch their wings before taking off. The soft feathers brushed his skin and caressed his lips, and he laughed even louder.

'Now, who is going to be next my beauties? Tell me who is next to confess?'

The sound became unbearably loud as the crows called to each other and him. They circled and swooped; the wind lifting their wings as they reverberated in the air. The noise carried to his ears as he listened to their words.

He nodded at their beating wings, forming them into words as they drifted off one by one. He made his way inside and sat at the table. Opening a bible, he turned to the Book of Revelations and read: *'I know your works, your labour, your patience and that you cannot bear those who are evil. And you have tested those who say they are apostles and are not, and have found them liars.'*

The words gave him comfort; he knew now that God understood his task. To rid the church of false apostles, those that dared to speak of God whilst acting on their evil natures. Yes, he felt holy and just as the next name entered the book. He knew that the crows were God's messengers. He would be taking confession again very soon, and adding to the list he wrote *Three for a funeral* in bold writing across the page.

It had been an onerous task and a difficult one to dispatch Father Kelly. He was not of a strong build but he had found his strength in the task before him. After initially stunning him, he had made him walk to his own grave as such, down to the dusty catacombs. Leaving unseen had been the easy part. Who would think anything of seeing a priest leave a church even if he had been spotted? He patted himself on the back for his foresight in keeping his robes. Understanding the nature of priests had been a useful tool to him as well. He thought of the times that he himself had sat in the confessional listening to people's perceived sins. What did they know of true evil? He had experienced it first-hand and had been called to his vocation of ridding the church of sinful priests. God had indeed chosen well in his advocate.

His crow family had gathered around him and helped him to carry out their punishments. Through the crows' eyes he saw the evil-doers as they really were. Most of all, the crows were sorely needed to carry their confessions to God. The pure one had taken it upon himself to take the penance from each one and become the sin-eater.

CHAPTER 7

'Crows will not pick out other crows' eyes.'

Romanian proverb

Sean took his frustration out on the desk by slapping it hard with his hand.

'Why do ye think we haven't found Father Kelly? After all, he left the other bodies out in the open for all to see! What do ye, think Connor?'

Connor looked at his boss; he was so grateful that he and Siobhan had been assigned to Sean on the last case. He knew that he couldn't learn from a better teacher and Siobhan had proved that by moving up the ranks already. He was teetering on the edge of his detective exams but he knew that he could learn more from Sean than any course or college could provide. He hero-worshipped him, and he loved the way that he was included in every aspect of the investigation, not just left to do the grunt work. Clearing his throat before speaking, he had pondered this question himself.

'I have thought about that too, boss. Maybe it's because he has left him where he can't easily be seen or moved him to a different location.'

'Connor, you are brilliant … yes … now, was the church thoroughly searched? I mean *thoroughly* searched? How about you and I go and have a poke around on our own? Ye never know, he could be in plain sight but just not obvious. I don't think he would risk moving a body, more chance of being seen, but if he was still alive, he *could* perhaps have moved him. To be honest, I think it is the former and after three days I don't think we are looking at finding him alive.'

Pulling his jacket from the back of his chair, he waited whilst Connor grabbed his notebook and coat. It had been quite cold lately and snow had been forecast for the weekend, so he hoped that they found Father Kelly before then. Mind you, he was convinced that Father Kelly was already dead.

'Let's crack on then.'

Heading towards the car park, he checked the boot for a working torch and lever bar. It wouldn't be the first time that he had gone to investigate and found none of the equipment working or missing. Climbing into the car, they set off for the outskirts of Dublin where the small parish of Maynside lay. On the way, Sean told Connor that he had spoken to Steve last night and had tried to get him to join their team on a permanent basis.

'Wow, boss that would be great if the old team were back together, wouldn't it? I never thought that it was fair what happened to DCI Ryan.'

'Not DCI anymore, back down to DI. No, I didn't think it was fair either, Connor; he is a bloody good detective and he earned his Chief Inspector. I hope he will be re-instated eventually; we need men like him at the top.'

They reached their destination – a small Victorian church built in the early 1800s with all of the Gothic architecture related to the period. Standing on the path leading to the church doors, Sean veered off to the left and indicated to Connor to go to the right. He had just turned down the side of the building and was examining a back door when Connor caught him up.

'Nothing much to see on the other side, sir. Just some old tombs with steps leading down into them which could possibly be accessed from inside the building too. Some of these older churches have catacomb-like chambers under the church for the burial of the richer families that often donated to the church.'

'Well, Connor, sounds like you are knowledgeable in church architecture. Let's go inside and see if we can get into anything from there. Go fetch the torch from the car.'

'I have been reading up about churches in the surrounding area, too – did you know for instance that this one was built on the site of a much older building? Hence the catacombs … they probably used it for smuggling rum or something.'

Sean laughed.

'You have a good imagination, I'll give ye that, Connor. Hurry up with that torch, now, I don't fancy slipping down some steps with my bad knees.'

First Connor showed Sean the outside steps leading down to, as he had described it, an underground chamber. The steps seemed to just disappear into the wall. They could see no entry from outside so they proceeded back to the front door. Upon entering the church, Sean took in a deep breath; he had seen too many churches lately and they all smelled the same: of piety and damnation.

Making his way towards the back of the church, he opened a door leading to a small anti-chamber. A row of hooks hung along one wall, each hook holding different coloured chasubles and robes. A small table sat along the other wall and held a bible, above it a small safe set in the wall. Sean presumed that it held the altar chalices and candle sticks. Robberies of church artefacts had been more frequent lately and most churches now had small safes to lock away any valuables. Two empty glass carafes sat on the small table either side of the bible and a plain wooden cross hung on the wall above them. At the end of the room, almost hidden by the robes hanging from the hooks, Sean found a smaller wooden door. He would have easily missed it if he had just opened the door to the room and glanced in. He found a handle and turned it; nothing happened.

'Connor, can you run across to the manse and ask for the keys for me, please? I think this might be the way into the outside chambers. It's certainly in the right place as it ties in with the outside area.'

Connor turned and Sean could hear the sound of his feet as he ran back through the church. Sean shivered and rubbed his knees. The cold weather certainly made him ache; he must be getting old. He made his way back into the church where he found a small heater that was on. He stood in front of it and chuckled: this little thing couldn't possibly keep such a huge church warm. He felt sorry for the parishioners and hoped that they didn't have to sit through too long a sermon. Then he thought that it probably wouldn't be Father Kelly delivering it any time soon.

Connor arrived back with a huge set of keys hanging on a large metal ring; they were old and large, most of them worn and rusting. Handing them over but holding one up separately, he said: 'I have been told that this is the one to that door. Apparently, they hardly ever open it. The wine for sacrament is kept just inside and there are a lot of steps leading to old burial tombs. No one it seems has been buried in there since the early 1900s when the last of the founding families passed.'

Placing the key in the lock, Sean was surprised at how easily it turned.

'This looks like it has been oiled lately and used,' he pointed out to Connor. Opening the door wide, he felt for a light switch. 'No electricity then, so be careful, Connor, and hand me that torch, will ye?'

Sean made his way down to the bottom of the flight of stairs. He stopped in his tracks and pointed to the floor. The air was damp and musty. He pointed to marks in the dusty ground that were clearly visible.

'Looks like drag marks and I can see some footprints. Please hand me your notebook so that I can mark the prints for forensics and can you please go back to the car and call in a forensics team? I don't want to disturb any evidence but I'm going to try to follow the trail. When you come back, please stay upstairs. I won't be long.'

Connor turned back up the stairs and Sean, treading on the opposite side to the dusty footprints, tiptoed toward the back of the chamber, following the trail of drag marks. The chamber opened out and several cave-like openings could be seen running around the circular chamber, each one filled with a stone tomb. The drag marks halted at what looked like a large brick-built structure inside one of the cave openings with a stone sarcophagus sitting on the top. Alongside the footprints and drag marks Sean could make out a circular imprint with a crisscross pattern inside it, as if something had been placed on the floor in front of the tomb. Most likely a light of some kind, he thought.

Suddenly, he heard a noise coming from the stone tomb; it sounded like scratching sounds, making him jump.

'Is that you, Father Kelly?' he called out. 'Help is on its way!'

He listened eagerly for any signs of life from within the tomb. The scratching sound was replaced by a different sort of fluttering sound which spooked Sean even more, and he jumped when he thought he heard a caw. Scanning the tomb with his torch, he could see that it was ornately carved and lichen had discoloured the stone which showed that at some point the tomb had been outside in the open, above ground. The torch beam alighted on something white sticking out of the crack where the lid and the base joined. Another note? He decided to leave it to forensics; he knew that James would be furious with him for coming into the chamber but hey … he had been careful not to disturb anything. Returning to the stairs, he stopped and listened; all was silent again and he shuddered before ascending quickly. Closing the door behind him, he found Connor and said:

'Well, if that is where Father Kelly is, I don't hold out much hope that he is still alive. Did you explain to forensics that lifting equipment will be needed? That stone lid is far too heavy to lift … so how the hell …?'

His sentence tailed off as he realised that the mark on the floor was probably from a small winch.

'Forensics are on their way, sir, so hopefully we might have some answers very soon.'

'I bloody hope so, Connor. This is turning into a serious case. We are definitely going to need some more help. I think that he has left us a note again, this time tucked into the tomb. We will have to wait for James to retrieve it. I will wait here for the team but can you in the meantime get a statement from the housekeeper and find out what ye can about that kid's rhyme? In case there's more of it on the note here? Oh … and who else worked with all three fathers at All Hallows or St Patricks. We need some names. There might be more priests in danger.'

The forensics team turned up twenty minutes later and Sean approached. Shaking hands with James, he briefly told him what he had found and his suspicion that the missing priest was inside the tomb.

'Right, leave it to us and you can watch from the side-lines. We need to photograph and document the chamber before we can bring in the lifting equipment so give me about thirty minutes for a preliminary. You have already left your big feet all over the crime scene.'

'Ah … but I *am* keeping ye in business lately with all this lot,' Sean said, pointing towards the staircase leading to the chambers below. 'I do actually think that Father Kelly is inside the tomb. I thought I heard something when I was down there … do you think he might still be alive?' Sean asked.

'No, those stone tombs are pretty air-tight when sealed and three days is a long time to be sealed up inside. The average size of a tomb …? Err, he would have been lucky to have lasted a day. Probably only five to seven hours depending on how much room was inside; some of these old stone tombs are quite roomy. It was probably a rat you heard.'

Sean shuddered.

'I hate rats! Let's hurry this up and open it, and then we can all get back for a cuppa. By the way, there seems to be another note stuck in the lid – can I have a look at it as soon as?'

James moved around Sean and started carrying equipment down the stairs.

'Make yourself useful and go suit up. I don't want any more of your DNA destroying my crime scene! And bring back the lifting winch, will you? Wait at the top of the stairs until I say it's OK to come down. I should have a few summary photos done by then.'

'Good. I want to be there when you open the thing.'

Sean trundled back up the stairs and, finding a suit in the back of his car, he put it on. He pulled up the zip and looked at Connor.

'Well, go on then, you too! There's another suit on the back seat. Ye don't want to miss this one, do ye?'

Connor smiled at his boss. He rushed to open the plastic bag and put on the white crime-scene suit. Struggling to carry the lifting equipment, he hurried after Sean whose back was just disappearing down the stairs. He heard him call out to James.

'OK detective,' said James. 'You may come down now; you were right, there is something moving inside the tomb so hurry up with the lifting gear.'

He waved Sean towards him and between the three men the hoist was soon in place.

'What do you think this mark was caused by, James? Is it where he used a hoist to lift the lid himself?' Sean pointed to the circular pattern that he had spotted earlier on the floor.

'No, I don't think it can be; the base isn't wide enough to take the weight … see how the legs are spread out on our hoist? I'm not sure what it is yet but I have taken some soil samples from inside the circle and pictures of it.'

The chain moving and the handle turning was the only sound in the room as the straps took the weight of the lid and became taught. All three men held their breath. The sound of stone grinding on stone stirred Sean into stepping forward and he placed his gloved hand on top of the lid to guide it as it rose. Soon a gap appeared between the tomb and the lid. Suddenly, Sean jumped back and shouted.

'Something touched my hand!' he exclaimed and the white piece of paper fluttered to the ground. James bent to retrieve it with tweezers and place it into an open bag.

'Jumpy, aren't we detective? It's just the note.'

Soon the lid was up high enough for the men to see inside. Shining a torch into the cavity, Sean gasped. Father Kelly, or what was left of him, and three blackbirds lay inside. One of the birds opened an eye and stared at Sean; he jumped back.

'It's still alive, poor thing; that's what I must have heard earlier.'

James gently lifted the black-feathered wing away from Father Kelly's face. It was Connor's turn to gasp: the bloody, pecked, scratched, eyeless and lipless grimace of what was left of Father Kelly's face lay beneath. Rushing back up the stairs to the outside, Connor threw up the contents of his stomach. Then, feeling a hand on his shoulder, he turned to see Sean who said:

'Well, at least you didn't add more DNA to James' crime scene. Time for us to head back to the station now, and leave him to do his job.' He started to peel the white suit from his shoulders. As they were leaving, James called out to Sean.

'Before you go, I thought that you might like to see the note.' He handed Sean the sheet of paper that had fallen earlier from the tomb as the lid was lifted.

Reading it, Sean said, 'Well, if nothing else, he is consistent.' Turning the plastic bag around to show Connor, he read out loud:

'*Three for a funeral* – another bloody rhyme.'

CHAPTER 8

'And the crow once called the raven black …'

RR Martin

Settling back into his chair, Sean looked at Connor.

'Two priests murdered could be a coincidence, but *three*? Now I believe that we have a serial killer who has a grudge against priests … which I might add could be any number of our finest citizens that were buggered by them as children … That, Connor, is what we are dealing with. I think we need to try and get a handle on this before he does it again. But I have a horrible feeling that he may already have.'

'It could be a woman, sir, couldn't it?'

'Yes, you're right, Connor, we must never assume anything but they would need to be extremely strong to overpower the priests. That is why I will err on the side of it being a man until anything leads me to think otherwise, purely from a physical point of view. If the marks in the dust were not from a hoist, I would love to know how the hell he lifted up that tomb lid!'

As he spoke, the telephone rang. Grabbing it, Connor called out:

'It's the morgue; they want you to pop down to see something.'

'Come on, then, we had better go see what James wants; hopefully he has finished the other two autopsies and has some news for us as at the moment apart from knowing that the killer is insane, I have no bloody idea.'

The two men entered the autopsy room. Connor was still having difficulty dealing with the smell of death and was passed a mint by Sean.

'Well, what do we have, then?'

Pointing towards the body of Father Kelly laid out on the table, James used a gloved hand to turn the priest's head.

'I wanted you to see this; it's not cause of death but it does explain how he was able to incapacitate them quickly. I checked and the other priests have the same marks. I would say from this that they knew their killer for them to be able to get close enough to do it.'

'Oh pity me miserable wretch that I am! I dared not speak – I dared not speak! We have put her living in the tomb.'

'Ah … Mr Edgar Allen Poe – *Fall of the house of Usher*, I do believe,' Sean said.

'Exactly that – entombed alive, just like our man here,' James replied.

Sean leant over the body, the face of Father Kelly in a rictus grimace still, the removal of the lips making it look like the corpse was grinning. Hands clawed, facing upwards, the finger tips bloodied and in places missing.

'Good job we don't need his finger prints for identifying him,' Sean smiled and then, sighing, he waved Connor over. 'What do ye see?'

Peering over Sean's shoulder, not wanting to get too close to the body, Connor's eyes opened wide.

'Burn marks? It looks like he used a stun gun, sir.'

'Easy enough to get off the internet nowadays … anything else, James?' Sean asked.

'I have got the full autopsy to do yet but you can have a look at the other two if you want. I have been a bit busy in case you hadn't noticed! I have this detective that keeps finding me dead priests to look at.'

Laughing, Sean said, 'Yeah, he's a pain in the arse, isn't he?'

Taking two folders from James, he thanked him and to Connor's relief they headed out of the morgue.

Settling back into his chair with a mug of steaming coffee in his hand, Sean looked at Connor.

'Well, ye could be right, Connor. If they used a stun gun to incapacitate them, it could easily be a woman … nothing can be ruled out at this stage. We have two connections: one, they are all priests, and two, they all worked together at some point. Let's see if we can find any other connections linking them, anyone that they all knew; it could even be another priest. My guess is that it's revenge killings and it usually leads us towards the inevitable when it concerns priests.'

Before Connor could reply, a young garda poked their head around the door.

'Excuse me, sir, I have had a missing person's report come in.'

'Don't tell me a missing bloody priest?' Sean almost shouted.

The garda looked confused.

'Not exactly, sir … apparently, he *used* to be a priest and he was staying at St Michael's – it's basically a homeless shelter. They were concerned as he had been behaving oddly and he hasn't been seen for over a week. Seems he had been suffering with his mental health.'

The garda finished and laid a piece of paper on the desk. Sean swung his feet up onto the desk, covering the paper that had just been left, and took a large slurp of his coffee

'OK thank you. We will visit St Michael's later.' He dismissed the garda.

'I just want to put that aside for a minute, Connor, while we get a moment to look at what we already have. This is getting over our heads. If he keeps on killing priests at this rate, we will never catch up. We need help! I wonder if Steve has thought anymore about what I said about joining us again? That would be grand, wouldn't it, Connor?'

Connor nodded in agreement, pinning the three notes found with the bodies onto the board. He turned to Sean and, handing him a sheet of paper, he said, 'I couldn't find an exact match to the words in the notes but I have found a children's rhyme about magpies, not crows. I'm still looking into it but the words seem to be in the same style. Perhaps it is his own version?'

Sean started to read from the sheet Connor had handed him.

'The Magpie Rhyme

One for sorrow

Two for joy

Three for a girl

Four for a boy

Five for silver

Six for gold

Seven for a secret never to be told

Eight for a wish

Nine for a kiss

Ten for a bird you must not miss.

Eleven for health

Twelve for wealth

Thirteen beware the devil himself.'

'I remember singing this as a kid every time I saw a magpie. I crossed meself and hoped that an diabhal didn't appear. We are a superstitious lot, but I don't see the connection to crows. We had this weird kid in school that used to go around cawing like a crow and acting the maggot. We always had a bit of craic at his expense but he was a sad case really; his parents died and he went to live with the Jesuit brothers … now what was his name? Ah well. back to what we have:

"One for malice

Two for mirth

Three for a funeral"

What do ye make of that, Connor?'

'Well, each one does relate to the priest or the way that they died, doesn't it? Ye couldn't be more malicious than cutting out someone's eyes. The *Two for mirth* bit could relate to the fact that Father Feelan used to dress up as a clown for the kids' parties, a bit jolly as such. And I think that Father Kelly being found in a tomb explains the *Three for a funeral*. The problem as I see it, sir, is that we don't know the rhyme so we don't know what comes next.'

'Well done, Connor. I wish we had been invited to the funeral – we might have caught the bugger then. I think that you've nailed it on the head; he is making the deaths suit his own rhyme. I wonder if Father Murphy had seen something that he shouldn't have?'

'Maybe he did see, sir, but turned a blind eye; perhaps that is why he took his eyes.'

'Connor, you are a genius! Now all we need to do is find out what that was and why he was killed. Easy, really.'

Turning back to the autopsy reports of Father Murphy and Father Feelan, he opened the first folder and reading from the page aloud he summarised:

'Death in each case was simple: the injuries sustained during the attacks led to both priests bleeding to death. In the case of Father

Murphy, it took a lot longer than Father Feelan to die so we can assume that the person who committed the attack was comfortable and secure in the knowledge that they wouldn't be disturbed. Father Feelan was more out in the open and practically in broad daylight. He inflicted the shape of the smile *post mortem*, but he must have been covered in blood, I would have thought, from the arterial spray from the cut throat. Slashing a throat is a messy job, you know, Connor … not that I have ever tried it, but I can think of a few throats I might like to slash. I reckon he is cleaning up in all senses of the word. Can you get the team to check bathrooms and laundry bins etcetera for bloody clothing at the seminary, please?

I still think it is all about vengeance. He certainly is one fucked-up individual! I had better let the superintendent know we have a serial killer on the loose. We won't hold the press back for much longer. The only reason it hasn't got out so far is the fact that these are small rural communities. This latest one, though, was right in the city and had a lot of witnesses at the scene. Better get ready for the press again, Connor.'

One thing this did tell Sean was that whoever it was, they were not worried about being caught, or could blend in to their surroundings … now who could blend in without being noticed in a church seminary other than a priest … or someone pretending to be one? His thoughts returned to the figure that he had watched sneaking away into a building at Father Feelan's murder scene … it could be nothing, but it was worth keeping an open mind about it. There was something about the figure that didn't seem quite right; maybe it was the way that he walked? Shaking his head to try to clear his thoughts, Sean surmised that one thing he was sure of was that anyone who could perform such terrible acts of depravity upon another human being must surely have suffered themselves.

'Right, we had better go check out this missing man from St Michael's and let's hope he isn't the next victim of "crow man".'

Connor chuckled as he followed his boss down to the car park.

'You make him sound like a superhero, sir.'

'Maybe he thinks he is … he might even think he can fly … being a crow and all.'

As they were about to climb into the car, Sean heard his name called. Turning, he saw a young garda chasing down the stairs, waving a sheet of paper.

'Sir, sir! Another one … another missing priest, sir!'

CHAPTER 9

'Crow calls you to awaken you to your true purpose … to remind you to follow your heart.'

Unknown

Steve leaned over the back of the sofa and kissed Meg gently on the lips. She stirred awake.

'That's not fair! You've been on the wine! Whoever declared wine unsafe to drink whilst pregnant should be banned from a nice bottle of red for life.'

Steve chuckled. 'Sorry, love, I will support ye in everything to do with being pregnant but a nice drop of Merlot will always win out.'

'Oh, ye will support me, Steve Ryan, will you? Well, will you wear one of those pregnancy bumps for dads? So that you can share the experience of what it's like to try to manoeuvre a bloody articulated belly through doorways?'

They both laughed and, sitting up, Meg kissed him back.

'Come on love, are ye hungry? I stopped at the deli to try to find something to tempt ye. After all, ye need to keep yer strength up to manoeuvre an articulated belly about; and I have something that I want to talk to ye about, too.'

'Well, if it's about baby names, no, we are not calling them Niamh and Oisín although my daddy would have loved it.'

Settling in a chair at the table where Steve had laid out all of his purchases, Meg laughed.

'How did you know that I've been craving pickled gherkins all day? Oh, and you got some chocolate coated ones too. Did I ever tell you that I love you? Where did you get chocolate coated pickles from?'

Steve smiled and pushed the empty pickle jar and the messy chocolate bowl nearer to the sink; he tried not to laugh as he explained.

'Oh, that new shop on the high street sells them.'

Meg turned her face towards Steve. He kissed her lips, then, pulling a face, he said, 'Yuck, you taste of pickles and chocolate – not a great combination.' She laughed and poking out her tongue, she looked at his face, so open and kind; oh, how she loved this man, but she knew that he was holding something back from her, something that he had been trying to say. She was worried now; she hoped that it wasn't bad news as he didn't deserve any more than he'd already had and neither did she.

'Come on, what is it that you are not telling me? Out with it.'

'A mhuirnín, how do you always know? Don't I have the best poker face ye ever did see? Am I that easy to read? Well, that's no good in my job. I shall have all the criminals knowing what I'm thinking.' He laughed. 'Seriously, though, yes you are right – I talked to Sean today and he is desperate for help on this new case of his: the priest murders. So much so that he has asked me to come over; he needs a new DI and he knows that I am miserable where I am … I said I would run it past you but that is all I said I would do.'

'Why didn't you tell me how unhappy you were? I thought that you were glad to be back … away from the memories? What are we talking about exactly? A permanent move to Ireland, or just a temporary one? Either way, I need to consider Romany as she's settled in art college here and I couldn't just leave her alone.'

'I know, love, it was just Sean and me doing our thing and thinking about the twins growing up on the farm … I'm sorry that I said anything … it's fine.'

'No, Steve Ryan, it is not fine and you don't get to do that to me; we promised to always be honest with each other. This is how the Sara bloody Dyson stuff started in the first place, by you not telling me everything.'

'You're right, I'm sorry.' Steve took a deep breath before ploughing on. 'I am so unhappy at work, being side-lined daily by Josh Hall … he blames me for Sara Dyson's death and I don't think that I can go on working in that environment. I need a clean start but I also need to make money, what with the twins on the way, so I can't afford to upset the apple cart. So, I bite my tongue and say nothing, every day. Hearing Sean say that he needs me over in Ireland, and that an opening for a DI has come up now that Siobhan has gone left me thinking about our future as a family. I would love for the children to grow up in Bally-Bay. It's as if, finally, I need to go home … if that makes any sense? For so many years I ran away and hid from what happened all those years ago … now I have faced my demons so to speak I feel the pull of Ireland and home. Maybe it's because I am going to become a father? I promised Sean that I would mention it … but it's fine, love, truly … before ye know it I will be back with my own team and this will be in the past.'

Meg looked at Steve. He had such a sad expression; how had she not seen his suffering before? She had been wrapped up in the excitement of the babies coming and moving back home. What with Romany settling into college and worrying about any after effects that she might be feeling after witnessing Sara Dyson's death, oh God, she hadn't even given Steve a thought. Yes, she had been relieved for him when he had told her that the disciplinary board had found that he had done nothing wrong but she had barely listened to him when he came home night after night frustrated and humiliated at having to attend courses on how to become a detective when he had been a really great one for twenty years. No wonder Steve was at the end of his tether – why had she not seen this coming? The thought of moving to Ireland was not as awful for her as Steve had thought it might be. After all, with the birth of the babies in the next few months she could do with her Aunty Sian's support ... she missed her mammy so much and the idea of going back to live in her childhood home was not as bad as she had thought it would be. It was a reminder of what she was missing in her life ... her mammy and daddy and Jonathon, her twin brother. Taking a deep breath, she took Steve by surprise when she simply said, 'Yes, yes! I would love to move to Ireland ... as long as Romany is happy to move in with Becky and the boys. She can come over in the holidays and we can rent the house out easily enough ... Yes, why not?'

Steve was overcome with shock and excitement and squeezed Meg until she almost popped. Grabbing the phone, he dialled Sean's number. Romany found them shouting down the phone and laughing loudly at the confused look on her face as she entered the room. After settling down and explaining to her what had been decided, they were all relieved when she said she was happy to live with Becky and the boys if they would have her, just till she had finished college, then she would come over to Ireland to do her degree.

'I can't wait! I can babysit while Becky has a night out. She deserves a break and I can just as easily catch a bus to college from there as here.'

Steve's smile nearly split his face in two; maybe this was the new start that he had been longing for. He would enjoy turning his old room in the farmhouse into a nursery for the babies. He suddenly had a thought.

'It's a good job that the agent hasn't found anyone to rent the farmhouse yet. I will have to call them tomorrow and take it off the market.'

'And I will have to call Becky and see if she agrees to have

Romany. Then call the estate agent to get this place let.'

'OMG, Mum! I will have actual Irish siblings!' laughed Romany.

'Nothing wrong with that,' Steve chuckled.

CHAPTER 10

'Night is a stealthy, evil Raven, Wrapt to the eyes in his black wings.'
Thomas Bailey Aldrich

He watched the elderly priest point animatedly at the trees above his head from his hiding place in the bushes that edged the church and cemetery. The younger priest nodded his head at the words being spoken to him by Father Reilly. He hated being tasked with this job. He would much rather be sitting in the study by a warm fire with a cup of tea as Father Reilly dozed in the armchair beside him. He was a rather lazy and slothful person and any physical task taxed his strength. Father Reilly was insistent that all of his young curates followed his orders to the letter and didn't leave the task to the gardeners who never did the job properly or cleaned up the mess of the eggs that smashed onto the wide walkway leading up to the church entrance when the crows' nests were destroyed with a long wooden pole.

Father Reilly detested the crows – the sound of their cawing and the mess that they made on the walkway. But every year they returned to nest in the tall trees that lined the avenue, as if to torment him. It was catching them at the right time. He prided himself on knowing the exact time to have the nests destroyed. Too early and they would re-build the nests, too late and the babies would have hatched and flown. He knew the exact moment when the eggs were laid and resting in their cosy feathered roost high up in the tree tops. An old farmer had told Father Reilly once how you could tell what kind of summer you would have by where the crows decided to nest; if the nests were made at the top of the trees, a fine summer would ensue; if nestled further down the branches, a wet and windy summer was forecast. The farmer hated the crows as much as Father Reilly as he lost a large portion of his crop to them every year.

He watched the priest give his instruction to the younger man as he had been given them himself years before. His mind returned to his childhood and he smiled to himself, remembering how his father never understood why the mawkin, or scarecrow, that he had made was always covered in crows. Little did he know that the boy filled the mawkin's shirt with seed every time that his father turned his back. He would watch them feed from his spot on the hill. The words to a rhyme came to his lips once again and he repeated them softly:

'One for the pigeons

One for the crow

One to rot

And one to grow.'

He always made sure that his crow brothers were fed well. He watched in disgust as Father Reilly made his way back to his soft armchair by the fire, leaving the younger priest to follow out his orders. Waving the long wooden pole with a hook on the end, he started poking at the nearest nest. Tears slid down the watcher's face as he witnessed the destruction, the sight of the pale blue eggs falling to the ground and smashing whilst the distraught parents dived and swooped at the black-robed figure.

Making his way around to the back door of the church, he knew that he would take revenge for what he had witnessed and that the perpetrator would be busy for a while, enough time for Father Reilly to give his confession.

*

He pushed the last egg into the flaccid lips of Father Reilly; it hit against his teeth, and then stopped, resting against the egg that already lay in his mouth. He had gasped his last breath a few minutes before, after the fourth egg had been forced down his throat. What was left of his tongue had rolled back into his throat cavity alongside the eggs and it didn't take long for his airway to be blocked. His eyes bulged and a blue hue tinged his skin. Satisfied that the priest was dead, he tucked the note into the edge of the black robes and the feather into his mouth. Patting Father Reilly on the chest as if leaving a dear friend, he made his way out of the building. As he hurried along the path, he witnessed the destruction of the last nest. The sky was filled with black forms screeching and swooping above the tree line. He looked up into the sky and called, 'Don't cry, my brothers and sisters, build your nests again; never again will your babies die, or your nests be destroyed. I have his confession, and his penance.'

Under the disguise of all of the chaotic and craven parents' calls and their railing of their attacker, he quickly made his escape. He congratulated himself; looking at his watch, he had been in, taken Father Reilly's confession and his penance in less than half an hour.

The young priest on the church pathway sighed; he hated this job and, leaning the pole against the wall of the church, he thought that he would sit with Father Reilly and have a cup of tea then finish the cleaning up later. He thought that he saw a black figure out of the corner of his eye. Shaking his head, he decided that it must have been his imagination as he headed inside to that nice cup of tea.

*

Sean stood over the body of Father Reilly.

'Now, this is just getting bizarre! You say he choked on birds' eggs? What kind of birds' eggs? No don't tell me, I can guess. Do we have the note too?' he asked James who was examining the body. Pulling a note from the priest's robes with a pair of tweezers, James popped the paper inside a clear bag and handed it to Sean, who read out: '*Four for a birth.*'

'I can't be sure which type of eggs till I get back to the morgue and run some tests, but the note looks the same as before. From what I can tell so far, it looks very much like he choked on the eggs as they were forced down his throat. Look – there is some bruising each side of the jaw, but I will know more later.'

Turning towards Connor, Sean asked him, 'Where did you put the priest that found him?'

'I left him in the church. He was a bit of a mess, not making a whole lot of sense. Saying something about the crows' nests; I think he's in shock, sir.'

'Well, let's go and talk to him and hope that he saw something. I am truly stumped; it just gets stranger by the priest. This is number four so I think we can safely say that we have a serial killer who hates priests on our hands … don't you agree? All I do know is he also is very fond of rhymes, or at least one particular rhyme.'

Sean approached the young priest who was sitting with his head in his hands at the front of the church. Sean couldn't help himself – he genuflected and crossed himself as he approached the altar. You can take the belief out of the boy, but you can't take the Catholic out of the man, he smiled wryly to himself. His own faith had sustained him through most of his life, through the good and the bad.

Discovering the appalling acts of depravity acted upon the girls and babies at St Theresa's in Bally-Bay, his home town, the cover-up by the church and the authorities in other institutions across Ireland, all done in the name of God, had sorely tested his faith, until it had got to the point of being practically non-existent. He could almost feel a certain amount of sympathy with crow man … maybe in his eyes the priests deserved to die in the most awful circumstances.

He could think of a few priests himself who had perpetrated terrible crimes against children even in his own school days under the guise of their priestly duties who deserved the same. Still, it was his job to catch whoever it was, and he was good at his job, but there was something about this case that his gut didn't like.

Reaching down and placing a hand on the young priest's shoulder, he gently spoke gently to him.

'Father, I am DCI Sean O'Dowd. Can you tell me what happened here this morning? Did ye see or hear anything or anyone strange or different than usual?'

The priest turned towards Sean, the shock still written clearly on his face.

'I was outside earlier with Father Reilly. He was giving me instructions to destroy the crows' nests along the walkway. He hates the mess they make so it is done every year … I don't particularly like to do it but Father Reilly was insistent,' he stuttered. 'He went in to make tea and I carried out the job … it was when I had finished and went inside to drink the tea that I found him … Oh dear, I need to finished cleaning up the paths, I haven't cleaned up the eggs and nests yet.'

'You can get back to your work in a minute, Father, but can you tell me did you see anyone outside whilst you were working? Or did Father Reilly have any visitors today?'

'No, Detective, no one … but I did think I saw someone out of the corner of my eye … no, it was nothing, just my imagination. I thought I saw a priest but it was probably just Father Reilly; maybe he forgot something.'

'Thank you, Father, you have been very helpful. I will leave Garda O'Brian to take your statement and you can get on with your day.'

Sean nodded to Connor then made his way outside. He started walking down the walkway that led up to the church. The pathway was strewn with the crows' nesting materials, guano, broken eggs and half-formed chicks. Looking up, he saw the distraught parent birds circling and swooping, calling out their grief at the loss of their young. Suddenly he stopped; bending down, he picked up an egg that had survived the fall intact. Rolling the egg in his hands he admired the delicate blue of the shell and the slight brown speckling across the ends, like freckles on a face. Whether it was the tiny fluttering from inside the egg or his brain piecing it all together but it dawned on him suddenly: the meaning of the words *'Four for a birth'*. Laying the egg gently back down, he instinctively understood what the killer was trying to say.

CHAPTER 11

'And may the crows feast on the unjust.'

Jim Butcher

He watched from a distance; he could see the enlightenment hit Sean's face as he pieced the puzzle together. He might understand the connection to his rhyme but he would never understand the reasoning behind it. Only the crows would know the truth; after all they had heard the confessions. One thing he did realise was that his friend the detective was not quite as stupid as he at first thought. He knew that Sean was beginning to understand, which meant that he needed to accelerate his list and if anyone got in his way, they would be giving their confession to him too.

Connor appeared at Sean's shoulder.

'Here comes James – let's leave him to it and head over to St Michael's to see what we can find out about our ex-priest with mental health problems. And we need to check out the latest details of that missing priest on the paper handed to me as we left. I also need to ring Steve. I need some bloody help here and I think I need to visit the Chief Super … Oh Jesus, Mary and Joseph; I can't believe that we have four dead priests and two others missing, all in a matter of six bloody days.' He stood back and watched as James supervised the removal of the body of Father Reilly into the coroner's van. 'My bloody to-do list is growing every time I inhale. I don't know about you, Connor, but I need a cup of tea and something to eat; I can't think straight when I'm hungry and I need to think a lot.'

Connor watched him rub his eyes and nodded in agreement. They were both exhausted: things were moving too quickly for the two of them to keep up.

'Let's go to that little café on Donahue Street for a bacon butty first, and a little breather. After all, if they have both been missing for a few days I don't think a few minutes more will make any difference.'

'Only the one with mental health issues has been missing a while, sir. The other call only came in as we left,' Connor reminded his boss.

'Well, I'm bloody starving and I need coffee,' Sean replied tersely.

Connor wondered how his boss could eat anything after witnessing the state of Father Reilly's body. The image of the popping eyes and the half-open mouth with the egg poking out on the priest's death mask had unnerved him. He couldn't begin to imagine who they were dealing with; who could perpetrate such tortures onto another human being? He also understood by now after working with the detective for a while that to keep Sean sweet and to keep his brain working he needed feeding regularly with bacon sandwiches and drip-fed strong coffee. If this didn't happen, Sean became HANGRY. He hoped that they caught a break soon as they were both exhausted and it seemed that the murderer was accelerating his kills, too.

*

Little did Sean or Connor know that while they were looking at Father Reilly's body, the killer was already with the next sinner. He had just finished sewing Father Quinlan's mouth together – his tongue now rested on the bedside table next to the glass of water which contained his false teeth. He raised the scissors and Father Quinlan saw them from the corner of his eye, descending towards him. The killer snipped the strong black thread and, satisfied, he stepped back and admired his work.

'There now, you won't be able to tell our little secret to anyone, will you? Just like you asked us all to keep yours a long time ago. I thank you for giving me your confession, Father, but I really need to leave … although we've had such a pleasant little chat.'

Father Quinlan watched in terror as the scissors plunged downwards towards him. Tucking the note into the bedclothes, the killer turned and left the room.

'Such a shame you had that stroke last year and couldn't move. I really enjoy it so much more when they wriggle.'

Placing his hand in his pocket, he felt the soft feather brush against his hand.

'Oh, I almost forgot – my brothers send their greeting, too.'

Pulling the long black feather from his pocket, he plunged it into the open eye staring up at him.

As he made his way down the corridor, he heard footsteps coming towards him. He ducked into the stairwell on the right … that was a close call. He knew that sooner or later he would be caught but he wanted to finish the task first. God had chosen him to deliver punishment to the sinners and to deliver their confessions to the sin-eater. Only he could do this, with the help of his crow brothers. Together, they wrought vengeance, with God's will, upon them all. Now he hurried away to take Father Quinlan's confession to the crows, along with his forked tongue, and to receive the next sinner's name. He was ready to move on quickly to the next one; the problem was, he needed to wait to receive their name.

Stepping over the body of the young nurse helper, left where he had removed her to get to Father Quinlan, he felt sorry that she had to die but nothing must be allowed to get in the way of his progress. As he rushed down the stairs, he heard a familiar voice.

'So, no one's been in to see Father Quinlan this morning? You say he has had a stroke and is unable to move, so why do you believe him to be missing, Father?'

'Well, Detective, the nurse always has him up, dressed and down to breakfast by now. When I checked his room earlier his bed was empty and there was no sign of his nurse. So, with everything that has been happening, I thought I had better give you a call. This is his room. As I said, it's empty ...'

He heard the door open followed by a gasp from the priest and DCI Sean O'Dowd. Chuckling to himself, he tiptoed quietly away down the rest of the stairs. Father Quinlan was laid back in his bed, the nurse's body sprawled across the floor as a pool of blood spread from a wound to her stomach. Bending down, Sean quickly took her pulse; her body was still warm but she was definitely dead. Turning around, he asked Connor to call James. Taking in the room, Sean's eyes alighted on the bathroom door. Rounding on the priest, he snapped: 'Did anyone not even think to check the bathroom when they looked into the room earlier?'

The priest stumbled on his words.

'I, I thought Father Peter had ... or one of the nurses.'

'So, how did ye know he was missing? For God's sake, forgive me, Father, but the killer must have been here the whole time with Father Quinlan, seeing as he had finished off the nurse. We probably only just bloody missed him.'

Sean's angry words reflected the frustration and helplessness that he was feeling. He knew that if the killer had been disturbed that he would most likely have killed that person, too. His anger was also directed at the killer himself, not for killing the priests but for interrupting his bacon butty. Before he could take his first bite, his phone had rung with yet another call about a missing priest. Also, because he would have to go back to the station and explain to his superior why he had the bodies of five, yes, bloody *five* dead fucking priests bodies in the morgue and not an inkling of who had killed them, but he now thought that he knew why.

CHAPTER 12

'For pride, avarice and envy are the three fierce sparks that set all hearts ablaze.'
Dante Alighieri

In the depths of sleep, his body twisted and turned, sweating and tormented as the images came in colour. Just as the film had that was playing at the picture house that day. He had stolen a shilling from his daddy's pocket when he had fallen asleep, in the drink as usual, and the boy knew that Father Benedict wouldn't wait for him as he very rarely had the chance to attend the film trip that was organised for the children on a Saturday morning. He raced through the village, his legs thumping as hard as his heart, and there to his relief stood the small school bus. The bus was past its best and held together with rust and a prayer. Black smoke belched out of the back as the driver revved the engine impatiently. Father Benedict smiled at him.

'Good to see ye today. I hope yer mammy and daddy are well; come on then, in ye go.' He lifted the boy onto the bus and followed in behind him.

The boy scanned the already full bus and Father Benedict pushed him gently forward.

'Come on then, find a seat. Else the film will be over before we get there. Steven Ryan, Sean O'Dowd, move yerselves over and let this lad squeeze in now.'

The boys were not happy but would never dare disobey Father Benedict or else they would be thrown off the bus. They moved over on the seat and made room for the boy. He was as reluctant to sit with his two worst enemies as they were to have him sit between them but nothing was going to stop him from going or enjoying this day as he knew he would pay for it later.

Digging an elbow into his side, Sean whispered into his ear: 'You stink and if ye so much as make a crow noise, I will beat ye black and blue, so I will.'

And just for good measure in case he didn't get the message, Steve dug his elbow into him on his other side. Smiling to himself, he didn't care. Nothing they could ever do to him could possibly be worse than what he received at home, and he was going to enjoy every moment of *The Lone Ranger* despite them all. Feeling the shilling in his pocket, he hoped that he might have enough for some sweets too or even an ice-cream in the interval. Nothing and no one was going to spoil this for him and he beamed at Sean and Steve.

'Yer bloody crazy, so ye are. I swear yer touched in the head,' Sean scowled.

His face shone as the film ended; he didn't want to move and he certainly didn't want it to end. He had never experienced anything like it in his life. The action seemed so fast and the characters so real and he never wanted to leave ever.

'Come on, now, or shall we pick ye up next month when we come again?' Father Benedict smiled; he could see how much the boy had enjoyed the experience as his face was split wide with the most enormous grin he had ever seen. Suddenly, the grin slid from his face.

'Daddy will not let me come again, Father. I will just have to remember every little bit. Tonto was me favourite, Father, I liked the feathers in his hair … like the crows.'

He woke with a smile still on his face at the memory of that day, one of a very few in his childhood that he could say was spent in pleasure. The day returned to its usual torment as soon as he arrived home to face the music. Still … he reflected on the awe and excitement that he had felt watching the film. Finding in himself a sense of belonging, there amongst the other children, as he joined in with their united laughter and joy if only for a couple of hours. For once he had a feeling of normality… a feeling of being the same. Looking up, he even managed a smile from Sean and Steven … even if it was because they were laughing at him; he didn't care. Today … today it was different.

He had awoken for once in a blissful state of happiness, the smile still plastered to his face even as the memory faded. Swinging his legs around, he started to get dressed. Standing, he put his hand into his pocket as if he could still feel the shilling in his hand from that day long ago. He remembered another day, too, when he had received some money for his birthday. This happened now and then: the parish fund would organise a small party once a year and all of the boys received a shiny new sixpence. He could still feel the pattern on the small coin as he rubbed his thumb over it. He loved the thistle printed on the front – it reminded him of the fields in Bally-Bay. He also remembered Father Byrne and immediately he understood the reason for his dream. Some of the older boys in the seminary would hide their parcels in the younger boy's dormitory. He never understood why until he himself became older and he would watch as Father Byrne confiscated the goodies sent by loving mothers to their sons.

Later, he would witness through the crack in the door Father Byrne tucking into the cake and biscuits meant for the boys and jangling the coins in his pocket that he had stolen from their parcels. Coins that had been sent by caring parents and in some cases saved with some difficulty, through hard times, to send as a birthday gift.

He was never one of the lucky ones as he had no one to send him any gifts of money or otherwise, but he felt the resentment from the other boys who did as they watched Father Byrne stroll around, claiming whatever he wished from their parcels. The same thing happened to the parish party sixpence – gathered up by Father Byrne as fast as they were given out by a kindly lady for safe keeping.

It was on one particular day that he had just been handed his sixpence and was in the middle of holding it up to watch the sunlight glint off the tiny coin as he turned it in his fingers only to have it snatched away by Father Byrne. He protested loudly – it was only the second time in his life that he had ever had any money to hold, the first being the shilling he had slipped from his father's pocket to pay for the picture house. He wasn't going to let it go without a fight. The woman had been about to hand a coin to him, the last boy in the row, when Father Byrne turned suddenly and muttered that the boy was a terrible fumble fingers and had dropped his coin already so he had better look after it for safe keeping and had then tucked it into his jacket pocket.

His anger was palpable … how dare he steal his money? He was about to jump onto Father Byrne's back and pummel him with his fists, but was held firmly by the two boys either side of him.

'Don't even think about it or we will all be punished!' they hissed into his ear, and the grand lady and Father Byrne passed serenely by.

Now, twisting his hands together, he felt every emotion from that moment wash over him. The joy, the happiness as he saw the shiny coin in his palm, then the humiliation and anger as it was snatched away from him. Well, nothing was going to hold him back this time; he was off to catch a thief. Just like Ali-Baba, he thought to himself except he was dealing with one thief not forty. God's message was loud and clear: 'Thou shalt not steal'. Father Byrne must be made to pay for his sins … time for another confession.

He turned to his bible, opening the book at Deuteronomy 32:21. He started to read: *'What are these vanities that have moved me to jealousy? With that which is not God; they have provoked me to anger.'* Scribbling feverishly across the pages, he wrote down his thoughts and vagaries of his mind. He would often get up and do the same in the night when awaking from dreams that battered his soul and made him question his sanity.

Only his belief that he was God's conduit enabled him to carry on.

'Six for a thief' he wrote in bold letters across the page and closed the book. He had not seen Father Byrne for many years and by all accounts his greed had caught him up. It was well known that he had indulged in the cardinal sin of greed, and his portly stature vouched for this. Not only did this obnoxious excuse for a man break God's holy commandments, but openly committed one of the seven deadly sins.

He was in a good mood that morning after he had indulged in a hearty breakfast before embarking on his little trip to Father Byrne's small parish in the village of Ennistree. He was also still holding onto the glow of his dream and the comfort that that trip to the cinema had given him for many years after. He thought a lot about a suitable punishment for Father Byrne whilst on his journey. The crows always divulged who was to be punished next and his dreams revealed why, but the *how* they were to be executed had so far been left to him. Making the punishment fit the crime had given him so much comfort; so far none of them had needed much persuading to confess their sins. He sighed; sometimes he wished that they did but he also knew that he would not then be carrying out God's will but indulging his own vanities and vengeance upon them, which would make them victims, too, something that he wanted to avoid if possible. He knew that the devil tempted him to make them suffer more, but his faith in himself to be strong enabled him to give them swift justice.

Coming up to the building, he tried the side door. He knew that Father Byrne was lax in his security and if anyone passing saw him, they wouldn't think twice about a priest entering the building, even this early in the morning. Tiptoeing as quietly as he could, he followed the small passageway to the front of the building and the hallway with the stairs running up to the next level centrally placed opposite the front door. Finding several closed doors along the landing, he panicked a little. *What if I open the wrong door?* He knew that Father Byrne had a live-in helper as he had watched from his hiding place the day before when had been wheeled about the grounds in a wheelchair. Listening with his ear to the door for any sounds from within, he opened the first one on the left which would look out across the gardens at the back. He figured that if the priest liked to be pushed around in the garden, he would want to see it from his window. His insight was correct and lying in the bed was the rather large mass of Father Byrne. He closed the door quietly behind him and, taking the gag from his pocket and the stun gun from the bag, he advanced on the sleeping figure.

He wiped the sweat from his brow. Who would have thought that this would be such hard work? Still, God had set him a challenge and nothing came easy; it always involved toil. It didn't help that Father Byrne had grown so large from his greed, so he really struggled to lift the body into the bath. Thank goodness for the hoist hanging from the ceiling. Even in a weakened state, Father Byrne had tried to struggle, making things harder. He pushed the saw back and forth through the bone. Blood still trickled from the priest's wrist wounds, but he had managed to drain most of it away as soon as he hit the artery. The bath itself, which held his body, was almost full but Father Byrne had stopped struggling after he had breathed in the bloodied water as his head sank under.

He had not waited for the bubbles to stop before he started to remove Father Byrne's hand; after all, he had to suffer, but not before he had confessed. He had led a life of greed and sloth. The vanities had been his undoing, and now he must make reparation for his sins. The bone splintered and gave way, forcing him to drop the saw into the water. It didn't matter now, anyway. He had his confession and, holding the hand in the air by the fingertip, he acknowledged Father Byrne's penance by praying for his absolution. That would make a fine meal for the sin-eater later! Making the sign of the cross, he stepped back, exhausted. Wrapping the hand in a towel, he then carefully placed the note and the feather onto the small table next to the bath after pushing the few toiletries aside, then turned on his heels and left, making his way along the dark corridor to the back entrance and silently slipping out. One thing he had been good at all of his life was making himself invisible – a valuable skill, so he had learnt.

He stepped out onto the pavement and watched the dawn sky begin to lighten and, looking down at his clothes, he slipped into a small wooded area that ran along the back of the houses via a small alleyway littered with dog shit. Trying not to step in any, he quickly pulled his wet and bloody cassock over his head and stuffed it into his bag after he'd pulled out some jeans and a sweatshirt. He needed to get going – the longer he lingered in one area, the more chance of being noticed. He hurriedly made his way along the road to the bus stop and, looking at his watch, he noticed that as usual his timing was impeccable the bus should be here any minute now.

CHAPTER 13

'Hearing a crow with no mouth cry in the deep darkness of the night, I feel a longing for my father before he was born.'

Ikkyu

Meg packed the last precious piece of her mother's china tea service into the box. She stood up and, straightening, she rubbed her back. Turning at the sound of someone entering the room, she pointed to the box and, smiling at the removal man, she said, 'That's the last one to go into storage; the rest of the boxes are coming with us to Ireland.'

Steve had looked doubtful as to whether it would all fit in the car when Meg had shown him all that she was taking with them, but he managed to cram the last lot into the boot and slammed it shut.

'Come on then, say goodbye. We have a long journey and we don't want to miss the night ferry. The removal firm will see to the rest and they'll lock up and drop the key into the agent's office.'

Steve put his arms around her now burgeoning waistline and, drawing her face upwards, he looked into her beautiful eyes.

'Are ye sure that ye want to do this, a mhuirnín?'

'Positive, come on!' She pulled his hand towards the car. 'Shall I drive?' She smiled up at him, her eyes sparkling.

'Not if we want to catch the ferry; it will take an hour to get that belly behind the steering wheel!' he teased. Laughing, they climbed into the car and drove off. Meg was tempted to look back but Steve could see the determination on her face as she kept her eyes forward and he smiled.

Meg grew weary as the miles flew by and even though they had booked an overnight ferry, the long journey took its toll. Arriving late in the afternoon the next day, Steve settled her into bed, pulled the covers up over her shoulders and he could swear that she was asleep before he left the bedroom. Unpacking could wait till later; he grabbed the car keys and headed into the village in search of groceries, forgetting that there wasn't a twenty-four-hour supermarket in Bally-Bay – something he was going to have to get used to. The shop was just pulling down the shutters as he pleaded to be allowed a quick run around the shelves. Giving him the OK, the owner called to him.

'I've done the till so ye will have te settle up in the morning. Just grab what ye need and we can sort it later.'

'But you don't know who I am! How do ye know you can trust me?' Steve asked.

'Ahh, but I knows yer face very well, Detective Ryan! Yer living up at the farm now, I hear, so I will know where ter come if ye do a legger! I shall know where te find ye.'

That was something else they would have to get used to – everyone knowing their business. He had forgotten how small communities worked. Grabbing what he needed, he rushed out of the door, thanking the shop keeper as he went. He didn't want to leave Meg for too long and he could order a proper shop online tomorrow; what he had would do for tonight. He waved at the old man as he pulled the last metal grill down over the shop window. One thing never changed, Steve thought; there would always be some little scrote trying to nick something, or smash shop windows, wherever you lived.

On entering the house, he found Meg nursing a cup of tea.

'I wondered where you had gone; I also hoped it was to get food. I'm starving.'

Steve unloaded what he had managed to grab.

'Sorry love, he was just closing up but he let me dash round and grab something just for tonight. I have to go back and pay him in the morning.'

'Wow! He is trusting! It's a pity that we didn't think to bring some of those chocolate-coated pickles with us. I just fancy one.'

Steve smiled to himself.

'Sorry, all I could grab was a cheese and tomato pizza and a bag of wilted salad leaves.'

'Well, that will have to do then. I might get Romany to get me some of those pickles and send them over.'

Steve looked stricken and mumbled something about not remembering where he had got them from. Meg took pity on him eventually and laughingly asked:

'You didn't really think that I believed that you had bought them, ye eejit? I saw the chocolate bowl and the pickle jar!'

They both burst out laughing and hugged each other tight. Steve kissed her.

'What, and ye never let on?' he asked, pulling away reluctantly.

'If I have a man who cares enough to do that for me, why would I spoil a good thing? Now, where is my gingersnap cheese cannelloni?'

They had both been through so much the last year, but they had also gained so much too, and the thought of becoming a father to twins could still put Steve in a panic. He prayed, like he hadn't done since he was a child, that he would have the patience of his father and the strength of his mother to help him cope with fatherhood. Sadness washed over him then as he recalled how the babies would grow up never knowing their wonderful grandparents. His sister, Bree, and Sara had made sure of that on both sides of the family. He also promised himself and Meg that he wouldn't wallow in what might have been but look forward to a new life and a new family. Rubbing his eyes with tiredness, he reached for the last slice of pizza.

'I'm exhausted. Let's get to bed and leave this lot till the morning.'

Meg didn't need to be told again as she had been fighting sleep for the last hour. Draining his beer, Steve dumped the bottle on the table and, turning, said, 'Race ye.'

'Ah, that's not fair!' Meg groaned as she plodded her heavily pregnant body up the stairs.

CHAPTER 14

'The crow wished everything was black, the owl, that everything was white.'

William Blake

As Meg and Steve drifted into slumber, so did the killer, until another dream prodded violently into his mind. He felt and heard the swish of the cane as it descended across his backside. He squeezed his eyes tight, so as not to see the smug look upon Father O'Grady's face as each stroke was laid on him. He could hear the whimper as it escaped his lips and the plea to Father Fitzgerald of his innocence.

'Now, are ye calling Father O'Grady a liar, ye sinful child? Do ye think that God listens to liars? Or do ye think that somehow you are special?'

'No, no, Father, I swear I'm not lying! I didn't do it.'

Father Fitzgerald smiled as the last stroke brought a scream from the boy.

'So, if you are so innocent, who did it then? Who called Father O'Grady that filthy name? Say his name and he shall be punished.'

He knew that he was beaten. If he gave a name, another innocent boy would suffer as much as he would, and also he would become a pariah to the other boys. He would be punished twice over for something that he didn't do. He looked up into the smirking face of Father O'Grady and in that moment he knew that however much he pleaded his innocence he was going to be punished. How long and how harsh depended on what he did next.

'I'm sorry, Father,' he whispered.

'Ah, the truth will out, my son, the truth will out! God detests a liar. Ye will never enter God's heaven unless ye confess yer sins. Heaven shall be forever closed to liars, son.'

He waited for the next blow to hit and the scream died in his throat as he sat up in bed, startled. Gasping for breath, the torments of the night receded slowly. He began to smile. The next two names, numbers seven and eight, had been given and, thanking God for his permission to punish them, he drifted back into a dreamless sleep.

Morning broke in two different places, each bringing joy to the hearts of two different people, but for entirely different reasons. Firstly, the killer knew that he would take as much pleasure in devising punishments for Father O'Grady and Father Fitzgerald as they had enjoyed meting it out to him and others back in the day; and secondly, Steve breathed deeply of the Irish air and felt that he had come home.

Picking up his phone that was now vibrating in his pocket, Steve answered Sean immediately. After the small talk subsided and they finished asking after each other's families, Steve arranged to meet Sean in the morning at 8am sharp.

'Enjoy yer day settling in and we can catch you up on the case when you get here. Connor is looking forward to working with you again; I haven't told him yet that it is going to be permanent but I know that he will welcome you as his new DI. I will tell him tomorrow.'

'That sounds grand, I'll see you then.'

Steve smiled to himself; it would be great working with Sean again. He had missed his friend. He pushed his phone back into his pocket and started making breakfast for his favourite girl. Balancing the tray on his arm, he pushed open the door to see Meg propped up in bed with her phone to her ear, talking to her aunt Sian.

'Yes, that would be wonderful, thank you; we'll look forward to seeing you soon!'

Steve raised an eyebrow.

'I was hoping it would just be you and me today, settling in. I don't want you to do too much and get carried away sorting things out. I was hoping to get the nursery decorated myself over a couple of weekends and the rest we can take our time at.'

'Aww, Steve!' Meg moved over and, giving him a huge cuddle, she looked him in the face. 'I know how much this means to you and I know how hard it is to let go of your parents' things. Don't forget, I have already been there with mine. But I can't live all cluttered up with two lots of furniture. I was hoping you could decide what you wanted to keep today as Uncle John has arranged to take away the rest to a charity for re-sale, if that's OK.'

Steve looked into Meg's face where only empathy and kindness were visible.

'I'm not sure that I'm ready to do this yet.'

'Yes, you are, love, because I will help you, and your mammy would love it that the babies are going to grow up in her home. Now, what have you made for me? I can smell coffee and I'm starving.'

Meg reached for the tray and Steve, knowing she was right, climbed in beside her, ready to start breakfast. He leaned over and kissed her neck.

'I know that you are right, a mhuirnín. What time did ye say they were coming?'

He reached for her and, cupping her breast in his hand, he leaned towards her. She laughed.

'Any minute now and I haven't eaten yet!' Steve pulled a face then they both burst into fits of laughter as at that moment Aunt Sian called up the stairs to let them know of their arrival.

'Another bloody thing I will have to get used to again is that no one locks the doors around here.'

A busy day ensued and Steve did not find that moving most of his parents' belongings out of the house as painful as he at first thought, so with John's help and enthusiasm the house was easily cleared. The furniture was strewn along the driveway, ready for Meg to decide what she wanted and where. Steve had decided it was probably easiest to let her choose to keep or leave whatever she wished. Except for one chair which had always been in his mother's room by the window. It was on rockers and he smiled as his thoughts turned to a memory: the sun shining on his face through the window, and his eyes closing as his mammy sang to him. He would fight sleep for as long as possible as he had longed for those moments to last, but always he succumbed within a few minutes. Unbeknown to him, his father would often come home and find them both asleep, curled up together in the chair, and he would stand watching them both with his heart full as they slept.

Steve gently lifted the chair into the nursery.

'I definitely want to keep this; I'm sure that it will be useful when the babies come.'

Meg looked up.

'Oh, isn't that perfect? And look at this, Steve!'

She held up an exquisitely sewn quilt.

'I've just found Mammy's quilt. It will go with the chair perfectly and then both our mammies will wrap them in love.'

Sian fingered the material of the quilt. -

'My own mammy sewed this over many years. Your mammy, Magda, and I would sit on the floor by her chair in front of the fire whilst Mammy sewed and I would brush Magda's hair. When she came over for Mammy's funeral, it was the only thing that she would take back with her to England.'

The day came to a close and, exhausted, Meg curled up on the sofa as Aunt Sian busied herself making the dinner. The two men lifted the last piece of furniture onto the trailer ready for John to take away. Steve turned and sighed.

'Ah, it's hard saying goodbye, Steven, but ye have a whole new life to look forward to, just as yer parents did all those years ago.' John patted him on the back and they turned towards the house, the smell of cooking churning their hungry stomachs.

Steve stood in the doorway and turned to face the hill. The faery thorn (or hawthorn) stood against the skyline, its branches a familiar comfort to him. He glanced at the two headstones poking through the grass beneath the tree and he knew then, in that moment, that he had come home. He was where he was supposed to be, in this place of his childhood where he too could make a family with Meg. Somewhere to put roots down, deep into the earth as his father and his father before him had. They had worked the land of their ancestors and here he would teach his children how to watch out for the lapwing nests on the ground in the summer and how they rose into the air, wheeling above you if you disturbed their home. He would show them how to find a curious dormouse in the hedgerow, feasting on the late summer blackberries – how sweet the taste of the juicy fruits! How if you ran to the top of the hill and breathed deeply, you could smell the salt of the Atlantic Ocean and hear its waves crashing on the rocks where the cliffs met the sea, the surf pounding, against the kelp clinging to the slate grey rocks. Yes, he would show his children the place that he loved and he would protect them from the evil that, along with the sea salt, had been hanging in the air over Bally-Bay.

CHAPTER 15

'No one is free, even birds are chained to the sky.'

Bob Dylan

He knew that he had been lucky so far; the gardaí didn't seem to have a clue. So much for the great detective, Sean O'Dowd, he thought. He stroked the feathers of the white crow that he held in his hands, the soft down parting as his fingers pushed through the leucistic feathers. The bird felt his fingers deepen the pressure and it made a squawk of protest. Cooing gently to the bird, he apologised.

'Sorry, my love, for allowing my anger to hurt you. Only the sinners shall suffer; I just need to work out their punishment. Thank you for your patience. I shall return soon with a morsel, a delicacy, a complete confession for you to eat.'

He placed the bird back inside the cage. A last look told him that he was as much imprisoned in his past as the bird now looking through the bars at him with his black eye tilted to the side. Climbing back through the loft window, he turned to the table where his ledger sat. He pulled the chair towards him and opened it to the most recent page. It was covered in writing that had been hurriedly scribbled, almost illegible; it stared back at him from the page. Picking up his pen, he carefully and clearly entered the next two names on the next blank page: Father O'Grady, and underneath, Father Fitzgerald. The pressure from the full-stop was so great that the mark had almost torn the paper.

He wasn't a patient man but he knew that his luck would run out soon and if he wanted to achieve his goal, he would have to be more careful. Last time he had almost been caught leaving Father Byrne's room; it had been a close call. He had heard footsteps and voices as he let the door close. He ran his finger down the poem till it stopped on the next two lines; skipping over '*Six for a thief*', he placed a large tick against the line and moved down to the next two.

'*Seven for a tale never to tell*'

'*Eight for Heaven*'

'*Number nine for Hell*' – Dante's final circle where betrayers met their fate for their treachery was reserved for a certain detective.

'*Ten for the devil wherever he may dwell*' would be for those left behind; they would forever be in Hell knowing that they couldn't have done anything to save the others, especially DCI Steven Ryan.

Father Fitzgerald had been convinced that by beating the sin from the boys' backsides he had reserved a place in Heaven for himself, but he had fallen a bit short. Laughing to himself at his little joke and the fact that he knew that he was destined for Hell himself along with Father Fitzgerald only made his revenge a little sweeter. As for Father O'Grady, research had shown that he was no longer a priest but had enjoyed a long life with a wife and family in Adare, Co Limerick, the seat of the Earl of Dunraven.

Quite appropriate, he smiled to himself; it was as if the name Dunraven was a gift, a sign that he was on the true path, the one intended for him by God. He was looking forward to a little trip thanks to Father Byrne. He should be quite comfortable whilst doing God's work. Picking up his mobile phone and scrolling through the pages, he found what he was looking for quite easily. He dialled the number for the Dunraven Hotel and booked a room for two nights in Father Byrne's name. Reading out the number from the credit card he had swiped from Father Byrne's bedside table, he hoped that the priest's account had enough money for a little luxury stay. He also intended renting a car for the journey from Dublin to Limerick. He could have flown into Shannon Airport and rented one there, but too many cameras. The less he was seen the better. He didn't want anyone stopping him before he had followed out his plan. No one would take any notice of a priest hiring a car unless they were looking for one. It was too far to take the bus this time.

Orchestrating a meeting with Father O'Grady had been a doddle: pretending to be an old boy from the seminary, catching up for old time's sake wasn't so far from the truth after all. Getting him to meet in a remote place would be the difficulty; he could always threaten to hurt his wife and family if he didn't come, but that was a last resort. No, he hoped that playing to his ego would be enough. Smiling now, his face was almost as smug as the last time he had seen Father O'Grady's when he was bent over the desk. Well, soon his confession would be his and whether he absolved him or not would depend on how much pain he could endure before death. *Yes!* An apt and fitting way to dispense justice, he thought. He also thought that Father O'Grady's sin was the worst of all of them because he encouraged another to sin along with him.

Pulling a suitcase from the top of the wardrobe, he started to pack. In his excitement, he nearly forgot the rhyme and feather. He folded the piece of paper with the line written on it and placed it with the soft black feather inside a book. He smiled as he looked at the cover: the illustrations of tortured bodies writhing in agony within Dante Alighieri's circles of hell gave him inspiration. Soon two more sinners would join them. He laid it reverently on top of the clothes and closed the suitcase lid.

He lay down on the small cot in the corner that substituted for a bed, then closing his eyes he waited and rested. He knew that he was beginning to tire; his physical body ached and he prayed for strength to carry out the last confessions. The sins of the others weighed heavy in his heart even though the sin-eater had done a magnificent job so far. He watched as the crow pecked at the severed hand now lying in the bottom of its cage. The flesh in parts had disappeared and white bone gleamed through in places. He jumped up suddenly, startling the crow, and it squawked its disapproval at being disturbed. Rushing out of the building, he made his way towards the shopping centre, his hat pulled down low over his face. He was dressed in scruffy jeans and a T-shirt that no one would connect with a priest. He hurried along the streets, head down and purposeful. An idea for his next confession had suddenly come and he thanked the lord for his help. Turning into the large department store, he was sure that he could purchase exactly what he needed in the cookery department. If not, he would try the plumbers along the road. Scanning the shelves, his eyes alighted on the exact thing that he wanted and, grabbing it from the shelf, he stopped to place an extra can of gas into the basket too. After all, he might run out before he had extracted the confession and he didn't want to have to stop before he had finished his work.

He returned to the abandoned building on the side of the derelict church that he now called home and placing the latest purchases into his suitcase, he turned to the cage. He put in plenty of water and food for the crow, then slipped his robes on and left to pick up the hire car.

If only his life had been different. An *if only* moment of an imaginary happy life that lasted for a second before the laughter bubbled up from his chest, into his throat and spilled from his mouth with the force of a river. Such ridiculous thoughts only served to strengthen his resolve; after all, which saint could anyone name that had not suffered terribly? He was doing God's work and if he happened to get some kind of justice for himself at the same time, who was he to argue with God's plan? He turned up the car radio and started to hum along with the music.

This time he hoped that he could take some time with Father O'Grady. Although he'd never actually laid a finger on the boys, he was often the reason for the worst punishments that they received.

He wouldn't be telling any tales anytime soon, only the one left to tell: his own confession. He wondered what kind of a father he had become as he was so settled now out of the priesthood. When it came time for him to punish his own children, he wondered if he did it himself or if he still told tales, perhaps watching as his wife meted out any punishment. Even if he had become a man of kindness and love, he needed to be punished for the sins he had committed when he held the power of life or death in his hands. Father O'Grady may hesitate to punish now – if he was a changed man – but he knew that he himself wouldn't!

Father O'Grady had turned a blind eye to the poisonous atmosphere in the seminary and the treatment of the children within its walls who should have felt protected and safe. Instead, he had instigated and encouraged the beatings – his punishment, therefore – would be just.

CHAPTER 16

'Everybody talks nobody listens. Good listeners are as rare as white crows.'

Helen Keller

Steve climbed out of the car and stretched his limbs; he would have to get used to the longer commute to work and back every day. It would be worth it; he was ready … ready for what this new case would bring, and ready for a new start. He headed across the car park to the entrance of the Garda station; it had been a while since he had been here and he was grateful to his old friend Sean and the superintendent for giving him the chance to start afresh. Straightening his shoulders, he headed through the door. Giving his name to the garda at the desk, he was soon passed through into the inner workings of the busy station. He followed the corridor through to the back as instructed and he could hear his friend's voice before he could see him. Sean was cursing as usual about the severe lack of coffee and staff as he entered the room.

'Nothing has changed then?' he asked. 'Sean still surviving on strong coffee and is a grumpy shite in the mornings?'

Connor suppressed a giggle as Sean turned to Steve and in a stern voice said:

'That will be grumpy shite Detective Chief Inspector to you, DI Ryan!'

Laughing, the two friends embraced and Steve gratefully took a cup of coffee from Connor.

'It's good to see you too, Connor. I hear Siobhan has moved on? Good luck to her. I'm glad we have the old team back together, though.'

Without any preamble, he asked, 'So what have we got, then?'

'Well, we won't have our Connor for too much longer. After he gets through his exams, he will be off after Siobhan to Dublin, I expect. What we do have is a lot of dead priests.'

Turning to the board, Sean quickly caught Steve up on the situation.

'So basically, you have a serial killer who has a great dislike for the clergy, one dead nurse, five dead bodies – all of them priests – and one ex-priest missing … correct? Any ideas yet? Apart from the obvious that he or she hates priests?' Steve asked.

'We have five priests and the only connection that has been found is that three of them taught at the seminary in Dublin. Father Murphy as you know lives in the small parish of Mornside next to Bally-Bay and has been there for years. The nurse, poor thing, just got in his way we believe. We have two of the autopsies back. As expected, they died of the injuries inflicted on them. We are still waiting for the other three from James. One thing he did show us was that all three of the first lot of bodies had been stunned first; I expect he will find the same on the other two as well. Probably to quieten them while he worked on them and boy, did he do a job on each one!

'He seems to have a macabre thing for crows and rhymes. *He* – we think it's a he merely because of the physical strength needed to commit each crime but we are not ruling out it being a woman. For the purposes of ease, we will call them *he*. He makes the mode of death suit his rhyme. He leaves us a line of verse and a feather on the body. The problem is we think that only he knows the rhyme; the closest we can find to it is that childhood one about magpies.

'He doesn't leave any DNA at the site which shows us that he has an awareness of crime scenes and he drifts in, does the job, then out again like a ghost. You would almost think that they were professional hits, but I think it is personal, some kind of vengeance killing. He also removes something from the body … a body part, so to speak. We have had eyes, tongues, lips, all removed from the body and the scene.' Sean sighed and slumped back in his chair. 'Not a lot really, nothing to go on; perhaps your fresh eyes can bring something new to the investigation.'

Steve flicked through the sparse paperwork of the case.

'Let's hope so although looking at what you have already, I doubt it! The problem we have is he is on a crusade and only he knows why, when and who. Each kill is different, the wounds inflicted vary. How are we sure that it is the same killer each time? As far as I can see the only thing connecting them is that they are all priests and also a tenuous link that some of them worked together years ago. For all we know it could be a gang of them … all killing priests.' Steve frowned at the pictures of all of the priests on the board as he finished speaking.

'Well, thank you for that bloody insight, DI Ryan! It's bad enough that we are looking for one bloody killer let alone a whole fecking gang of them. We had a call about another body. A Father Byrne – perhaps you could go with Connor to check it out whilst I go visit the super to bring him up to date? The ex-priest with issues can wait for now; let's concentrate on them one at a time and hope no more reports come in while you are gone. Give me a call when you get there. Father Byrne was quite elderly, just as all of them have been, and has been living in the small parish of Ennistree. Meet back here for an update in three hours after I have seen the super and I will pop down to the morgue to see if James can tell us any more. Oh, and bring us back a sandwich; there is a nice village bakery in Ennistree. I shall need something after a visit to the morgue. Now, bugger off.' Sean picked up his mug and, taking his coffee with him, he tapped on the superintendent's office door.

Steve and Connor looked at each other then they both burst out laughing before heading out of the door.

'I think our Sean is in great need of a bacon butty, don't you think, Connor?' Steve said and they laughed again. When they reached the front desk, a young garda called to him.

'Excuse me, sir, you might need this if you are going out.' He handed Steve a badge inside a wallet; it had been a while since Steve had held a badge with the gardaí. He held it open in his hand and read *City of Dublin Western Division* stamped on it. Staring at it, he tucked it into his pocket.

'That makes it all real somehow. Do ye mind if I just call Meg before we leave, Connor? I will be quick. I just want to check she is OK.'

'Oh yes, of course. Congratulations on the babies, sir, and welcome aboard.'

After calling Meghan and checking in, Steve felt more on top of things. He was excited to jump into the investigation although what he could actually add to it as yet he didn't know. Sean had covered all of the basics which was actually an incredible feat given the short passage of time and the number of staff that he had. Back in Cambridge, he would have had a team of at least five not including himself. He had forgotten how good Connor was at the mundane research and as they got into the car, he praised him on his work.

'Sean is the messiest of workers but he has an amazing brain and is an excellent detective. Thank goodness he has had you to sort the paperwork and get the board up and running. I appreciate your organisation skills, Connor; I hope I can be of some help even in a small way.'

Entering the address for Ennistree into the sat nav, he pulled out of the car park. He chatted to Connor on the way and asked him to describe each of the crime scenes in as much detail as possible. He stopped him several times to ask questions but generally wanted an eyewitness view, a first impression. As they were driving, a call came in over the radio: a young priest had called in to ask when someone would be coming as he had discovered Father Byrne's body in a bathroom over three hours ago.

'Oh well, Connor, looks like I am going to get my first look at the priest killer's latest crime scene for myself.'

'Well, I'm warning you, sir, he certainly does a good job. I didn't think I was squeamish until I saw his handiwork.'

'Well, ye don't have to come in on this one if ye need a rest but saying that, I would really appreciate a second eye on the scene if ye can bear it. Can ye also call James and tell him we have another customer for him?'

They arrived to a flurry of activity at the scene. A young priest was sitting with a blanket around his shoulders, shivering in wet robes while a woman was handing out tea.

'Good morning. I'm DI Ryan. I presume that you are the person that found the body? Do you think that you could show me where it is? You seem to be wet; I heard mention of a bathroom. Was it flooded?'

'I got soaked trying to pull Father Byrne from the bath; it was horrible! The water was full of blood … why … how could *anyone* –?'

'So, you touched the body, Father …?' queried Steve.

'Father Ryan, actually. Err … like yourself, Detective … Yes, I tried to lift him out but he was too heavy. At first I thought he had had an accident … but then I saw the arm.'

'Well, we will probably need a DNA sample from you to eliminate you from our enquiries but the water might have contaminated it. I will leave it to the forensic team if they wish to take one. Are ye willing, Father?'

'If it helps, of course.' He pointed to a door. 'If you don't mind, I won't come in again.'

'No, that's fine we can take it from here, thank you, Father …'

After all, you have already contaminated our crime scene, Steve mumbled under his breath. Connor, catching his words, smiled but the smile soon disappeared as they entered the room.

Lying on his back, half in and half out of a bloody water-filled bath tub, was Father Byrne. He was completely naked and obviously dead. Water had splashed onto the floor but whether from the struggle with the killer or the attempt by Father Ryan to remove the body was as yet unknown. Hanging over the side of the bath lay Father Byrne's arm. The forearm just above the wrist had been amputated and by the look of the raw uneven edges of the wound it hadn't been done with any great skill or care.

Steve stood back and surveyed the scene.

'What do ye make of that, Connor?' he asked the young Garda.

'Personally, I would say we definitely have another one on our hands. … pardon the pun,' he said, pointing to the missing arm. Steve smiled to himself; young Connor seemed to be picking up Sean's sense of humour. It was the one thing that they had found helped carry them through investigations that were so horrendous such as this one was turning out to be. The thing was, Sean was so much better at it than he was. Connor continued speaking.

'It seems to be the same killer. There have been missing body parts from all of the kills and I can see a black feather and what looks like a note on the small table beside the bath. One thing, sir, he must be extremely strong to lift a man the size of Father Byrne. It certainly seemed that the priest likcd to indulge.'

Steve raised his eyes towards the ceiling.

'I think you might find that might have helped a lot,' he said, pointing to the electric hoist and rail which ran across the ceiling. Connor hadn't noticed it before. *Observation!* The one thing he was still learning about in his quest to be as good a detective as Sean and Steve … it seemed he had a way to go. Steve noticed the despondency in Connor's face.

'Don't be too hard on yourself, now … there is a lot to take in with this scene.' As he finished speaking, James arrived with his small forensic team that consisted of two other people.

'Ah, Steve so good to see you again! I thought that you had come to keep that partner of yours in check, not join him in finding bodies.'

Steve smiled. 'I will leave ye to it. Do ye think it's the same as the others on first impression?' he enquired.

'Too early to say but at first glance I would say yes.'

Moving over to the letter and feather, he picked them up with tweezers and placed them into a bag and sealed it up.

'Well, he seems consistent. *Six for a thief.*'

He held the note up for Steve to read. Pursing his lips tightly together, Steve looked once again at the bloated body of Father Byrne and the raw, hanging mess where an arm had once been …

'That might explain the missing hand; in some countries the punishment for theft is losing a hand,' he uttered.

'That's barbaric!' said Connor.

'A thief might steal from anyone; *why* he is stealing from *you* is what you need to understand,' quoted the pathologist with a smile.

Steve nodded to Connor and they headed back out to the car to leave James to do what he did best, informing Father Ryan on the way that someone would be back to take a statement from him tomorrow. Climbing into the seat beside Connor, Steve mused: 'It takes some kind of a person to hack off another one's arm. Perhaps he has medical or butchery training, but to be honest it wasn't done very professionally.'

'I think we are dealing with some sort of madman, sir!' Connor replied.

'He or she might be quite mad, Connor, but we should never underestimate someone who has managed to kill six priests right under our noses and leave us without a clue,' Steve replied.

'If we want to be politically correct, sir, we should call them *they,* not *he* or *she*. I have just been on a course where we have been learning about gender fluid and non-binary personnel and how to correctly address people according to their wishes,' Connor replied.

'Well, for Jesus' sake, don't mention it to Sean! He has enough trouble addressing anyone with anything other than a grunt,' Steve smiled.

On their return, they found Sean slumped in his chair with a frustrated look on his face. After explaining what they had found and the condition of Father Byrne, his frown increased.

'So, we have a sixth priest murdered by the same person. The Chief is talking about bringing in the big guns from Dublin if we don't make any progress in the next forty-eight hours. I told him that now you are here we will have it solved sooner.' He turned to Steve smiling. 'Well, I hope you have more bloody idea than I do at the moment?'

'Sorry, Sean, we have been discussing it all on the way back and unless he slips up forensically, or we get an eye witness, we don't have a hope in hell.'

'What did James have to say? At this stage, anything that can help is welcome.'

Steve patted his friend on the shoulder as Connor passed him a cup of coffee. Connor had already placed a copy of the latest rhyme on the board against Father Byrne's picture.

'James didn't have a lot of time to talk but said that as all of the bodies had been stunned first, he expected that Father Byrne would prove to be the same. He found no fibres, prints or DNA on the bodies that couldn't be accounted for and that all of them had died of the injuries inflicted on them. Each received a line of the rhyme and a corvid's feather was placed at the scene. He identified the circular mark on the catacomb floor at Father Kelly's crime scene as possibly from a metal bird cage – the shape and form of the marks fit. He also found droppings from …' Sean picked up a paper from the desk and read from it. '…*Corvus corone* – a carrion crow – on the floor. This also ties in with the three crows' bodies found inside the tomb. The single feathers left with the notes from this and all of the other killings plus the eggs from Father Reilly's were from *Corvus frugilegus* or the common rook but both birds are from the *Corvidae* family. According to James who apparently is a bit of a twitcher, the carrion crow lives mainly in suburbia and is usually a loner, and rooks mostly live in open fields and woodland. Both nest in tall trees and do so in social family groups. He thinks the carrion crows were caught and starved before being placed in the tomb with Father Kelly. Either way, all it tells us is that he has a bloody crow fetish and hates priests.'

Sean slumped back into his chair, looking despairingly at Steve and Connor.

'So, can we just re-cap?' Steve asked. 'We have six priests, all murdered and no forensic evidence to help. Father Murphy – eyes poked out, found in the confessional. *One for malice*. Possible motive – looking the other way. Father Feelan – throat slit, clown's nose on face, found in the grounds of St Patrick's Seminary College. *Two for mirth*. Possible motive –interfering with boys whilst dressed up for events. Father Kelly – beaten and buried alive in a tomb in the catacombs of Maynside parish church, eaten by crows placed inside the tomb with him and eventual suffocation. *Three for a funeral*. Possible motive – unknown as yet. Father Reilly – choked to death on birds' eggs forced into his mouth, found at home in his parish. *Four for a birth*. Possible motive – poking out the nests and killing the crows along the path, hence the eggs. James confirmed that crows eggs were used. Father Quinlan – had his tongue cut out and bled to

THE PRIEST: A CONFESSION OF CROWS

death, stabbed with scissors, mouth sewn shut, found in bed in his care home in Ennistree. *Five for a secret.* Possible motive –keeping a secret, or not, as the case may be. And last but not least, Father Byrne – had his hand removed just below the elbow, found at home in his own bath. *Six for a thief.* Possible motive – some countries remove hands for stealing but theft of what?

'I think it's pretty self-explanatory and clear that the rhyme foretells the mode of death for each murder, but what is unknown at this time is what slight they are being punished for and whom it was against. We have one tenuous connection to them all … Connor, have you managed to confirm that they all, at one time, worked together in later years? Some also taught at the seminary and some retired to their own parishes. They are all fairly elderly now so I would assume that they are being punished for whatever took place a long time ago. I don't think the killer has finished his poem yet so maybe we should concentrate on finding any other priests still alive that were with this lot.'

He pointed to the list of names on the board.

'I am working on that connection now, sir,' Connor replied.

'Well, it's certainly a puzzle,' Steve said. 'But it'll have to wait till tomorrow as I have a very pregnant lady who needs feeding; she is a nightmare when she is hungry, almost as bad as Sean. It's as if she really is eating for three. I will see you all bright and early.'

Picking up his jacket from the back of the chair, he headed for the door.

'Don't forget the chocolate pickles,' Sean called after him.

Popping his head back around the door, Steve replied, 'She bloody told ye!'

'Yes, she did.' Sean and Connor burst out laughing.

'Et tu, brute?' Steve said to Connor, smiling.

103

CHAPTER 17

*'It's better to fall among crows than flatterers, for those devour only the dead –
these, the living.'*

Antisthenes

It was dusk as he placed the bag inside the boot of the car.
Turning, he took a deep breath in as he watched the sky turn
colour. He looked back at the hotel, the windows lit making it seem
warm and welcoming. Where he was going would not be so. He had
slipped the cassock back over his other clothing to keep up the
pretence of being Father Byrne. The collar seemed to cling a little
tighter and he put his finger under the white stiff plastic tab collar
and wiggled it. He was excited for the night to come; he had his
fingers crossed that the former Father O'Grady would keep his word
to meet at the castle ruin. He had worked hard to convince him that
he had a package from his old friend Father Fitzgerald and that time
was limited as he was passing through so he could not dilly dally.

'To be sure, he had begged me to bring it along for him. He sends
his kind regards, and as I am not stopping, the pull-in that serves as a
car park for the castle ruin is the most convenient. I can always return
it and wait until another person is passing to bring it for ye if it isn't
possible to meet me at such short notice. The last thing I want to do
is be a nuisance now.'

He thought back on his words; curiosity killed the cat, so they
say. Let's hope that this time it does the same to a priest, or ex-priest.
He wanted to arrive a little early to put some items in place and to
check out the remoteness of the place. *Google Earth* had given him a
fairly good idea how far he was from the road but he also needed to

make sure that he wouldn't be disturbed. Pulling into the quiet lane that led to the ruin, he smiled to himself. It was perfect! The ruins were approximately fifty yards from the end of the pull-in and if he went right to the end, he was completely hidden from the road by tall hedges and trees. After all, it would be a slog to carry Father O'Grady's body very far. He hoped that he wasn't as heavy with sin as Father Byrne! He was happy – he couldn't have planned it any better. He got out of the car and, taking the bag up to the ruin, he hid it behind a large fallen rock. Suddenly, a small light caught the corner of his eye and he ducked down behind the rock. He watched as a dog walker came ambling along the track further down the hill on the other side. He held his breath; he didn't want to be seen. He hoped that the dog didn't catch his scent. Luckily for him, the owner called the dog in the opposite direction. He watched tentatively as they passed out of sight over the crest of the hill. No sooner had he moved position than he saw headlights making their way along the small lane. Climbing down from the rocks in the ruin, he made his way towards the other car. Smiling, he held out his hand to greet his old adversary and torturer.

'Hello, you must be Father O'Grady.'

'Not been called that for a long time now. It's just plain old Mister, now. I'm very curious to find out what Father Hugh has sent me.' Eagerly, O'Grady stepped forward and shook the hand proffered to him. He smiled curiously – something about the face was familiar. 'Do I know ye, Father … from before, I mean?'

'Yes, I'm afraid ye do,' came the reply and as quick as a flash his hand withdrew a stun gun from inside his robes and O'Grady slumped to the ground. Picking up the dead weight, he was thankful that O'Grady had never been a large man, and as he hoisted him up and over his shoulder, he whispered, 'Father Byrne sends his regards.'

O'Grady woke to see, above him, the stars, clear in the night sky. Groaning, he found that his head hurt as he moved; what could have happened? Had he fallen somehow? His head cleared slightly and a look of panic swept across his face as he remembered … something about a priest? Suddenly he screamed as he felt his arms jerk upwards and his shoulders seemed to be pulled out of their sockets. He looked up and saw a rope attached to his wrists and he was being hauled upright, against a stone wall.

'Perfect; you're back with me just in time for some fun. Now, we can't have you making lots of noise while you give your confession, can we?'

'I know you!' he mumbled as he felt a piece of cloth being forced into his mouth and another placed around his face and tied tightly at the back. He could hardly breathe and was finding it hard not to gag on the cloth in his mouth.

'Yes, you do, Father, and before the night is out you will remember lots of other boys that you tortured with your tale-telling. Time to make reparation, time for a confession.'

O'Grady's eyes followed the man, now dressed in dark clothing, as he removed something from a bag. Anger and helplessness showed in their dark blue colour, as well as puzzlement and then recognition. As the man turned to face him, this was replaced with fear and panic when he saw what he now held in his hand. The hissing sound that followed made him let go of his bowels and the stench hit his nostrils at the same time as the fire touched his flesh.

CHAPTER 18

'Deep into the darkness peering, I stood there, wondering, fearing. Doubting, dreaming dreams no mortal ever dared to dream before.'

Edgar Allen Poe

The next morning, Steve arrived to find the place in a flux. Sean was on the telephone and Connor was adding a new face to the board.

'What's happening? Do we have another body?'

'Possibly. I will let DCI O'Dowd, I mean … err, Sean, fill you in. We're not sure yet.' Connor turned, placing a cup of coffee into Steve's hand as he spoke.

'I see Sean has got ye well trained in coffee provision. Thanks, Connor, sometimes it's the most important part of the job,' Steve said, smiling. Just as he sat down, Sean finished his call.

'Morning, Steve. I don't know what to make of this one. I will run it past ye for an opinion before deciding if it's worth a trip to Adare. I have just received a telephone call from a DI Hughes from Munster southern division. He received a report this morning from local Garda that a dog walker had found the body of a man in some castle ruins near Adare.'

'Well, I don't understand the connection to our case. Was it a priest they found?' Steve said, and frowned.

'He said it was a rather horrific find, and that the dog walker is traumatised. They have never had to deal with anything like it before. It seems it's not the usual murder that they deal with as it's a rather quiet country village. The victim had been strung up and tortured, and whoever did it apparently took their time. They chose a rather remote spot so as not to be disturbed.

'They managed to identify the body from the registration of a car left near the scene. And *no*, he wasn't a priest but DI Hughes had heard about what we are dealing with here and after calling at the victim's address, the wife confirmed that her husband had gone to meet an old friend and that he had not returned, which was out of character, and – wait for it – he was also an ex-priest, a Father O'Grady.

'DI Hughes thought that it might have some interest for us as after the forensic team arrived and started to remove the body, they found tucked into the victim's clothing … wait for it again … a feather and a rhyme.'

They all looked at each other.

'He said that he would send all of the photos they have of the scene and the note etcetera through to us and we can decide if it's one of ours before they do any more.'

'Sounds like one of ours with the feather and the note but something has changed – perhaps the method of killing will give us a clue? It could just be a copycat who found out that this man used to be a priest. We need to find out where he trained and if there is any connection to the others,' Steve said.

'Connor, if you could start on that … Steve, could you take a look at the photos with me and we can make a decision whether one of us travels down to see for ourselves.'

Sean collected the paperwork that was spilling out of the printer and started laying it out on the desk. The first picture that he picked up was of a piece of paper. The words *Seven for a tale never to tell* were boldly written on it, just as all the others had been, and laid underneath it was a feather, blood still glistening on its black softness.

Steve picked up another picture. He turned it and squinted to make sure that he was taking in what his eyes were seeing. It was a figure, arms tied above the head by a rope which was pulled tight. A further picture showed it had been tied to a wooden joist sticking out from a stone wall. The metal hinge that attached it to the wall had almost rusted through but it still allowed the wooden beam to swing away from the wall. A rusty hook served to hold the rope in place and it looked to be a possible light or torch holder at one time, or even a spit to roast meat upon as the clear insert in the wall behind looked like an old fireplace.

Steve's eyes returned to the figure hanging from the beam. The latter, he thought, as he studied the picture of what was left of what once had been a man but now resembled a piece of roast meat. The flesh was charred and black in places, the fingers and toes either curled beyond recognition or completely gone; the same with the facial features. Steve threw the picture away from him in disgust.

'Yuck, this one is worse than the others! He has really gone to town on him. Obviously, his sin was the greatest of them all. Do you think that it is significant that all his identifying features have been destroyed?'

Sean picked up another picture and showed it Steve.

'See how his mouth is in a grimace? At first, I thought that was because he had been burnt, but if you look closer, I think he has cut off his lips – that's why his teeth are showing. Jesus, Mary and Joseph, the man must be completely insane.'

'I don't know about insane but his behaviour is certainly accelerating,' Steve said. 'Anyway, we are not yet sure that it is a man responsible for this; it still might be a woman.'

'Well, it must be a woman with a very strong stomach. I know I couldn't do that to anyone,' Sean said and reached for the picture, and grimaced.

'Never underestimate a woman; look at Bree, for example,' Steve answered softly.

'Yeah, but she was not the full shilling.'

'Exactly my point. Well, someone definitely needs to go down south and visit the crime scene; apparently, it's a ruin of a 13th century castle out near Adare. He chose his spot well; the only visitors to the area are dog walkers and the odd tourist stopping to take a look. It has no facilities for tourism nearby and is not heavily trafficked by the locals.'

'I know that you would rather stay nearby for Meg, Steve … so I will go in case it entails an overnighter; but I'm having me bloody coffee before I set out.'

A disgruntled Sean mumbled about bloody dead priests under his breath as Connor handed him a steaming mug of coffee.

An hour later, he popped his head into the chief's office to bring him up to speed on events and warn him of possible expenses for a night out. Sean soon found himself heading down the Naas Road and out of the west Dublin outskirts. Turning the radio down, he thought that the journey to Adare would give him some thinking time. Unless forensics came up with something, he was at a total loss as to his next move. Obviously, he didn't want the big boys from Dublin central to take over so he needed to find something, and quickly. Hopefully not another dead priest. Something was bothering Sean about the whole case; it was nagging away at the back of his mind. Every time that he thought he had a handle on it … the something… whatever it was, slipped away. The more he tried, the more it evaded him. Perhaps it would come back to him by the time he returned. It was something to do with a figure that slipped away behind the trees and a name … a familiar name but he just couldn't grasp where he knew it from. He shook his head in exasperation.

'You are getting too old, not as sharp as ye were,' he told himself, the niggling of an idea continuing to annoy him as he drove towards Adare. 'The whole bloody thing is a feckin' catastrophe from start to finish,' he exclaimed. 'Feckin' crazy!'

Steve and Connor were having similar thoughts as once again they went over the work that had already been done in case anything had been missed.

'The problem as I see it is that whoever is doing this is killing their victims so fast that we are barely able to keep up. We need a break; let's see if we can turn anything up from the statements given at each crime scene and see if anything jogs the memory.'

Steve picked up the first folder that was lying on the desk; he hadn't had time yet to fully catch up with all of the other cases. He had definitely been thrown in at the deep end with Father Byrne's case as soon as he arrived. Turning to Connor who was sitting at the computer, he asked: 'Maybe you could concentrate on finding more background on all of the priests, Connor? Perhaps there is more that links their deaths than we realise.'

'On it already, sir,' Connor called back from behind the screen.

Steve smiled at the young Garda; had he ever been that keen all those years ago? He was glad that Connor was so conscientious – he didn't think he had been so interested in his work at the same age.

In fact, Sean and himself had been a bit feckless; just counting time most days till they could get out to the pub. Perhaps that was more down to his DCI at the time who was just waiting to retire and didn't really give a shite if he solved any of the local crimes or not. He mostly left them to their own devices as they were pretty rural and not a lot of criminal activity took place. It was more about kids feckin' about or thieving from shops, plus the odd burglary. His sergeant … now, he was one to remember! He tipped back in his chair and recalled the great hulk of a man whom he had admired greatly. Then of course his mind turned to the day that changed his life for good, and the carnage that he found in the church in Bally-Bay all those years ago, and the effect this had on his life and that of many others.

Bringing himself back to the present time, he continued reading through each file while he waited to hear from Sean when he arrived in Adare. Hopefully something would jump out at him but as he returned to the third file, he didn't hold out much hope of that happening anytime soon. The rest of the day was taken up with trawling through witness statements which gave them exactly nothing new. Connor decided to go through seminary records for St Patrick's. The online ledgers listed thousands of names of would-be priests who had passed through those hallowed walls. Sean on the other hand had a long journey ahead of him. He was tired and was beginning to feel old. His knees ached in the mornings – he was nearer to fifty than forty. Driving long distances for hours didn't help and he decided to take his time with a few stops along the way. The priest could wait; he certainly wasn't going anywhere soon.

CHAPTER 19

'Abashed the Devil stood and felt how awful goodness is.'

John Milton (*Paradise Lost*)

He rolled over onto his back in the large bed and stretched; he had slept like a baby. Such comfort had beguiled him into resting a little longer than he had intended. He could get used to this luxury but he knew that Father O'Grady's body would soon be found, if it hadn't been already. He also knew that as much as he hated the detective, Sean was certainly not stupid and any sightings of a priest in the area would alert him immediately. There had been no doubt in his mind that he would be told about this latest one by the local gardaí as there had been plenty of publicity in the newspapers about the gruesome murders. It wouldn't take an idiot to put two and two together, even without his calling card note and feather.

So far, he had been opportunistic with his chances of getting to his victims … no, *victims* were what these evil bastards had left behind them over the years. No, he preferred to think of them as his missions. He had been tasked by the holy Lord himself to rid his church of the malignant evil that had been rotting away since Eve ate that apple. He was also finding that each killing gave him great satisfaction, and renewed strength and vigour to carry on. He also felt the calling of the sin-eater in his head. The pain was often unbearable and he held his ears as if he could shut out the sound of the crows calling to him. Only when he embraced the sound and elevated himself to the highest points did he feel connected to God through their voices.

'Hurry, brother, that we may feast upon the sinner's flesh,' he heard them cry in his head, above the noise of life going on around him.

He took his time showering and dressing; it had been a while since he had had access to such luxury and he found his own body odour offensive at times, only stopping to wash away the blood from himself and his clothes upon return to his eyrie. His bloodied robes from last night's adventure now lay in the boot of the hire car waiting to be washed. Now dressed and clean, he had changed into the ordinary clothes that he had packed in his case and was about to sneak out of the hotel via the back door. His stomach rumbled … what a pity that he didn't have time for breakfast. He hadn't eaten anything since he had left the city yesterday morning. Perhaps he would stop on the way home and grab a sandwich … He felt in his pocket for some change and pulled out a handful of euros. *Well, that won't buy anything much*, he thought. He put it back in his pocket again. Did he dare use Father Byrne's credit card again? He knew that the more he exposed himself to life, the easier he would be to catch. *He* wanted to be the one to choose when he was caught. He still had so much more to do and could clearly see the end. His thoughts and visions burned in his mind's eye. It burned almost as fiercely as the gas torch flame that he had used on Father O'Grady two nights ago. It was surely burning as brightly inside him as in the seventh circle of Hell.

Once free of his restraints as an ordained priest, he had been able to choose for himself how he interpreted God's words. He knew that others would think that he had lost his mind and his way … strayed too far from the path for redemption now. His thoughts strayed again to Dante: '*Midway along the journey of my life, I woke to find myself in a dark wood; for I had wandered off from the straight path.*'

Only he knew what others didn't … that God had given him a mission and as long as he stayed within its boundaries, he would provide him with all that he needed to complete his task.

He emerged from the back of the hotel into the staff car park and hoped that the exit door had not set off any alarms inside as he opened it. Passing the bins, he reached his car and threw his case into the boot and climbed into the driving seat. He only realised that he had been holding his breath as he left the village behind him and headed for the motorway entrance. Taking a deep breath, he wondered how long his luck would hold. He hoped until he had taken at least one of the detectives' lives. First, he needed to concentrate on the task at hand: his final priest. *Eight for heaven* – Father Declan Fitzgerald.

As he drove, he passed a small rural service station. Pulling in, he slipped the priest's robe over his head and stepped out of the car to put fuel into it. He was hoping to grab some sandwiches and drinks to sustain him on the journey and was sure that he wouldn't be asked for a pin number for his card when he played the bumbling priest that had forgotten it. He was right as usual – the indoctrinated populace of Ireland would never so much as question a priest. Grabbing a few packs of sandwiches and drinks, the unsuspecting man at the till had even offered to carry it to the car for "Father Byrne" as he returned the card.

'Ah, 'tis unnecessary, my good fellow. Thank you for the offer and good day to ye.'

'Safe journey, Father,' came the reply.

Throwing the food onto the passenger seat, he drove as quickly from the forecourt as was reasonably possible and headed about a mile up the road. Pulling over, he breathed a sigh of relief as he jumped out of the car and pulled the robe over his head before getting back in.

Sean, meanwhile, was sitting in his car nearby, distracted by his own thoughts and the rumbling in his stomach, meaning he didn't take a lot of notice of the parked car on the side of the road and the hastily removed black robe being flung into the back seat by a man dressed in dirty jeans and jumper. Something that he would regret missing later on.

Back in civilian clothes, the man drove off, heading back to drop off the hire car. In his rear-view mirror, he saw a car that seemed familiar to him. Panic set in … had he been seen? Was this it? He slowed a little and waited to see if the car behind him stopped and turned around. Dreading the sound of the siren and the flash of a blue light, he sighed with relief as the BMW continued on its way, the back of Sean's head distinct through the car's back window. *That was close*, he thought, and as the car climbed the incline to the motorway, he grabbed for a sandwich. The fear had made him hungrier. Tearing at the wrapping with his teeth and stuffing a sandwich into his mouth, he bit into it with delight. The adrenaline still pumping in his heart made it beat faster.

No time to waste, he thought. *I have an appointment with a priest and another with a couple of detectives.*

He flung the keys to the car through the hire firm's letter-box and hurried back to his crow friend. He had missed him and he also had a present for him. Father O'Grady had talked a lot during his confession … that was until he had peeled his lips from his face. They now lay inside the bag that he carried with him, a feast for the sin-eater to enjoy.

Watching the entrance to the abandoned church for at least fifteen minutes, he approached the large board covering the fence. Glancing up and down the street, he slipped into the gap between the old building and the fencing. He wasn't used to using the entrance during daylight hours and was usually extremely cautious. He had perhaps relaxed a little since he could feel the end approaching, so he didn't see the pair of rheumy eyes that followed his progress down the street and saw him slip inside the building.

Home at last, he made his way up the stairs to the small garret which he had been living in for the last six months. As soon as he realised that the dreams he had been having, or should he say nightmares, were actually memories that he had been blocking out for years, he had left the parish in Maynooth where he had been teaching new seminary students. He had tried to struggle on as usual, tried desperately to behave normally, when all he wanted to do was scream. His mind had been declining during his last few months at the seminary, to the point where others had noticed. He had struggled with his understanding of his life, and his faith had been sorely tested to the point where he was unable anymore to perform his priestly duties.

At first, he had been appalled by the revelations in the nightmares. Each one felt as if he was re-living the horror of that moment. It was only later when he realised that the return to his mind of these deep and evil experiences was to awaken him to God's task. Now that he understood, he welcomed each new revelation. It was his sacred message, information from the Lord, as to his wishes. So far, he had carried them out to the letter. The crows were his messengers from God and his connection to them since he was a child had now been utilised.

Dropping the bag on the floor, he hurried to the door that led to the roof garret where he slept. In his hand, he carried a bloody rag wrapped around the parts of Father O'Grady that he had offered up as his confession. The sin-eater would feast tonight as Father O'Grady's sins had been plentiful. Upon approaching the cage, he gasped as he saw the small black and white body laid on the floor of the makeshift aviary, its form stiff and cold. Sticking out from its beak was a large strip of sinew torn from Father Byrne's hand that had become stuck in its throat. He cried out as he cradled the small body in his hands, tears falling onto the now unmoving feathered breast. He sunk to his knees as the impact of what had happened finally sunk in. God's message was loud and clear: if the tasks set before him had been onerous before, at least the burden had been shared with the sin-eater. Maybe he had displeased the Lord in some way. What lay ahead of him now was much more burdensome. He realised the impact and consequences of the crow's greed. The mantle of sin-eater now passed to him and rested squarely on his shoulders alone.

Laying the small feathered creature down, he turned back inside where, sitting on the side of the small cot, he opened the parcel and, staring down at the bloody, fleshy lips, he started to recite:

'Through the holiest of spirits, may I take on your sins and may you have forgiveness in this act, as I reconcile that my soul is forever burdened with your sins. Amen!'

His hand moved gently towards his face as his mouth opened to receive the offering:

'The blood of Christ and the flesh of his body,' he muttered as his teeth sank into the flesh.

CHAPTER 20

'To hatch a crow, a black rainbow. Bent in emptiness over emptiness.'

Ted Hughes

'That is one twisted murderer!' Connor exclaimed as he threw the picture back onto the desk. 'Why, just *why*?'

'We will only know the answer to that once we catch them, I'm afraid. We are not psychiatrists and I think even they would struggle with this one. Let's try and concentrate on the next target, shall we? Hopefully he has slipped up with this latest one and we might get a break, although I won't hold my breath.'

Steve returned to the pile of files on the desk and, sighing, he opened the last one. He had found nothing new for them to work on, though Sean and Connor had done a thorough job. Sean would pick up the coroner's report on this latest murder later which could contain something to add to the rest. Steve opened the last file – it only contained one sheet of paper with a small amount of writing on it. Reading it, he frowned.

'What is this, Connor?' he asked.

Glancing briefly over his shoulder, Connor replied:

'Oh, that's the missing ex-priest reported after the second murder by Father Michael. I just chucked it at the bottom in case it was relevant to anything. Apparently, he had a few mental health issues and dropped off of their radar, but we haven't actually had time to follow up. Father Michael said he wasn't really worried as he had done this before and turned up at another parish miles away, but he hasn't been seen in the usual homeless shelters or church halls for a few weeks. He used to be Father Doyle but had a bit of a breakdown a couple of years ago and has been sort of looked after in different parishes ever since. Do you think it is something we should be looking at?' the young garda asked, afraid that he had missed something and made a mistake.

'Don't worry,' said Steve. 'We can follow it up tomorrow. We will probably find out that he is in a parish shelter by the sea with his feet up if he has any sense. Let's call it a day; my head hurts from thinking. I'm not looking forward to the drive home tonight. We've got to go to dinner with Meg's aunt, Sian, and her uncle John. I haven't spoken to them properly since … well, you know, since we had to tell them the terrible news about finding the dead babies and her sister. Oh well, at least I won't have to cook. Night, Connor.'

Picking up his jacket and stretching his back, he made his way towards the door, then stopped.

'What did you say that missing priest's name was?'

'Ex-priest – Father Doyle. It could be anything now. Night, sir.'

'Now why does that name sound familiar …?'

Shaking his head, he ducked out of the door.

Sean decided he would save all calls to Steve till the morning so his meal with Meg's aunt and uncle was not interrupted. He would text him to let him know that he had arrived safely and that the scene was as gruesome as they expected it to be – and tell him to enjoy his dinner while he "relaxed" in the mortuary waiting for the coroner's report.

On his way past the superintendent's office, he saw that the light was still on in his room. He hadn't spoken to his new boss as such since he had arrived back; he had been a tad busy. Knocking tentatively on the door, he thought no time like the present to get re-acquainted. He had met him on the last case when he had been seconded over to Ireland to help Sean with the mess in Bally-Bay. Now he was back and after only a few hours he was once again in the deep end of a murder case and loving every minute of it. He hadn't realised how bored he had been back in Cambridge after his demotion, doing mundane tasks. He had felt dead inside. There was nothing like a good killing to get his thinking muscle working again.

'Come in, for Jesus' sake!'

Steve opened the door carefully. The super sounded pretty stressed.

'Oh, Steve, it's you! Sorry about that, I was just coming to see if you were still around or had left for home. That was the bloody press office, nagging again about a statement. I can't put them off any longer I wanted to wait for Sean to get back before making a statement to the press but they are pushing for something in the morning. What do you think, have you had time to catch up?'

Steve sighed and thought carefully before replying. He understood the pressure the super was under and didn't want to add to it.

'It's certainly a complicated case, sir, and I will be honest, any help from the public would be good. Perhaps we could put out a general appeal for sightings of suspicious persons loitering about or any witnesses in the area at the time of the killings to come forward with any information, etcetera. After all, we need all the help we can get and it will appease the press at the same time.'

'The only problem with that, Steve, is the nutters will be out in force and all and sundry will be ringing in. We'll have to set up phone lines and staff to man them and that costs money.'

The superintendent looked worried.

'I know it's tough on the budget, sir, but sometimes it's worth it. At least we will be being seen to do something.'

'You're a wise man, Steve, a wise man … how is your lovely Meghan doing? The babies must be due quite soon?' the super asked.

'She's doing grand, thank you, sir, just grand. We are going for dinner tonight with her aunt and uncle. Do you remember the case of the babies at Bally-Bay and the one we couldn't identify? I haven't really seen them properly since we came back although they helped clear the house the day we arrived, but we never really had time to talk. I feel rather awkward, to be honest, sir.'

'I'm sure they will only be thinking about the new arrivals – now get off home or you will be late. I will see you in the morning. And Steve? Welcome home, it's good to have you here.'

'Thank you, sir. Goodnight.'

He closed the door behind him and thought about what the super had said … welcome home … and yes, now he felt like he *was* home.

Steve had agreed to meet Meg at Sian and John's cottage. He entered tentatively; the last time he had been there he had bad news to bring. Finding out that Meg's aunt, Sian, had also been a victim in the tragic case that he had been part of last year concerning the young girls and babies at St Theresa's had been a tragedy for them all. She had been accosted by the paedophile priest, Father Benedict, and had secretly given birth to twins who subsequentially died and were buried in the graveyard. He cast his mind back to the horrific sight of hundreds of babies' bones lying uncared for that had simply been tossed into large pits at the back of the cemetery, the little bodies piled on top of each other, year upon year. He was proud that he and Sean had found via DNA each and every one of the babies, and often the bodies of their own mothers at the site, too, and returned them to their families to be buried with love and dignity. The painstaking process had taken months to complete but the hard work of the geophysics and forensics, plus Sean and his own team, ensured not one little body was left behind or unidentified.

Taking a deep breath, he walked into the room where Meg was ensconced in an armchair, her feet resting on a stool. Her protruding stomach was heaving and moving as if in time to an unseen dance.

'Ow! Now look here you two, behave yourselves, your father's here.'

Leaning over to give Meg, a kiss he laughed.

'It looks like they are having a céilí,' he said and gestured to her belly and gave it a rub.

'Well, they have been at it all afternoon.'

He looked up and greeted John and Sian, hugging them to him. He realised how much he missed his own mammy and daddy and he could understand why Meg had needed to be near her aunt for the birth of the babies. He also realised that there was no awkwardness and Sian even showed him the small wooden box with the glass front that now resided on the shelf near the fire. It held the small rubber duck, discoloured and dirty that he had found in the cemetery where it had been placed by Sian in remembrance of her children.

'I will be forever grateful to ye, Steve, for bringing me peace. Now we can always talk about them … no more secrets.'

He held her hand for a little longer than he intended, and jerking himself out of his reverie, he said:

'What's for dinner? It smells delicious and I'm starving, ye know.'

Sian was grateful for his tact in not mentioning the subject any more. She laughed and nodded as she called John to get Steve a drink while she served up dinner.

Sitting at the table later on, his appetite replete, he looked around the room and savoured the warmth and comfort that it offered him; it felt good, it felt right. At last he was at home and he cursed the wasted years that he had not spent with his own family here in Bally-bay. He hoped that one day his children would have a happy, summer-filled childhood as carefree as his own had been. Meg had a hospital and midwife appointment tomorrow morning and he was hoping again to see the babies on the scan. His fascination with the life now growing inside her amused Meg. Perhaps it was anathema to the terrible things that he saw in his job that made that spark of life even more precious to him. Or maybe it was because he was the one responsible for it … with a little help from Meg, of course, in bringing this new life into the world.

Standing up, he pulled Meg to her feet.

'Come on, time to head back. Thanks for the meal, Sian. I think Meg was about to give out at me if I gave her any more pizza or takeaways.'

They all laughed and headed for the door.

'Oh, by the way Steve,' said John. 'Aidan Doyle sends his best. He says perhaps ye can meet at the pub one night to wet the babies' heads.'

Steve stopped in his tracks at the mention of Aidan's name.

'That will be grand. I need to catch up with everyone but I have just been so busy with this case … can ye tell me, did Aidan have a brother? I seem to remember a boy a bit older than us at school who was a bit strange named Doyle.'

'No, no brother but he had a cousin … I think he went off to be a priest after the terrible tragedy at the farm. Youse will have to ask him when ye have that drink.'

'Sure I will.'

Steve helped Meg into the car and, settling into the driver's seat, his head was a long way away … back to when he was a child with the boy in the playground that Sean and he had teased mercilessly. Red bloomed on his cheeks as he thought about the treatment that they had dished out and the guilt that he now felt. Luckily, it was dark and Meg couldn't see. She lay back in the seat with her eyes closed as a face that he hadn't thought about for probably over thirty-five years swam into his mind's eye, and shame lay on his shoulders like a weight.

CHAPTER 21

'Grief is a thing with feathers.'

Max Porter

No time left to grieve his feathered half, he placed the tiny body into a box. He deserved a burial in a holy place for the suffering that he had had to endure during his tiny lifetime and for the sin and suffering that he had swallowed to allow selfish and cruel humans their repentance. He would make sure that the bird was placed in holy ground when he went to finish his last and final service. He wondered if Sean O'Dowd had done enough in our Lord's eyes to gain forgiveness and whether he would repent at the last.

First thoughts were to re-group and deal with the last one. Father Fitzgerald! Would he be strong enough to carry out the necessary absolution? He had come so far but he had up to now relied on the sin-eater to finish the task, except now he had to do it himself. The thought of what he had just done played on his mind and he felt the need to vomit. Forcing it down, he moved on quickly to planning his next task. Turning the pages in his book, his eye caught the writing on the last page and reading it aloud to himself only hardened his resolve.

'Through me is the way into the city of woe, through me is the way to eternal pain, through me is the way to go among the lost.' Dante was right; yes, I am truly in hell, he thought.

He picked up a pen and held the book in his hands reverently. Feeling the cover, he smelled the oldness of it and the blackness of the leather it was made of. His fingers lingered and hovered over the lettering on the front, tracing the path of the large golden letters spelling out the words: *The HOLY BIBLE*. Then, turning to a page indiscriminately, he read from the book. *'And we know that for those who love God all things work together for good, for those who are called according to his purpose.'* Romans 8:28. He often found God's messages amongst the pages and this time it was no exception; he knew the glory would be his as he did God's will.

Writing the words "Father Fitzgerald" and his list of many sins beneath the name, he closed his eyes. Thoughts rushed through him and he wrote blind with his eyes shut as if God were using him as a vessel. His face lit up beatifically in the light from the lone candle that had almost burned to a stub sitting on a dirty plate. Congealed matter lay on the plate's surface along with dried blood that the flies were now attempting to investigate. The odour pungent and unpleasant went unnoticed by his nose. He did not falter, his words poured from him, let loose onto the page via the pen held in his hand. The hand that still had remnants of dried blood, now smeared and staining his fingers. Exhaustion soon overcame him, and dropping the pen, he slumped onto the small bed in the corner. He pulled the fetid blanket over him and he fell into a deep slumber.

He woke a few hours later, the taste of blood still in his mouth, looking for some water to wash the foul taste away. He stumbled across his book which had fallen to the floor.

'At least they will all understand in the end,' he thought as he picked it up. He didn't need Dante Alighieri to tell him that he had entered through the gates of Hell as he had done all that time ago, but willingly. Seven circles he had travelled and was about to embark on the eighth. Father Declan Fitzgerald waited to give his confession. The ninth gate would only be entered when he was ready to see Sean. The ninth circle was reserved for the detectives alone, treachery and betrayal being their sin. *'Abandon all hope ye who enter here.'* All hope had been abandoned a long time before, back before even his own birth but certainly since.

Cleaning himself up, he went onto the roof just as he usually did before embarking on his next endeavour. He had always before sought the company of the sin-eater before leaving. Tonight, he just sat there watching the sun sink slowly as night fell, reflecting on his achievements and losses. He had no care for his own life and knew that it was inevitable that when the time came, he would be ready to do what was needed. The loss of his companion had hurt him deeply and although he understood God's reason for taking him, his resentment was growing. His beautiful white crow didn't deserve death; he had earned his life-time over after the sins that he had to endure of others. He had been hoping to release him into the wild again where he would be able to stand up to the bullies now that he was strong. That had been taken away from them both as a reminder of who was driving this force but maybe he had shown vanity in its execution and needed to be punished for his sin. Asking God for his forgiveness, he stood up, ready to face the next one.

Father Fitzgerald opened his eyes; had he heard a noise or were his old ears and rheumy eyes playing him up? He thought he saw a dark figure move towards him … yes, there was definitely someone there.

'Who are you? What do you want?' he called, trying to rise from the comfy armchair that he had been dozing in. The blow was so unexpected that he fell backwards with a groan. Returned to his sitting position, he tried to open his eyes but was blinded by the blood now pouring into them from the large cut across his forehead. The figure spoke; he recognised the voice and confusion etched deeply into his face.

'You!'

'Yes, Father, do you remember me now? The boy that you beat till he couldn't stand up and the cuts and scars that you inflicted on me are still evident on my body to this day. Well, all of the others have given their confession so now it's your turn! I wonder what piece of you shall we take in penance?'

Before he could scream, a filthy rag was pushed deep into his throat as he was tied to the chair, each and every boy remembered as he took his confession. After each one was named, he was revived enough to say the name of the next until his heart gave out and beat no more. It was held now in the hands of his killer, still warm as he moved it toward his lips. He didn't care if he left DNA behind; he had no intention of running away from the gardaí, just avoiding them long enough to fulfil his task. Then, throwing the organ down, he pronounced the soul departed for which his sins he would bear. Washing his hands off quickly in the sink, he made his way from the darkened room. He needed to get back to the abandoned church before daylight.

Standing an hour later on the roof near the crow's cage, he held the bucket of water above his head and poured. The water trickled down over his head as the blood washed away. It had covered his body and dribbled down his chin from the heart as he had sunk his teeth into it. Taking tentative bites at first, he thought he could feel it pulse in his hand. Becoming bolder, he soon devoured most of the large organ, abandoning the rest to the floor. There was no need to take the heart with him for he had become the sin-eater.

He had no feelings left; numbness seeped throughout his body and overcame him. This was due partly to the cold water that he now splashed up his arms and across his face. He felt no disgust at himself for what he had done, just a deep satisfaction that he was now nearing the end.

A fire burned within his chest as he recollected the confession he had taken from Father Fitzgerald. A righteous all-consuming inferno raged within him. Holding his arms above his head, he called to the cawing black birds that had been his companions throughout his trials since childhood. Their blackened feathered bodies swirled about him like smoke, an Indian ink stain spreading and covering his nakedness as they swarmed over him.

Seeking their warmth, he slumped down and succumbed to their ministrations as they soothed him with the sound of their voices and nestled over his body which now was curled into a foetal position. He passed into a glorious sleep ... only to awaken in a darkened night, cold and shivering, his feathered companions long gone to roost. He must have slept the whole day away, he thought. The starry sky above him was perfect indigo velveteen, which seemed to blanket him in its glow. Time slowed, passing overhead in what seemed like eons ... or maybe just in a blink of an eye.

CHAPTER 22

'The scariest monsters are those that lurk within our own souls.'

Edgar Allen Poe

He climbed back in through the access window and found himself some clothing. Once dressed and beginning to warm up, he realised how hungry he was – after all, he hadn't eaten for twenty-four hours, the last thing being Father Fitzgerald's heart; just a small snack, he chuckled to himself. He *had* been able to do it! He smiled; he was about to indulge in the deadly sin of pride when he stopped short. He was only doing what was expected of a sin-eater, nothing more, nothing less. Pride before a fall, so they said, and the biggest mission of all lay before him.

Careful planning was needed for this one: Sean was no elderly priest. He was a hardened police officer and he was also a rather well built one. He needed a strategy that enabled him to catch him at a vulnerable moment. Sean would definitely have to be on his own as he would never in a million years tackle both of the detectives together. He had marvelled at his strength when needed, such as lifting the priests' bodies, and especially the strength that he had needed to push off the tomb lid. Luckily, he had discovered a little secret to opening the stone sarcophagus a little more easily. A catch had been installed just to release the air seal and free the lid. He thanked God for his strength and the Victorians for their ingenuity and their fear of dying. He had been able to slide the lid open enough to push Father Kelly inside. His companions were too busy enjoying the feast to try to escape. He could still hear the muffled screams as he slid the lid shut, and could see the terror in Father Kelly's eyes just before the birds plucked them out.

Edgar Allen Poe had been his inspiration for Father Kelly's "funeral" inside the tomb. He hoped that he had suffered as justice was carried out by his crow brothers for the death of his pet all of those years ago. He remembered he had been reading Poe when Father Kelly had caught him. An old and battered copy of the *Master of Poetry* had been passed around amongst the boys. It had been banned by the fathers so it was one of the books sneaked into the seminary, another being *Lady Chatterley's Lover* which all the boys enjoyed because of the sex and the swearing. To be honest, he had read *The Murders in the Rue Morgue* and been so terrified that he had never finished any of the other tales in the book. When he was caught with it in his possession, he had been about to pass it on to Patrick Thomas..

Dante Alighieri's *Inferno* was allowed and was a firm favourite of Father Kelly's. He would delight in reading passages to the boys of the Hell that they would endure if they strayed from the path. The horrific descriptions and pictures depicted within the pages of the tortures that the sinners endured was enough to scare the bejesus out of them all. In fact, they were all convinced that they were bound for Hell. The battered copy held in his hand now had once belonged to Father Kelly and it was too much of a temptation not to take it away with him for inspiration.

Running his fingers down the list of names, he recalled each one and the manner of their deaths. He felt a great freedom in the choices he had made. Although lives were taken in the name of God, he was no longer tied to the dogma of Catholicism and the priesthood. His imagination could run wild if he wanted it to, but each and every death needed to mean something for the sake of the confession or he would just be killing for his own pleasure. He had not been the only one to suffer at the hands of evil men disguised as God's servants so he needed to take their confessions for them too. That is all except

Sean O'Dowd and Steven Ryan; they were for himself alone.

He already understood that now he would never receive the rewards of Heaven; by taking the place of the sin-eater, he had condemned his own soul and was now headed for Hell. So, he would take Sean with him, and Steve too if he could. How that was to be done he was still unsure but what he did know was what method of death they would receive, and where it would occur. That is if everything went to plan, a plan which he was yet to make.

Picking up his copy of *Inferno*, he turned to the second canto and ran his fingers along the list of deadly sins on the mountain of purgatory, and compared them to each one of the dead priests. All of them had been lustful but Father Murphy had been spiteful with his *pride*, thinking that he knew better than a child. Ignorance was certainly better than the truth.

Father Feelan had abused his power by dressing as a clown to lure the innocent; his sin was *lust*.

Father Kelly had killed his pet crow with his bare hands in front of him, *jealous* of the bond between them. It had attacked Father Kelly whilst trying to save the boy.

Father Reilly's *pride* meant that he would not allow any mess from the crows on the pathway beside the church. Thus, he was an instigator of murder.

Father Quinlan had forced his *envy* of the boys' young bodies upon the boys themselves, making them keep his sordid secrets.

Father Byrne's thievery was surpassed only by his *gluttony* and greed.

Father O'Grady lied to get the boys punished; his *sloth* at tasking others to do his work was renowned.

Father Fitzgerald's *wrath* knew no bounds; he beat the boys' very souls from their bodies while telling them that they would never go to Heaven.

Each and every one of them deserved to die. In fact, he had saved them from themselves by killing them and taking their sins upon himself. God might be forgiving at judgement time … but he hoped not.

Turning back to his bible, he read from Deuteronomy 32:21:

'What are these vanities? They have moved me to jealousy with that which is not God; they have provoked me to anger with their vanities; and I will move them to jealousy with those which are not a people. I will provoke them to anger with a foolish nation. What are these vanities of pride, greed, lust, envy, gluttony, wrath and sloth?'

He knew exactly what they were: he had witnessed them as a child and as a man, and so he destroyed them in each person by his own hand.

CHAPTER 23

'Crows are not always available to give warning.'

Carlos Castaneda

Sean left the crime scene in Adare none the wiser as to how he was going to stop the killer. He had even had second thoughts about handing it over to the Dublin crew. It would have been easier to just wash his hands of it all. There had definitely been a cross-over in some areas with a couple of the killings. Somehow though he felt a deep connection to this case, a gut feeling that he wasn't seeing all of the picture, that he was missing a piece of the puzzle; he just didn't know what or why yet. His gut was not happy as something was wrong. He also knew that he had been selfish in asking his friend to give up everything to help him with the case. The last one they had worked on together had been bad enough for them both, but particularly for Steve. The babies would be arriving soon and he wanted to sort this out before family and other distractions drew his friend away. The problem with gut feelings is they are not fact based and the justice system only worked on facts

After viewing the body, which was in a much worse state in the flesh than any pictures could ever show, he read the coroner's report; he knew and understood that the killings were escalating and the perpetrator would stop at nothing to achieve his goal. What that goal was neither of the detectives had yet to grasp. What had become clear to Sean was the urgency of the case, which led him to his decision to return immediately, rather than stay over for the night. He arranged for the body of Father O'Grady to be sent on to James in the hope that he could find something that perhaps they had missed, some clue as to who and what they were dealing with. Mostly the *why*?

Finding a small café on the road home, he ordered himself something to eat and settled into a quiet spot at the back. He wasn't sure how he felt about eating just at that moment but also knew he had a long journey ahead of him. He had always prided himself on his strong stomach while others, Steve included, would heave out their last repast after a particular nasty find. He was always robust and laughed at their discomfort, heartily tucking into a large breakfast in the canteen back at the station. This time though he only managed a mouthful before pushing his still half full plate away from him. Picking up his mobile, he rang Steve's number to bring him up to date on the gruesomeness of the crime scene and his decision to return.

Steve surprised him with his next question.

'Do you remember that kid at school who we teased a lot, someone to do with Aidan Doyle … a cousin or some such? Something about him has been bugging me and I can't put my finger on it. If ye don't mind, I am leaving now to meet Aidan at the pub. I'll ask him.'

'Sure, we'll catch up when I get back. I'll go and grab a couple of hours sleep and meet you early, say 7:30am? Night … and hang on, yes! I *do* remember him! We called him crow-boy as he cawed all of the time … wait … *crows*?'

'His name was –'

Too late – Sean had lost his signal and whatever Steve was trying to tell him was lost in the ether.

Sean shrugged his shoulders; he remembered the small skinny dirty kid who stank and he also remembered how mercilessly he had bullied him, and his final act of betrayal towards him when he had told Father Benedict what he knew. He remembered the words that the boy had screamed at him in an effort to ward off the cruel jibes and punches that Sean was inflicting on him in the hope of scaring his persecutor. It wasn't so much the words that he had uttered about what he had done that scared the boy standing over him, but the truth in his eyes as they flared with hate and condemnation.

He never knew what had happened to the boy; he had never even given him a thought in all these years. He had just disappeared one day and was never missed by anyone. The adults in the small community, including his own parents, had whispered about the tragedy at the farm for a couple of weeks, out of earshot of their children, but this fizzled out as soon as Aidan Doyle's parents took over the farm and moved into the house. Why had Steve suddenly thought about him? It had been so long ago. Steve never knew of Sean's betrayal so why would he remember the boy now? Whenever the boy was mentioned, Sean had just avoided or changed the subject.

Climbing back into the car, he felt the shame crawl back over his skin, along with the feeling of fear which had driven him to tell Father Benedict what crow-boy had said to him that day. He had made a promise to Father Benedict not to reveal their conversation with anyone, including his parents, and not long after that the boy disappeared. The memory of that time seemed so distant now. For over forty years he had never even told Steve, his best friend and mucker. His thoughts returned to the conversation with Steve before they were cut off. The further away from the city, the less reliable the phone signal, even today.

He smiled to himself as he thought about the huge clunky first Nokia mobile that he had saved and saved for. It weighed a ton but it had impressed Roisin, the girl behind the bar at his local, enough that she married him, only later to find that just like the Nokia, a new and much more reliable model would soon be available. The old version didn't seem to work as before; it spent too much time at work or the pub, only returning when he was so far removed from the man she had married that she didn't recognise him.

Sean had given up the demon drink now and was well on the way to recovery after years of AA meetings, but sadly it was too late for his marriage and his relationship with his children, which he was still trying to re-build years later.

He focused on his driving now; the sooner he got back and found some answers the better. He rubbed his eyes hard – tiredness was kicking in – but he saw the lights on the outskirts of Dublin and he was determined to get back home as soon as he could.

He didn't remember crawling into bed but the shrill tone of his phone awoke him. He was unsure where he was for a moment and he saw that it was still dark outside – he hadn't even drawn the curtains. He literally had climbed into bed practically fully dressed. He wasn't getting any younger and this case was giving him so much grief and sleepless nights. He grasped for his phone on the bedside table.

'For fucks sake!'

He put the phone to his ear and gave a grunt. He listened as the sergeant at the station apologised for the lateness of the call. He thought that Sean wouldn't want to leave this one till the morning. Local Garda had secured the scene, and he had informed the CSI unit that they had another one.

'Jesus and Mary,' Sean said as he rubbed his eyes. He looked at the phone as it lit up – it was two-thirty in the morning so he had been asleep for only forty minutes.

He couldn't believe that they had yet another murdered priest. The killer was working even quicker than they had thought.

'Bugger!'

He flung his legs out of bed, mumbling.

'No time for a shower, a clean shirt will have to do. Let's hope he left us something to go on this time as so far, I don't have a bloody clue.'

He shivered in the chill early morning air as he pulled on his clothes, wondering how on earth they were going to catch a killer that drifted in and out unseen like air. He phoned Steve who offered to go and visit the scene to give Sean time to get back to sleep.

'Nah! I'm awake now. Let's just see what he has left us this time, shall we? One thing I think we can count on is we will have a rhyme and a feather … you come in a bit later. I can deal with this.'

*

Steve found it hard to get back to sleep so decided to go downstairs and again go through what scant evidence they had. He like Sean's gut … He felt that they were missing something, he just wished he knew what it bloody well was. Trying not to wake Meg, he slid out from under the covers and, grabbing his clothes, retreated to the landing to slip them on. Meg had been restless last night; her back had been aching and the twins had been restless too, kicking her and moving around, causing her discomfort. There was hardly any room left, Meg had been complaining, and he felt helpless to ease the burden of the pregnancy and future birth. Consequently, he hadn't been asleep long himself before Sean's call.

He picked up the laptop and made his way into the kitchen. He placed it on the old farmhouse table. Rubbing his fingers along the grooves in the wood and scratches of wear and tear, he smiled to himself. He was so pleased that Meg had loved it as much as him; it held such memories for him. His whole world revolved at one point in time around this table, back when he was a child and his mammy and daddy were sitting around it. Mammy had usually cooked a mouth-watering feast for them and Daddy would sit and talk about the price of grain or how the hay was drying nicely in the field. It was comforting in its normality. His parents had loved him; he had loved and been loved. In his job he had often seen how unfortunate some children were. His daddy might not have been his blood parent but he was as real as any father could be and he had loved him so … that he was sure of!

He hoped that he could be even half the father that his dad was to his own children. His parents had been a gift from God. '*'tis a pity it is only now that I realise it,*' he thought. Placing the kettle on the range, he settled down in the chair and opened the laptop, wishing his mammy was here to share a cup of tea with him like they used to.

CHAPTER 24

"Take thy beak from out my heart, and take thy form from off my door!" Quoth the Raven, 'Nevermore.'"

Edgar Allen Poe

Entering the room, Sean was unsure of exactly what he would find. He had been shocked at the viciousness of the attack on Father Hugh and hoped that Father Fitzgerald had not suffered the same fate. He saw James in his white suit kneeling down next to an armchair and placing something into an evidence bag.

'I won't say a good morning as so far it bloody well hasn't been,' James stated, holding up the bag for Sean to see.

'Hello to you too. What is that? Another body part? Has he left it behind this time? Perhaps he was disturbed.'

'Something is definitely different this time.' James pointed to the bag. 'Let me introduce you to Father Fitzgerald's heart, or what is left of it. Instead of taking the body part away this time, he snacked on it here.'

Sean gagged.

'What? Oh, Jesus Christ, Mary, mother of God! What are ye saying? That he *ate* it?'

'I am almost one hundred percent sure of it – yes! I can see teeth marks on the remains, and I can assure you that the human heart is a lot bigger than this. I will get it back to the lab and see if I can get an imprint or any DNA.'

Looking over at the remains of Father Fitzgerald sitting in his armchair, Sean decided there was nothing more he could do there and was essentially in the way of the crime scene team.

'I'll get out of your way,' he said as he turned to leave. 'Can I expect a summary later today? Oh, I just remembered – is the usual note and feather on this one?'

'Yep.' James held up a plastic bag with a blood-splattered piece of paper inside and another with a black feather inside. Peering at the writing, Sean read out '*Eight for Heaven*'.

'Well, there's nothing heavenly about this case. I wonder how long his fucking rhyme is?'

He headed back to his car, his stomach churning. Sean was too sickened to head back to bed and called at the twenty-four hour service station for a double espresso shot from the coffee machine before turning the car towards the station. By the time Steve joined him at seven, he was buzzing.

'What's going on here? Do you have news? I stopped and grabbed you a coffee but by the look of ye, ye are jacked up already.' Steve marvelled at Sean who was practically jumping in his seat.

'Well, the other priest last night was a Father Fitzgerald. I am sure that James will fill you in on the details; he will be performing the autopsy later this afternoon. Let's just say even *I* lost me stomach a wee bit.'

Sean related to Steve last night's horrific discovery of a partially eaten heart, now bagged and in the mortuary awaiting forensic examination. Then, turning back to the desk and picking up a file, he continued.

'The best bit is I have been working all night and I think I might have found a small break. Connor has been working on trying to link all of the deaths apart from the three common factors that: one, they are all priests, two, the feather, and three, the note with the rhyme. For some bloody obscure reason, my gut kept telling me that it was related to the Bally-Bay case. I couldn't connect why or how it involved St Theresa's or even Father Benedict, but after going through everything from the beginning and looking at who had been murdered, I found it ... a connection. I never understood why Father Murphy was the first killed or even if he had any connection to the other priests that were murdered, but he did have a connection to Bally-Bay. I have managed to look into some of the church archives that we had in the basement relating to the last case in Bally-Bay and I think that I may have found a link between all of them.'

He pointed to his desk that now looked as if a paper bomb had hit it. The musty smell of old box files animated from the pile.

'Apparently, they all attended the same seminary as Father Benedict and left in the early 1970s. Some such as he went to their own parish but all of the others went on to teach at ... of course, you can guess *where*? Tenuous, I know, and they were not at the same seminary or college all at the same time which is why Connor came up against it ... that is until 1981, when they *all* taught at St Patrick's Seminary College.'

Steve watched Sean visibly deflate in the chair; it was as if he had been waiting to pass on what he had found before he collapsed with exhaustion.

'That is at least *one* fantastic bit of news – well done you! You have established that the link to the killer is in there somewhere and you have had our first breakthrough. Why don't you go and get some rest? I will get Connor on to it and we can meet up later. What time is the autopsy? I'll meet you there. Come on now, go get yer head down a wee time, we need ye at full strength.'

Steve cajoled Sean into leaving for home and rest. Patting his friend on the arm, he watched him stand and make his way to the door.

'Only if ye are sure? The autopsy is at three,' Sean replied.

'Go now, get away with ye.' Steve held up his hand as he sat at the desk vacated moments earlier by Sean. 'I'll get meself up to date and see what I can turn up.'

He watched Sean go out of the door and walk across the carpark and climb wearily into his car.

'Oh bugger! I forgot to tell him what Aidan told me about his strange cousin. Oh well. I can tell him later, it will keep,' he mumbled to no one in particular.

Connor arrived soon after and the morning went by in a flash. They discovered that not only did the priests on their list teach together at St. Patrick's but that they had also been named in the early 2000s in an investigation into historical child abuse claims. Nothing was proven and because they were all elderly, they were all shifted away to small parishes to retire quietly, except for Father O'Grady who had left the priesthood years before and had subsequently married and had a family. They were also able to add their most recent body – Father Fitzgerald – to that list. Finally, they had a motive … a tentative one to be sure … but better than nothing. It had to be the reason for the killings; either that or they would never find a reason for the killer's actions – until they caught them, that was!

Asking Connor to dig out the file on the abuse investigation, he later left to meet Sean at the mortuary for the latest autopsy, although it was pretty evident what the cause of death was; it really was a task in evidence gathering. He didn't expect a DNA match as so far, they hadn't had one but if and when they caught the perpetrator, they could use it as evidence if a match was found. First, though, they needed a small breakthrough, a little clue as to who the fuck and why? Although the latter Steve believed was beginning to make itself very clear from what Connor had turned up from the abuse allegations. Hopefully when they returned after the autopsy, they would have some names from the statements in the file. It was something to work from, anyway. Making his way across the carpark, he entered the building. He hated this place; the smell hit his nostrils immediately. Pulling open the large glass doors and seeing the long corridor leading to the morgue, he popped a strong mint into his mouth and pushed his way through the plastic screening leading into the autopsy room. He saw that James had already started and Sean was chewing gum and leaning in towards the chest cavity of the body on the table as James pointed something out to him. Glancing away quickly, he swallowed deeply and popped another strong mint into his mouth before greeting the two men and joining them at the table.

'Look, Steve, he practically ripped the heart out of his chest!'

Sean's glee was quickly left behind when James pointed to the jagged edges of the wound.

'It takes some force to actually inflict such a wound; if you look here, the edges on this side are much straighter and deeper. I would say that a sharp instrument such as a knife was used to start the process and marks on the ribs tally in with this. But pure strength was used to rip the heart from its place in the body. Another thing is that Father Fitzgerald was alive awake and his heart was still pumping up until this point,' James clarified.

Steve was about to lose his last cup of coffee when he felt his phone vibrate in his pocket. Using it as an excuse to leave the room, he waved his phone at Sean who just smiled back, making gagging gestures with his fingers down his throat at his friend.

Once out of the room, Steve glanced at the phone and saw that the call was from Meg. Panicking he answered it, quickly establishing that he was urgently needed at home. The backache from the night before had progressed into full-on labour. He cut the call off in his haste and returned to Sean, his sickness now forgotten as he relayed that Meg was in labour. Shouting to the two men that he had to go, he turned and bumped into the next body lying on a trolley awaiting its turn for James's administrations. Apologising to the cadaver and patting it on the sheet that covered it, he ran from the room shouting that he was going be a dad. This was followed by laughter from Sean and James.

'One out, and one in, isn't that what they say?' James said as he pulled the sheet up over Father Fitzgerald's body.

'Or in this case, eight out, two in,' laughed Sean.

Holding up what was left of Father Fitzgerald's heart that now rested in a kidney bowl resting on top of his body, James said: 'I will swab this for DNA. Hopefully we will get some from the saliva and take some impressions of the bite mark. At least this time we have a bit more to compare to any suspects that you might bring in. I will get the results back to you as soon as they are in but I am not hopeful for a couple of days at least.'

'Thanks, James. I will get back into the office and catch Connor to see what he may have turned up whilst I was out earlier.' As Sean turned to go, James put a cautionary hand on his arm.

'Don't underestimate this killer, Sean; the priests were all older men and easily overpowered but it takes super-human strength to do this,' he said pointing to the body cavity. 'Take care of yerselves.'

Sean gave him a weary smile. 'Do ye think we're dealing with the devil hisself, James?'

'I'm not so sure with this one, Sean. We have dealt with some pretty awful cases over the years but this … what has been done to these priests, sinners or not, is pure evil.'

CHAPTER 25

'He was already dead. He died a year ago.'

Eric Draven (*The Crow*)

Sean headed back to the office and gave Connor the good news about the babies being on the way. He also sent Steve a good luck message and a hug for Meghan.

Sinking back into his chair, he brought Connor up to date on the autopsy report, not sparing him any details as he wanted the youngster to understand the importance of catching the perpetrator sooner rather than later. He had relied on Connor's clear thinking several times during this and the last case that they had worked on together with Steve at Bally-Bay. The girls' faces on the pictures and the bodies of all the wee babies that they had found within the grounds of St Theresa's Orphans and Girls Home still haunted him. It also is what drove him to think that there was a tenuous link to this case, too. *Why?* He couldn't say, but his gut was not happy. Like Steve had said, everything seemed to link back to bloody Bally-Bay and this case especially was turning out to be as difficult as the last.

Call it gut instinct or just his own long experience kicking in, but having another serial killer on his patch again worried him more than he was letting on to Steve or Connor. He was becoming weary of watching the parameters of his life disappear with each and every horrific thing that he had been forced to confront over the last couple of years.

He could understand a little now of the horror that his school friend and partner Steve had been through. Starting with Steve's first horrific case as a young trainee Garda when he had found a half-crazed girl covered in blood and a murdered priest inside the church at Bally-Bay, only later to find out that she was actually his twin sister who had been left behind in St Theresa's to be abused and tortured until the only way that she could escape her abuser was by killing him.

It would have made a saint question their belief in any kind of God that could allow such abuse of children. So, he could understand his friend's reluctance to acknowledge any religious fealty. He himself was struggling to hold on to his own religious beliefs. He also believed that that somehow was why he was dealing with this all over again. It certainly would explain why the priests had been targeted. Could his killer be a survivor of such abuse, he wondered? And if so, why did they wait so long before taking revenge? All of these questions mulled around in his head until Connor brought him yet more coffee and placed the file on his desk that he had dug out from the archives concerning the allegations of historical abuse of boys by the fathers at St Patrick's Seminary in the early 2000s.

Sipping his coffee, he opened the file Connor had placed on the desk. The information was in date order of when the statements were taken of past and present students at the seminary, tthe names of the priests accused of such conduct at the back. Scanning the list of named abusers, he could easily relate the names to his case. Each and every one of the priests that had been murdered and were now lying in the morgue refrigerators were on the list. His guess at the reason for the murders had obviously been correct, but the multitude of names of accusers meant it would take a lot of work to track down each and every one of them to ask them, 'Oh, by the way have ye murdered any old priests lately?'

Seeing the amount of names, he wondered why no kind of prosecution of the priests had taken place. He turned to the last page of the report and the answer to his question was revealed. A short statement read:

'The Bishop of Mornside, Father Declan Murphy who oversees St Patrick's Seminary and its students' welfare and religious guidance, has assured the Assistant Commissioner that a full-scale internal investigation has taken place. The result being, that though one or two of the Father's means of disciplining the boys have been rather over exuberant, the boys' concerns have been addressed and the fathers involved now, I believe, have been singled out and sent for re-training on appropriate chastisement methods for younger pupils. All of the fathers concerned were of a mature age and hopefully the re-training will bring the methods used now to an acceptable and up-to-date, more modern way of thinking.

I am satisfied that the Bishop has everything under control and has shown that an excellent training and student welfare programme at the seminary is exemplary and no further action is necessary.

Signed: Chief Superintendent, AJ Donnelly, Mornside Western Division'

A large faded ink stamp covered the document, stating Garda National Bureau of Criminal Investigation. Now he knew why! Someone on that list was his killer, he was sure of it, but trawling through over a hundred statements would take time and he was beginning to feel weary. The coffee buzz had worn off long ago so he told Connor to call it a night. They would start on the list of names in the morning.

'Perhaps by then we will be Uncle Sean and Uncle Connor. I'll give Steve a call as soon as I'm home. He left the morgue in a right old panic! I bet the wee ones haven't even been born yet. Poor sod! I wouldn't want to go back to all those nappy changes and sleepless nights. Talking of which, get a really good night's sleep and we can start again fresh in the morning. Goodnight, Connor.'

'Goodnight, sir,' Connor replied.

Before he left the station, Sean walked across to the other side of the room and added the latest murdered priest's face to the board. The picture of Father Fitzgerald looked down at him along with all of the others.

'I will get ye justice, just as I would for any other victim. I swore an oath to uphold the law whatever the costs but I hope that every single one of you bastards rots in Hell!'

He looked each picture in the face and, switching off the light, Detective Inspector Sean O'Dowd left the room, snatching the folder from the desk as he passed by. He searched in his pocket for his keys then started out across the car park. Weary and deflated after his coffee buzz, he decided that he needed to grab something to eat; he had been getting the shakes for over an hour. And then he would get a hot shower. He would grab a few hours sleep and get up early to go through the file. It was almost dark now and the lighting in the parking area was abysmal. Nearing the car, he pressed the key fob and opened the passenger door to place the file on the seat as he did so, he felt it fall from his hand onto the tarmac. He clutched at his chest. A pain in his head and a tightening feeling in his chest was the last thing he remembered before passing out and a vague sense of falling onto the front passenger seat of the car.

CHAPTER 26

'Abandon all hope ye who enter here.'

Dante Alighieri (*Inferno*)

Not a lot was left of the inside of the church that had been attached to St Theresa's. It had been abandoned in the scandal that followed the finding of the babies' and girls' bodies; all that remained were the stout stone walls and parts of the vaulted roof. He had visited it often at night, knowing that he was only a stone's throw from his family home. Everything inside the building had been taken by ghoulish visitors to this place of death, and the crumbling walls had been graffitied by kids leaving their tag on the place. The floor was littered with old rubbish, empty bottles and used drug paraphernalia. He smiled to himself at the thought that no one ever came here, apart from the dregs of society but even they had abandoned the place lately and he had no fear that anyone would interrupt his plan.

Stopping in the area where once the altar had stood, he watched the naked figure swing gently from side to side. He checked the ropes around the man's ankles and wrists and he poked the body to make it swing more, hoping that it would be enough to awaken him.

'You haven't kept in shape, now fella; just look at that weight around your waist.'

His arms ached from carrying the dead weight. He rubbed his muscles vigorously. Now that he had him tied and helpless, he could take his time, even rest if he wished. The excitement and anticipation of seeing him open his eyes and then for recognition to spread throughout his face was too much for him. Holding open the jaw, he reached into his pocket and, releasing the lid of the tube in his hand, he squeezed a line of glue along each lip. Then he pressed them firmly together. He tied a gag in place as extra insurance and repeated the process with the backs of each of the man's hands. He proceeded to tie them too with plastic zip ties to a board that ran across the swinging figure's back, his arms outstretched. Giving the glue a few minutes to completely set, he sat back on an old crate and watched the figure swing gently. He laughed out loud.

'The roles have been reversed now, Sean O'Dowd! No more beating on smaller weaker boys or telling tales for you.'

He reached into the black holdall he had carried with him and grabbed hold of the stun-gun. Earlier he had used it to incapacitate Sean in the carpark, along with a blow to the back of his head which had rendered him unconscious long enough for him to tie him up and bring him to Bally-Bay where it had started all those years ago.

'Time to wake up now, Sean. I wouldn't want you to miss your school reunion now.'

He turned the dial on the stun-gun and held it to Sean's chest. The hanging figure convulsed and danced on the end of the rope that was holding him upside down.

Sean tried to scream but realised immediately that he couldn't open his mouth. Pain shot through him when he tried and he writhed in agony at the pulling on his mouth. He also realised that he was in a terrible predicament, one that he didn't think he could get out of. He couldn't see much as it was quite dark. He needed to let his eyes adjust. He also felt disoriented. He watched as a small light moved towards him, held by a dark figure in a long robe.

'Shit! I'm in trouble now. Mary mother of Jesus have mercy,' he thought as he squinted his eyes towards the dim light, trying to see who was approaching but it only reflected back the terror he was feeling. Somehow, he knew that this was the end.

It wasn't how he had intended his last moments to be. He always thought that they would be on a sunny beach with a pint of black in his hand. An involuntary chuckle tried to fall from his lips at the thought of an alcoholic dreaming of a drink whilst hanging naked upside down. The shock hit home … yes, he was fucking naked! He could feel the cold air on his skin forming into goose-bumps. And why couldn't he open his mouth to speak? He would give the feckin' bastard a piece of his mind. He writhed and twisted, trying to free himself as each thought ran through his head. Suddenly, he stilled as understanding hit him like a punch in the gut.

'Welcome to the ninth circle of Hell, Sean! You should feel right at home here, it is the one reserved for betrayal and treachery. Something you would know all about and the reason for you being here.'

Sean tried to speak but a silent scream hurtled at speed into his head as pain ripped through his face at each try.

'Save your words for God. I don't need to take your confession, Sean, as I was there when your treachery took place. Still not understanding, Sean? Not sure who I am yet? Let me take you back nearly forty years to a school yard in Bally-Bay where there was a young boy who was different from everyone else. A young boy who was bullied, teased, beaten and abused, just for that sole reason. Who after a day of suffering at school went home to a nightmare and to more of the same treatment … That is until one day the boy turned on his persecutors and took pleasure in extinguishing their lives.

'Then, emboldened by this feeling, he screamed his secret at the boy who was still beating him in the hope of scaring him off, only to watch with satisfaction as the truth of what he had just told him dawned on the bully. The satisfaction wasn't to last long, though, was it, Sean? Instead of the longed-for peace that he thought this revelation would bring, the boy – whose only desire was to spend time with the crows – was sent away, to be abused some more. The boy's real family, you see, were the corvids; they never judged him, always cared for him and they were the only ones that ever loved him. No, that bully took his secret to Father Benedict and told tales of the boy and what he had told him.'

Sean's eyes popped as the reality of his situation hit him full force. Why had he not seen it, how had he missed it? All of the clues were there, and being a party to it, he was the only one left who knew. The only person in the whole wide world that knew that the man in front of him had killed his own parents, and Father Benedict, swearing Sean to silence, had covered it all up. Assuming that the boy had been removed to St Patrick's Seminary, Sean guessed that he was one of the hundred or so boys on their list abused by the priests over a period of years.

His betrayal of the boy all those years ago had led him to become the monster that now stood in front of him. His head dropped to his shoulder in shame; he had been the reason for the deaths of eight priests and when he died too, he would take that knowledge with him.

'Ah, I see you are beginning to understand the consequences of your betrayal, Sean, and your own predicament at this moment in time. I shouldn't take it to heart – they all deserved exactly what I did to them and so much more. It's just a shame that I only remembered about your betrayal and how you were the cause of all of my pain and suffering when I saw the names in the paper. Ah, the great Detective Sean O'Dowd and his friend, Detective Steve Ryan – the *heroes* of Bally-Bay!

'You needn't think that your friend will appear to save you this time, either. No one except you and I know where you are and why! So you see, Ryan won't work it all out but don't worry, his turn will come. Hell, the final circle, waits for our Steven.'

Sean knew the truth of his words but he couldn't even speak to try and negotiate with him. No, his fate was sealed and that realisation lay heavy on him. He would never see his kids again and he hoped that the same fate didn't wait for Steve too. If he hadn't been so tired, if only he had been paying more attention as he left the office, the killer would never have been able to take Sean even with a bloody taser! He looked disparagingly at the slight frame of his antagonist and noticed that he walked with a limp. He was one hundred percent sure now that he had seen him that day, sneaking back into the building at Father Feelan's crime scene dressed as a priest. Sean had known all along that the only person who could safely move freely around all of the murder sites was a priest, or someone dressed as one.

To be fair, he had almost worked it out, and he hoped that Steve did too after talking to Aidan the other night. Perhaps that is what he had been trying to tell Sean when the signal had dropped out on his mobile phone. It must have slipped his mind after that and he just hoped that Steve made the connection and caught this bastard, even if it was too late for him. His only regret was that he wouldn't get to see Steve and Meg's babies and the look on his friend's face when he became a father.

A tear slid from the corner of his eye and, seeing it, the killer laughed.

'Having regrets, are we? I will leave you to think about your confession for a while. It will prolong the agony and I will delight in each and every minute that you think about what I am going to do to you, Sean.'

Pushing his captive till he swung back and forth, he prepared to return one last time to his roost on the rooftop of the abandoned church. It would give his next confessor time to contemplate on his sins, but first he would have a little fun with his old schoolfriend.

CHAPTER 27

'A lucky man is rarer than a white crow.'

Juvenal (Roman poet)

The birth was over quite quickly compared to the ordeal that his friend Sean was enduring, unbeknownst to Steve who now sat in a hospital chair with a baby in each arm whilst Meghan slept. Looking down at the faces of his new born children, softness overcame his features as a feeling of overpowering love filled his whole being. A tenderness that every man felt on becoming a father entered his heart. He couldn't wait to share his luck with his best friend Sean and he was hoping that Meg would allow their son to be named for him, but agreement on names had yet to be decided. They had argued a little as Steve didn't wish to use the name Magda after his last case, let alone hear it again, but Meghan's mammy had been called Magda, making the decision harder for Meg.

'Let's wait till they arrive and see what suits them, shall we?' he had suggested.

One child stirred in his arms, his tiny hands clutching and waving in the air. Steve held his finger out towards the tiny fist and smiled as he grasped hold of it tightly.

The babies opened their eyes abruptly and simultaneously at the same time as a loud beating on the window occurred. Steve startled too, and the babies began to cry. The sound of what seemed like a scream could be heard and the banging on the window pane continued. Walking towards the glass, he wondered how it hadn't shattered at the strength of the knocking and the wing beats. A large black crow continued to bash itself against the glass and Steve realised that above the wailing babies, the screaming sound that he had heard was emanating from the crow.

'Dear God, is it the morrígan herself at the window?' Meg cried out as she lifted the babies from Steve's arms. Trying but not succeeding to hush and comfort them both, she moved away from the noise further back into the room just as the glass cracked. As suddenly as it had started, the noise stopped. The crow faltered as its wings slowed their beating, then stopped; it dropped from the sill to the ground where it lay still. Steve rushed from the room and, running out of the hospital building, he reached the bird's lifeless body. Looking at the bloodstained beak, he stepped back, then noticed the white markings on its under-wings, now displayed pointing outwards in a cruciform on the ground.

'What in the name of our Lady happened there?' he said, nudging the bird's lifeless body with his shoe. He looked upwards to see black clouds gathering in the sky, blocking out the sunlight apart from a single beam that hit him full in the face, blocking his vision. He raised his hands, shielding his eyes just in time as several black feathered forms dove straight at him, beating their wings and attacking him with their sharp beaks and claws. He ran towards the building and aimed for the exit door that he had left open when he had run outside earlier. He just made it inside as the last claw scraped down his back and he practically fell inside the door backwards, shielding his face with his arms. He ran full pelt along the corridor as panic swept over him and he could feel blood trickling down his forehead next to his right eye, his back and head stinging in several places.

He stumbled into the room to see Meg and a nurse, each with a baby in their arms. The twins slept peacefully as if nothing had happened. Relief washed over him and he slumped into the chair as the nurse placed the baby in the plastic cot by the bed and rushed to tend to his wounds. Meg sat staring into space, still stunned by what had just occurred. The nurse wheeled a trolley next to the chair and asked Steve to remove his shirt then bathed and dressed each wound.

'The one on your eye needs a little Steri-Strip tape, but it will peel off by itself in a few days; I'm hoping it won't scar too badly,' she reassured him.

'I don't think anyone would notice if it did with this lot already here,' Steve smiled, wryly pointing at the scars from where his sister's claw-like fingers had raked his face during capture a couple of years ago. The nurse looked embarrassed as she whisked the trolley away.

Standing up and walking towards the bed, he took Meg's cold hands in his and rubbed them gently.

'Well, if that was a bloody banshee, it sure scared the feckin' bejesus out of me,' he said, trying hard to bring humour to a situation that he couldn't explain. Meghan fell into his arms and the sobbing started, soaking his shirt or what was left of it in minutes. In between sobs, he heard her say, 'But a banshee brings death to the house!' and she sobbed even harder.

Holding her and the babies even more tightly, his urge to protect them grew stronger. What he was protecting them from was a complete mystery to him. His detective instincts were useless to him now as there was nothing tangible for him to work with. No facts or clues as to why he had been attacked by a load of bloody crows. Maybe it was just one of those weird phenomena that occurred once in a while. But his instincts which were the only thing that he could rely on said it was related to the case – no matter how strange that sounded. He vowed to settle Meg and the babies and as soon as the visitors started to arrive, he was going to pop out and call Sean.

Settling Meg back in bed, he lay down beside her, stroking her hair. She leaned back into his chest, feeling a comfort from his arms around her. Both twins were fed and sleeping peacefully in their cribs. Meg looked up at Steve and she gently kissed the taped wound left by one of the crows.

'Please tell me what the hell just happened here today, Steve? I'm so scared. I know that you pooh pooh all of my superstitious stuff, but I could swear that the morrígan was clawing and wailing at our window. You know what they say when a banshee screams? Someone is about to die! What if it is one of the twins? Oh God, Steve, what if it's the babies?' Meg cried out as she sobbed into his shoulder.

'I really don't know what to say, my love, but I am here and I promise that I won't let anything harm the babies or you.'

'But how can you? You are only a man, Steve. What happened today was way beyond our understanding. As soon as I am out of here, I will leave an offering to the morrígan high on the hill where the crows nest; maybe that will appease her.'

He stayed silent – after all, he had to agree with Meg, he couldn't keep her safe, it was out of his hands. He had never felt so helpless, and he had no explanation to give. He just held onto her tightly; he wouldn't pray as he had seen enough misery to not have faith in anything that wasn't tangible. This time, though, he wished that he did; he could definitely do with some divine help.

They were both drifting off to sleep when Steve felt his phone vibrate in his pocket; at the same time, there came a small knock at the door. Slipping quietly from the bed, he opened it to see Sian and John standing there, laden with beribboned gifts and flowers.

'Come in. Meg is asleep at the moment but the babies are due to wake for a feed at any moment, so get yourselves comfy.' He pulled out a chair for Sian to sit on. 'I'll just pop out and find another chair. I'm sure Meg will be thrilled to see you both.'

Hugs and kisses followed then Steve slipped from the room before he could be questioned on the dressing on his head and the blood on his shirt. He thought he would pop down to the car and change it as he always kept spare clothes in the boot. You never knew when a suspect would spew on you or you would slip in the mud traipsing over a field to look at a crime scene. It would also give him time to see who had been calling him; he hoped it was Sean so that he could share his good news with him.

Pulling his phone from his pocket and glancing at the screen, he could see it wasn't Sean, just the station. Well, they could wait – he was needed here at the moment and that's where he should be. He had made a promise to himself that as soon as the twins were born, he would stop working all of the hours God sent. No time like the present to start putting it into practice, a decision that he would come to regret later on.

CHAPTER 28

'I walk along the wind-blown path
With leaves strewn at my feet –
The trees are bent from nature's wrath
There's someone I must meet.

And as the thought comes to my mind
A wind-song brings a crow
Which lights upon a branch and I'm
To learn what I must know.

'It's time,' she says, 'for you to fly
You've been given many a feather.
Try out your wings and touch the sky
You've long lost any tether.

Leave all your sorrows of long past days
Rush now, the future's calling
All wounds have healed, now turn your gaze
There is no risk of falling.

Remember that it's me the crow
Who's helped you find your wings.
I'm there when soft or strong winds blow
No matter what life brings.'

Doris Potter (*Discoveries in the Dark*)

Connor was frantic. Unable to raise either Steve or Sean on the phone, he was unsure what his next step should be. He couldn't stall much longer – he would give them both one more try in half an hour and then he would be forced to go tell the superintendent. He understood that Steve was with his partner Meghan at the hospital but he had been unable to raise Sean since he had left the station. Perhaps he had decided to pop into the hospital to catch up with Steve …

James had worked most of the night on the autopsy report on Father Declan Fitzgerald and, finally, some DNA results had found a familial match. James had managed to extract a good sample from the heart and the teeth-mark mould would help identify their suspect, if and when they arrested someone. This time the perpetrator had been careless, or perhaps he just didn't care anymore. Either way, Connor hoped that at last they had been given a breakthrough. He really looked up to Sean as a mentor, and the detective's humour and quick thinking had helped turn Garda Connor O'Brian into a competent and intuitive future detective. He would always be grateful to Steve, too, for bringing his brother Collum's murderer to justice, giving closure to his parents and restoring his brother's reputation. He understood as well what it had taken Steve to do that as the person responsible had turned out to be Steve's twin sister. So, a little covering up for their absence would not be a problem until it became one.

He would use the time to ring around and see if they could find the missing priest with mental health problems. After all, he could already have become the next victim of their killer. They had been a bit over-whelmed with the rapidity of the bodies piling up. One thing they all knew was that this killer meant business. Connor decided to make a start on the list of names of the former pupils of the seminary that had made abuse allegations back in the 2000s.

Picking up the telephone, he turned the page till he found the number for the St Michael's homeless shelter and whilst waiting for it to ring, he flipped through the small file of information on the desk concerning the missing priest. It consisted of just one page with a couple of short sentences and named the missing person as an ex– priest called Father Doyle, with the person reporting it a Father Michael, the shelter manager. As he finished reading the report, a voice answered.

'Hello, St Michael's.'

He explained why he was calling and got ready to add any notes to the almost empty piece of paper.

'So, you haven't seen or heard from Father Doyle since you reported him missing?' he now asked. 'And you say that this has happened before? Can you tell me when Father Doyle disappeared before, was he gone long?' Pausing to wait for a reply, Connor continued jotting notes on the page before continuing to question Father Michael. 'I see from the report that you gave that he has been gone for a month now. Is this quite usual behaviour for him? I guess what I am trying to discover is the state of Father Doyle's mind and, to be blunt, is alcohol an issue?'

Satisfied with all of the answers given, Connor felt pleased; he didn't think that Father Doyle was another victim of their priest killer. Relieved, he put the folder to one side. He was sure that Father Doyle would turn up sooner or later. Father Michael had explained that he had left the seminary and the priesthood after what you could only term as a complete mental health breakdown, and had been drifting from church to church, but refusing any kind of help or counselling apart from food and shelter. He had not been seen for possibly three weeks or more but had gone missing before on several occasions. So really, Father Doyle was no longer a priest but he had been at the seminary during the time of the abuse accusations.

Walking over to his desk, Connor pulled the heavy folder taken from records a week ago towards him. Flipping through the pages of statements, he noted all those attached to any of the dead priests' names. His list was growing and time hurried on at pace. Upon reaching the last page, he found – as Sean had – a signature from the chief superintendent at the time of the allegations. He flipped the page in frustration and a small piece of paper slipped out.

It was a page from a garda's notebook. Written on it was: 'Interview with Father Doyle concerning allegations of abuse during the time he was at the seminary. NO KNOWLEDGE OF ALLEGATIONS – NO ALLEGATIONS AGAINST.'

This one small slip of paper could as easily have been missed, but frustratingly all it did was affirm that he had not been involved in abusing boys at the seminary. What it didn't show was if he had made any allegations himself. It did, however, confirm his name and that he had been there at the same time as the dead priests.

Next, Connor decided to try to get hold of Sean and Steve in that order. Picking up the phone again, he dialled Sean's phone. He let it ring for a long time before it was finally answered.

'Hello, sir, sorry to bother you, it's Garda O'Brian.' He waited for Sean to reply for a few seconds and then, when all he could hear was heavy breathing, he asked if Sean was hurt. 'Are you alright, sir, do you need help?'

Suddenly a voice … not Sean's … spoke.

'He is beyond help. Now he is burning in Hell where betrayers belong. Tell Detective Steve Ryan I am waiting with his friend where it all began; he knows where to find us.' The voice was cold and hard and it sent chills along Connor's spine which made him shiver. He stared at the screen as the red phone icon blinked out.

Flipping open the note pad on the desk, he found Steve's number and dialled, praying that he would answer; he knew that he needed to do something as Sean could be injured or, worse, dead. A bad feeling had begun to sit in the pit of his stomach as the phone continued ringing.

'Mother Mary, please make him answer!' he pleaded. After a while, it clicked into answer phone and he left an urgent message for Steve to contact him. He looked at the clock – four o'clock in the afternoon. He had not seen Sean for almost twenty-four hours now and he had been trying to get hold of him all day. He hoped that he wasn't in any trouble but now there was only one thing to do. Standing up, he started walking towards the chief super's office when the phone on his desk rang. Rushing back to grab it, he was relieved to hear the comforting voice of Steve on the end of the line.

'Hello, sir, I am so relieved that you answered!'

'Are ye calling to congratulate us? The wee ones are here! Where is Sean? I bet he is waiting to wet the babies' heads with a cola?' Steve joked.

'That is just the problem, sir. I can't get hold of Detective O'Dowd. I thought he must have sneaked in to the hospital to see the wee ones but I have been trying to get him on his phone for hours. To be honest, sir, I was getting really worried and was on my way to the superintendent's office when you rang. I just tried his phone for the last time about ten minutes ago and a man answered – a man who said that he had a message for you. I think Sean is in terrible trouble, sir. He said that Sean was burning in Hell and that he was waiting for you, *where it all began.*'

Steve's heart jumped into his mouth then sank to his gut. Yes, Sean was in trouble, alright, big trouble by the sound of it.

'Connor, listen to me carefully. I am on my way in. Go to the super's office and tell him exactly what you have just told me. When did you last see him? It's really important that we pin down how long he may have been gone.'

'Well, I said good night to him about five last night and he was heading home for some sleep. He took the folder with him with the list of names of the abused boys in, just to see if any names rang a bell. Oh Jesus, sir, I should have told the super earlier but I was trying to give Sean a break. I thought he was with you at the hospital. I tried to get you too but obviously you weren't able to answer your phone there.' Connor almost sobbed as his last words hit home.

'No, Connor, I was just as culpable as I turned my phone off – I knew you were trying to get me but I thought it could wait. Now, go do what I said, and Connor, start a trace on Sean's phone and car immediately. I will be with you soon.' Pressing the red icon, he began to panic. 'Oh Mary and Joseph … Sean, man, what have I done?' He rushed back into the room where Meg and her uncle John and auntie Sian were sitting with her. She could see immediately that something was wrong.

'What is it, Steve, what has happened?'

'It's Sean, love. He's missing and I think our killer has got him.' He looked around frantically, at all of their faces – then terror hit him full on, reflected back in their eyes.

'Go, love, quickly, go now and be safe. Our babies need a father. Please be careful!' Meg started crying. 'See, the morrígan *was* here! Oh God, please be careful.'

John stood up and put a comforting hand on Steve's arm.

'Come on, I'll walk you out.'

Steve nodded and, kissing Meg, he left her being comforted by Sian as he almost ran out of the door.

'Please don't worry about them, Steve; Sian and I will look after them till you come back. But listen to Meghan and don't do anything stupid, stay calm and do your job, don't take any risks.' John turned to go back to Meg and the babies as Steve turned towards the car.

Racing back to the station, all kinds of thoughts ran through his head. Where was the killer … somewhere that he knew? Did he even have Sean and if so, was he dead or alive? Dear God, he hoped for the latter. One thing he didn't understand – why Sean? He wasn't a priest – nothing like a priest. He rushed back, breaking all speeding records, and was greeted at the door by Connor and behind him a room full of gardaí. Walking quickly towards the superintendent, they shook hands as he was filled in on the situation.

'We are treating it as a kidnapping, Garda O'Brian. We've looked at the camera footage covering our carpark from last night about the time that Sean left. Although it is grainy, it appears that Detective O'Dowd was incapacitated in the car park as he was placing something in his car and was then shoved into the front seat while the perpetrator climbed into the driver side and drove away. We followed the car on street cams to ascertain what direction he went but so far there is no clear image and after a few miles, we lose him. It looks very much like they left the city.'

Steve looked stunned; left the city? Where? Bloody hell, *where*?

'They could be anywhere now, sir; did Connor tell you about the telephone message? It must be someone in our past but it could be anyone! Over the years, we have put away a fair few criminals. I have been wracking my brains to think of something we were both involved with and apart from our garda training, we only worked together last year on the St Theresa's case in Bally-Bay.'

'Well, one thing for sure, he had some neck kidnapping a senior officer right in our own station carpark; that alone doesn't look good for us, or Sean.'

Steve turned from the superintendent searching for a clue, a link. He literally jumped then banged the palm of his hand on his forehead.

'Connor!' he shouted. Where is that file on the missing priest? What was his name again? Was it Doyle by any chance?'

'Yes, sir, Matthew Doyle, ex-priest. He hasn't been seen for almost three weeks now. I also have a DNA report marked *urgent* back from the lab. They have a familial match to an old case and a mountain of reports to look through from the phone-line that the super set up after the press conference this morning.'

'You had a press conference, sir?' Steve asked the superintendent.

'Yes. I was being pressured from above to get a handle on it. The killing of priests doesn't go down well with the upper echelon of the constabulary, or the public. We simply asked for the public's help … if they saw anything suspicious, etcetera. I will get a few bodies over to help sift through the calls. Obviously, we will have the usual crank calls, but hopefully we will find a diamond in the rough. Any information at this point in time would be helpful in finding Sean. Well, I will leave you to it, Detective Ryan; if you need anything just call me … and Steve …we will have Sean back in the fold tonight. Gardaí are out searching abandoned buildings and waste areas as we speak. Have faith in our Lord.' The super turned and left.

'Faith … bloody faith! The only thing that could save Sean now is good police work! come on, Connor.'

Steve charged to the desk, slumped in a chair and picked up two folders. He briefly read the small file on the missing ex-priest, Matthew Doyle. Then turning to the other folder, he flipped the page to read James's report on the bite-mark on Father Fitzgerald's heart. Slumping back, then exclaimed.

'Fucks sake, why didn't I see it? I bet Sean put two and two together. The missing link is Aidan Doyle. Connor, I know who it is; I know who the bloody killer is!'

Quickly Steve explained how Aidan's DNA from the last case in Bally-Bay was a match for the bite mark DNA. It indicated he was either a first or second cousin rather than a close match.

'We took everyone's DNA in the village, do you remember, Connor? We wanted to try and match all of the babies in the pit. It's *Matthew* Doyle … he's Aidan's cousin; he was a couple of years older than us at school. Sean ragged him terrible. He was a pathetic little creature, really. Something happened and his parents died in an accident or something. I remember him being in hospital for an age after the accident then he was whisked away when he recovered. That's when Aidan's daddy took over the farm. We were only boys.

Could that be the connection? I haven't thought about him in years. We used to call him Crazy Doyle and he used to caw like a crow … Oh my God, it's him, so it is! Crow Boy has become Crow Man, the priest killer!'

Before any reply could be made, Connor rushed up, waving a paper in his hand.

'Sir, sir, we have information. Sean's … err Detective Inspector O'Dowd's car has been spotted parked in Angel Street off the main Dublin Road. Also, I Google searched the area and there are some abandoned buildings along there awaiting demolition, including an old church. The word is that the area is well known for homelessness and drug use. There used to be a soup kitchen and shelter in the church building up until last year, when it was declared unsafe. We also received a report via the phone line that a suspicious character has been seen sneaking in through the hoarding late at night and lights have been seen at the very top of the old church on the rooftop. Is it something we should maybe check out?' Connor asked.

CHAPTER 29

'If this is the distorted one, then many corpses will ensue, cries resound in the walled courts, ravens shall feast on men's feet.'

Dante Alighieri (*The Divine Comedy*)

He sat on the dusty pile of rags in the corner of the room. Looking through the broken window of the church, he could see that it was late afternoon.

'See, they haven't missed you much. It has taken all day to find out that you were even missing and then I had to tell them myself. No one cares about an old detective past his prime, let alone a dead one. Where is your old friend now to see you pay for your perfidy?' he called to the figure swinging naked, upside down, arms splayed outwards and hands tied across a wooden board. The face and shoulders had turned black and blue where blood had pooled to the lowest point on the body, where livor mortis was present. Rigor mortis had started to pass. He knew that it wouldn't be long before Steve Ryan found them, especially after leaving him his cryptic clue and looking through the file that Sean had on him when he had captured him; he knew it wouldn't be long before he put two and two together.

He decided to rest for a little while. After all, he was exhausted from his night's work. Give Sean his due, he hadn't given his confession easily and he certainly had had to work for it. He was pleased he had reached his pinnacle, had fulfilled his task in the name of God and it was all over. Steve would finish his rhyme for him; he would be dwelling in Hell with the devil once he found his friend and realised that he was too late to save him. Lifting a small sleeping bag from underneath the rags, he curled up on it as he whispered his last prayer and offering as a sin-eater. He knew that his own time was drawing near but he smiled to himself as he asked God to be merciful; he had performed his tasks well, and had sent on the souls of the sinner and the fathers to be judged.

He woke a little while later; it was pitch black and his ears immediately attuned to the noises around him. Something had woken him. He listened but all he could hear were the noises of the night. A raven alighted at the window, then, turning its eye to him, bravely hopped onto the sill then landed on Sean's feet tied by the rope and nailed to the board that joined the piece across his shoulders forming a crucifix. Tentatively eyeing the man watching him from the corner, who nodded to him in acknowledgement, the bird moved sideways. He pecked at the underside of one foot. Then, becoming braver, he clung to the rope and his large beak tore into the flesh.

He watched silently as the bird feasted for quite a while, then found that he was quite hungry himself. So, standing up, he walked towards the swinging figure. The raven took flight, though reluctant to leave its food source.

'Don't worry, I won't be gone long. I think we have a few hours yet to feast until that stupid detective works it all out. He always was the last in all the class tests at school.'

He then disappeared out of the door leaving the raven perched on the stone sill and the body of Sean O'Dowd swinging upside down, naked, from the rope.

He went to Sean's car which he had hidden from view behind the overgrown bushes, out of sight of passing traffic. Turning the key, he started the engine and without any lights he slowly travelled down the overgrown driveway. Hopping out, he unlocked the padlock holding together the rusted gates of St Theresa's Church and quickly left Bally-Bay.

He knew that he was safe from discovery for a few hours yet and he wanted to return to clean up and to fetch the body of his faithful brother crow, the sin-eater, so that he could bury him in consecrated ground. He deserved that at least for all of the work that he had done for our Lord; he didn't want his death to be any less celebrated than his life. He had been his constant companion for a while and had kept his secrets safe. He also wanted to retrieve his book and to dispose of Sean's phone along the way. He knew that they could easily trace him by the phone but he didn't want to make it too easy for them. He drove a few miles out of the village and removed the battery then flung the phone as far as he could out of the window. The cold night air hit his lungs, causing him to gasp as he quickly put up the window. He had been numb before to any changes in temperature – maybe it was because he had fulfilled his promise to bring those that had sinned against him back to the fold. As a priest, he had certainly played the part in the taking of all their confessions. He shivered, the damp night air had chilled him like never before. The blood-stained clothes that he wore clung to his body – still, he would soon need them no longer.

He parked Sean's car around the corner and walked quickly to the building. He admired the old carved stonework now crumbling and covered in lichens. Dirty grey clung to everything and rot and decay had set in, common in this part of the city where buildings such as this were to make way for clean, concrete tower blocks and shopping malls. He was so familiar with the building that he needed no light to find his way. The moonlight was bright enough. Squeezing his way through the wire fence, he made his way in through the broken boards. No one had disturbed him in his eyrie in the tower of the old church. Climbing the stairs to his living quarters, he first washed, changed his clothes, then he sat on the small camp bed in the corner. Eating his meagre repast of bread and cheese washed down with a glass of slightly brown-coloured water from the rusty tap in the old water tank high on the roof of the building, which had been a life saver. He toasted his cup. Was this his last supper? he wondered.

'I'm weary, Lord. Have I proved to you my devotion? May I rest now?'

He laid his head back onto the tiny cot bed which had served him well over the last few months and dropped into a restless sleep. In his dreams, he felt the softness of feathers as his dark angels surrounded him, caressing his face and touching his body, the black down enfolding around him as he drifted on the soft cloud. Blackness engulfed him but he wasn't afraid, in fact quite the opposite. It was as if he had come home. A blissful peace filled his soul and he slept deeply.

He was back in the tree, a child again. He looked down and a small blue speckled egg lay in his hand. Popping it into his pocket, he carefully climbed down the trunk, his fingers gripping and clinging to the rough surface of the bark. The parent birds took no notice of the nest robber, only acknowledging him as he threw them some corn taken from his pocket. On reaching the ground, he scanned the surrounding fields. He could see his mother in the farmyard feeding the chickens, and over in the far field he watched as his father sowed the first spring crop, his tractor followed by a host of hungry, black-feathered birds. Like a funeral cortège, he thought, and suddenly wished that it was his father's funeral and that he was the one driving the tractor.

He made the sign of the cross, then ran as fast as he could across the field of barley which was already growing and up to knee height. He glanced up several times to check where his parents were. Luckily, they were still where he had last seen them. His fingers curled around the small egg in his trouser pocket. He thought that he felt small movements inside the shell. Hopefully it would hatch soon, he thought. Dashing into the barn, he found the hen that he had been watching for the last week. She had been brooding a large clutch of eggs and, slipping his hand underneath her carefully whilst keeping her busy with a handful of the corn, he placed the tiny egg amongst the others.

For weeks, he snuck out to the barn. The egg had indeed hatched and the tiny pink wrinkled chick had turned into a soft downy black baby crow. He had hidden it well at the back, away from his father's eyes. Holding the small bird carefully in his hand, he fed it small amounts of food stashed or stolen from his mammy's larder. Stroking its soft back, he cawed softly to it and it nuzzled his face and replied in small squeaks. He told it how beautiful it was and that soon it would have fine glossy feathers with the colours of the rainbow in them. He then told it how they would shine with God's light in the sunshine, an iridescent glow of purples, greens and a deep, deep blue.

'I love you,' he said as he placed it gently back in the small nest that he had made for it in the hay.

His father had watched the boy and seen where he was going night and day, sneaking off instead of doing his chores. He stood by the wall, watching him now as he came out of the barn, scanning the area before running full pelt back to the farmhouse. He watched him enter the door then started walking towards the barn. He stood in the doorway for a few moments, looking to see if anything was amiss. Listening intently, he was about to leave when he heard it – the smallest of sounds emanating from the back of the barn. He followed it to the nest …

The next evening, the boy practically skipped his way to the barn, throwing caution to the wind in his excitement at seeing his friend, the crow. His scream echoed for miles as he ran into the night, into the darkness, his small body shaking with a barely contained fury, the body of the baby crow cradled in his hands; he ran till he could run no more, then he crawled under the hawthorn tree. The crows above in the branches called out their sorrow and his father's figure was lit up in the doorway, calling out his name. His mammy was trying to hold him back till she was flung back inside. He woke, startled, just as his daddy's hand reached through the branches of the sceach ghael – the hawthorn – to grasp his hair.

It wasn't the dream that had so rudely awakened him, but loud voices calling to each other and feet climbing the stairs to his tiny garret. Jumping up, he seized the book just as Steve and two gardaí burst through the door. He climbed quickly onto the roof terrace through a small access hatch leaving Steve to follow closely on his heels. He backed towards the edge of the roof then turned, smiling at his pursuer.

'Steve, how nice to see you again! You won't find what you are looking for here. The last piece of the puzzle, you see, was meant for you, but I'm afraid that you arrived a little quicker than I thought you would. We have ended our little game early, not that we were ever friends at playtime, eh, Steve? I have left a little gift for you on the table; it's a shame that I couldn't give it to you personally.'

'Where is he, Matthew?' Steve started forwards, hands out in a gesture of good faith.

'Stop where you are, Steve!' He started to back away from Steve, nearer to the roof edge. He climbed up onto the ledge and turned. 'You still haven't worked it all out, have you?'

Steve stopped; he knew that one more step would send him over the edge and he would never find Sean or get the answers he craved.

'Why, Sean? He isn't a priest?' Steve asked.

'Why *Sean*, why *me*?' he mimicked like a whiny child. 'You two made my life another kind of hell in the only place that I could escape from the other one. It wasn't the bullying that Sean needed to confess to! No, it was the telling Father Benedict of my little secret … that I had killed my own parents.

'Ah, I can see by your face that he never told you about that. The day when I screamed it at him, trying to put the fear of God into him in the hope of some reprieve from the beatings, and it worked for a little while. But Sean was no priest, he couldn't hold a confession like that to himself, so he betrayed me to Father Benedict and I was sent on yet again to live a different kind of hell with the fathers in the seminary.

'I had lost most of the memory of that night, and here I need to thank you and Sean as seeing your names appear in the paper brought it all back. The *Heroes of Bally-Bay* where it all started eh, Steve? My life of misery and Sean's … well, let's just say he's finished up where he started.

'They all deserved exactly what they got and now my job here is done. You will be the tenth and you'll dwell with the devil.' He made the sign of the cross and, putting his arms out, he leaned backwards off the edge.

Steve rushed forward, grasping at Matthew's clothing. Matthew firmly held his arms at the elbow. Shaking his hands off, Steve nearly toppled over the edge himself but was held tight by a strong pair of arms about his waist. He felt Matthew's hands slide downward towards his wrists, trying to pull him with him over the edge. Steve desperately tried to hang on to him but felt him slip quietly away. He made no sound as he fell. Steve heard the impact as the body hit the ground and he leaned over the roof edge to take a look at the body, now splayed out on a pile of rubbish down below. Blood seeped from a large wound at the back of Matthew's head where it had struck the masonry of the tower on the way down.

'Where you belong, Matthew Doyle. May you be the one to rot in Hell.' Steve stepped back from the edge, Connor carefully grasping him by the arm.

'That was very close, sir, thank God I had hold of you, or he would have pulled you over. We have found a note on the table for you. There is a rhyme and a feather the same as the others. It says: *'Ten for the devil wherever he may dwell.'* He seems to have missed out number nine, sir. We have up to eight on the priests' bodies.'

Steve stared at Connor in a daze.

'Number nine? Number nine? What are you talking about?'

'The rhyme, sir. Each number related to a body and their presumed sin; what about number nine? It's missing, if you're number ten. Do you think he intended killing you, like the others? And where is Sean? Is this the place, sir, that he wanted you to meet him? Do you know this place?'

'No. I have never been here before. This isn't where he meant me to be. Yes, Connor, I think he intended taking me with him over the ledge. I think we thwarted his original plan. I do believe he hoped to lure me to where Sean is and finish me off too. That is why he took a chance to take me with him. I have a good idea where Sean might be, though. He practically told me in a roundabout way. Come on, Connor, we need to get to Bally-Bay quickly. I am sure that Sean is there.'

Racing down the steps, he stopped long enough to inform the superintendent and to arrange for the forensic team to come. He walked over to the body of Matthew Doyle splayed out on the ground, a bible lay next to him that had fallen from his hand.

'Make sure that is bagged too, please, and anything else upstairs.'

He left instructions for James to follow on afterwards as he was certain now what it was that he would find in Bally-Bay.

CHAPTER 30

Dante's 9th Circle of Hell

'The last circle was dedicated to betrayal, those who committed the ultimate sin of treachery, betrayed their loved ones, friends, countries and even their masters.'

Dante Alighieri (*Inferno*)

Dread pooled in Steve's stomach the closer that they came to home. It settled there like lead, and he felt sick. His stomach roiled like a turbulent sea and he stopped the car just in time to lean out of the door and vomit on the road.

'Are you alright, sir? I'm not surprised that you were sick. It's the shock, sir. He nearly killed you, too. Would you like me to drive?'

'No, thank you, Connor, and what did I tell you? We are a team and you can call me *Steve* when we are not at the station.'

'That's exactly what Sean would say …' Conner tailed off taking in the enormity of what he had just said.

If what Steve thought he would find in Bally-Bay was true, how could he ever call this place home again? The whole of his life had been a conscious effort to escape from this town and yet he was always drawn back again. No matter the trauma, no matter the hell that being back here seemed to cause, he eventually ended up back here again and again.

Meg was part of this story in Bally-Bay, too; so, he felt that fate had had a hand in bringing them both together for this reason. Steve also knew that he would find his dear friend dead now; he was unsure how the hell he had escaped this thing … this wrath … this bloody war. Yes, he felt that he had been fighting a battle with evil for a very long time. Meg had been right – the morrígan needed her pound of flesh and he hoped that Sean's death in battle would be enough of a sacrifice. Yes, they were both involved in a battle, he for his and his loved ones' lives, and Sean for his mortal soul. He prayed that Meg and the babies were OK.

He drove on silently through the night. The battle for his own life may be over, but the battle for his soul was about to begin. Matthew had been right to leave him the tenth rhyme: he had been dwelling with the devil in Hell since that fateful day as a young garda when he had found the girl screaming in the church in Bally-Bay … all those years ago. He had been fighting his own demons for most of his life

The blue lights reflected back from the puddles on the country lanes; the rain had dampened them earlier in the night. He took his time – he wanted to get there safely but also he didn't really want to arrive. When he did, it would all become a reality and the longer that he could pretend that all would be well, the better. Sean had been gone for twenty-four hours now, so no way could he still be alive. Delaying his arrival that would lead to the discovery of his friend wasn't really a selfish thing to do. He knew that Sean was in no danger now. He had let him down badly; he should have answered his phone sooner. Now he would have to live with that. The inevitability of it all came crashing in on him the minute the headlights hit the stone walls of St Theresa's and the abandoned church. Leaving the headlights on, he climbed out of the car.

'Where shall we start looking, Steve?' Connor asked shyly, still uncomfortable at calling his superior by his name rather than his rank. Lifting the boot, Steve passed Connor a large torch and took one out for himself.

'I know exactly where he will be, Connor. Where would a priest, or ex-priest, be most comfortable but inside a church. Don't forget he wanted me here to see his work. Well, he is getting his wish even though the bastard is dead.'

Stepping forward, he turned to Connor.

'You don't need to see this if you don't want to. Neither I nor Sean would think any the less of ye.'

Connor nodded to Steve in assurance that he would be right behind him. He understood it would be Steve who would need his support once they got inside, not Sean. Taking a deep breath, they pulled the huge wooden door open. It swung more easily than they at first thought; silently, it opened on greased hinges. Obviously, Matthew had visited and prepared for his finale which is what Steve was sure this was. It's just that Sean and he were not willing participants.

The smell hit them first, and then the metallic tang of blood hit the back of their throats making them both gag. Then the awful smell of decay and decomposition hit next. Steve's hand shook as he held up his torch and the beam of light hit the figure hanging from the ceiling. The raven startled them both as it took flight away from the beam of light, away from the people intruding on its feast.

'Oh my Lord Jesus!' Connor exclaimed at the sight that befell them before turning and running out of the door, retching. Steve, not feeling brave or good, continued on into the building. Looking up, he exclaimed.

'Jesus, Mary and Joseph, God in heaven!'

It echoed around the empty space. He could see what had once been his dear friend, hanging upside down from a rope. His tortured, twisted and naked body, or what was left of it, reeked with the stench of death. He knew he should leave it there till the forensic team came, but he just had to get him down and cover him. After all, they know who'd killed him now. Sean didn't deserve to be found naked and abused. He was a hero and he deserved dignity in death, as well as life. Grabbing the sleeping bag that Matthew had left in the corner, he untied the rope that was holding his hanging friend and gently lowered him into his waiting arms.

Weeping quietly, head bowed over his friend's body, they found him a few minutes later. James led the team in to gently lift Steve away from Sean's body and out of the door.

'Keep him covered, James!' he shouted out behind him. 'Please keep him covered.'

Connor led Steve to the car and, taking the keys from him, drove him back to the city.

'What now, Steve? Do you want me to take you back to the station?'

'No. Drop me at the hospital, I need to see my family … I need to tell Meg … I just need to …'

Steve couldn't find his words, he felt numb. Sean's death had not really impacted him yet and he started to shiver.

'That's fine, sir, I think that you should be checked out for shock anyway. I will inform the superintendent and leave you for a few hours. I will collect you in the morning, sir.'

'Thank you, Connor,' Steve said, then shivered. '… and stop calling me *sir*.'

At the hospital, Steve climbed out of the car, assuring Connor that he would be fine after he grabbed a coffee from the vending machine. He thanked him and walked towards the entrance. Looking up, he had wanted, hoped even, that this would be a night that he would always remember, but not for the reasons it would now. Choking back his emotion, he turned and watched Connor drive slowly away toward the hospital exit. An ambulance with blue lights flashed passed Connor, then screeched towards the open hospital doorway amidst the chaos of ambulance doors being flung open, voices speaking in calm but officious ways, and trolley wheels rattling.

Steve took a moment to just breathe.

Life was precious. Didn't his wee babies prove that? In this place of life and death, he also felt torn; he was the one still alive and able to enjoy time with his children. Life would go on, it was the way of the world but without Sean in it, his was going to change in a big way from now on. He closed his eyes and images of Sean hanging in the church where they had laughed as children and sang in the choir floated in his mind's eye. He swallowed down the vomit reaching his mouth and headed towards the lift to take him up to the maternity unit.

The hiss of the doors opening seemed to awaken him from his stupor. Pressing the button automatically, he shook his head and, rubbing his hands over his face, he wiped the smell and tears of death away from his life. He knew that he needed to be strong for Meg and the babies.

Entering the room, he stood in the doorway, the light seeping in as he watched his beloved sleeping peacefully, a baby in each arm. He approached the bed and one of the babies stirred. He lifted the boy gently into his arms.

'Hello, Sean, my boy. Your daddy needs a bit of comfort, so he does.'

The baby looked up at him, blinking in the small amount of light with the largest and bluest eyes Steve had ever seen. Watching his son's face, he found it hard not to smile at the faces he was pulling. Holding him tightly, he laughed out loud as with a tremendous push up of his legs the baby shit himself.

'Yes, sir! Uncle Sean would definitely have approved of you.'

He quietly wept as his son wriggled in his arms. Meg, watching from the bed, held out her hand and gently took Steve's in hers. There was no need to say anything; he was here with his family where he should be. Understanding his loss, Meg said nothing; he would tell her when he was ready.

Meg took Steve in her arms and he wept tears for his old friend Sean; he wept more tears for his mammy and his daddy, but mostly he wept for himself.

CHAPTER 31

'People once believed that when someone dies, a crow carries their soul to the land of the dead. But sometimes, something so bad happens that a terrible sadness is carried with it and the soul can't rest.'

Eric Draven (*The Crow*)

Connor arrived promptly at 8am to find Steve waiting at the hospital entrance. Climbing into the car, he found Connor sitting with a folder and a takeaway coffee ready to whisk him off to the station.

'Thanks, Connor. Did you manage to get any sleep at all?'

'A little, sir. That is the preliminary report from James. He stayed up to do Sean's autopsy. I'm so sorry, sir, it doesn't make for great reading. I wish I had gone to the super earlier … perhaps we could have saved him. The super has asked that everyone meet at 9am for a briefing.'

'No, Connor, Sean would not want you to blame yourself … we could all say *if only*. I should have answered my phone or I should have rung him earlier, the day before, to finish telling him about what I had found out about Matthew Doyle. Or Sean should have been more cautious … we all *should have* …'

Sighing, Steve took a large gulp from his coffee to cover up the quiver in his voice.

'By the way, Steve, I haven't had time to congratulate you on the birth of the babies. I hope that Meghan is well too?' Connor smiled and turned his head towards Steve.

'Thank you, yes, they are all doing grand. I can't believe that they will be coming home later today. Then it will all become real,' he replied.

Glancing at his superior, Connor watched as a conflict of emotions raced across his face. His grin had turned to a frown immediately he had made it.

'Don't feel guilty at being happy about the babies, sir. Sean wouldn't want it any other way,' Connor said.

'I know, Connor … and don't call me sir till we reach the station.'

Steve smiled. Bringing his attention to the folder, he took in a deep breath before turning the page. As he glanced over the first few paragraphs, he read the list of injuries that James had found on Sean's body.

'The bastard!'

He threw the document down between his legs to the floor, unable to read any more about the injuries to his friend.

'If it's any consolation at all, James said that he went down fighting and that Doyle wouldn't have been able to incapacitate him without the stun gun.'

Connor looked over at Steve who now sat, head in hands.

Lifting his head, he used his anger to push away the images in his head of Sean as he had last seen him. Also, anger helped him keep a lid on his other emotions and he had composed himself by the time that they pulled into the carpark of the garda station. He was a professional and Sean deserved his respect as such, to write up his report and deliver to the team everything that they had discovered about Matthew Doyle. He was looking forward to seeing James and taking a look at anything they had found in the abandoned building that Doyle had been using as a home. He especially wanted a look at the book that had fallen from his hand when he had hit the ground.

It obviously was precious to him for him to keep hold of it as he fell.

Steve climbed out of the car with Connor following. They both visibly straightened and took a deep breath on entering the building. A hush fell as they entered the station and all of the staff nodded in acknowledgement. The superintendent greeted them at the door.

'At least he is at peace now,' he said quietly.

'Your bloody faith didn't work, though … sir,' Steve replied in a tone he'd not used before to a superior officer.

Ignoring it in understanding of Steve's grief, the super called everyone into the room. Addressing them all, he told of his own grief at losing one of the best officers Ireland had ever seen, of his own frustration that the perpetrator of Sean's death would never be brought to justice, and that if anyone needed help and support in dealing with the loss of their finest, then counselling would be made available. This last piece of information was directly spoken towards Steve who actually flinched at the words. He knew that no amount of counselling could ever replace his friend or help him feel less guilty about his death … no, he'd been more than a friend – Sean had been the brother that he had never had.

The superintendent finished speaking and asked Steve to follow him to his office where he turned to address him.

'I know how hard this is and is going to be for you, Steve. Sean was not only a colleague to you but an amazing friend, with a lot of history between you both. I know that at the moment you are grieving and are probably unsure as to what you want to do next, so I am going to suggest that you take some paternity leave and spend time with your loved ones. I am also going to recommend to the board that on your return you step up as DCI. You are more than capable as you have already been in the role, and we would be lucky to have you … and I believe it is what Sean would want. I also wanted you to know that I have contacted Sean's family. Perhaps if you feel up to it a word with his children might help their loss.'

Steve was flabbergasted; he wasn't expecting that … he also was unsure how he felt about taking Sean's job or even continuing as a police officer.

'I don't know, sir, I … I …'

'Take your time, Steve. Now, go home and hold your new babies, kiss their mammy and just breathe in that sea air for at least two weeks … then you can let me know.'

'Thank you, sir. I think you are a very wise man,' Steve replied.

'Oh, and by the way, Steve, I expect an invitation to the christening.'

Dismissed, Steve returned to his office where sitting on his desk, waiting for him, was the report from James, and the last of the notes and feathers found with Sean's body. Lifting the folder up, underneath it he found two books, one of which Matthew had been holding onto as he fell. Picking it up and turning it over, he read the title: *The Divine Comedy* by Dante Alighieri. The second, as expected, was *The HOLY BIBLE*.

Steve took the book carefully from the sealed bag, and flicking through the pages he thought that maybe something would jump out at him to give some small comfort. Instead, inside he found the ramblings of a madman. Most of the writing was illegible but what words he could make out confirmed his and Sean's belief that Matthew Doyle had been the victim of abuse at the hands of the fathers at St. Patrick's along with hundreds of other boys in the seminary. Nothing that Matthew Doyle could have suffered, however, could compensate for the evil that he inflicted on them later and also on his dear friend.

He turned the pages and a folded piece of paper fluttered out and dropped onto the desk. Opening it, he turned it around in his hands until he could make sense of what he was seeing. Upon the paper was a very detailed drawing of a mountain made up of terraces, with the title: *The Mountain of Purgatory*. Each terrace was named for each of the deadly sins and against each sin a name had been added. Each of the names tallied with the names of the murdered priests. Surrounding each terrace was a series of concentric spheres with the named planets surrounding the Earth.

'Hey, Connor, what do you make of this?' Steve called, holding the piece of paper in the air.

'I'm not sure, sir, but James sent a note explaining what he *thought* it was,' Connor replied.

Placing the drawing and the book back on his desk, he once more turned to the folder Connor had given him earlier with James's preliminary findings. Quickly skipping over the first couple of pages concerning Sean's physical injuries, he found what he was looking for: two sheets of paper with a note attached in James's handwriting.

'Steve, I believe the piece of loose paper that depicts a drawing of a mountain and planets in our solar system to be based upon Dante's Divine Comedy poem which has three parts:

Part one: Inferno – Hell

Part two: Purgatorio – Purgatory

Part three: Paradiso – Paradise / Heaven

The mountain represented the terraces of Hell which must be gone through before reaching earthly paradise / purgatory. Each terrace held a different torture for souls, depending on the sin that they had committed in life, such as:

EARTHLY PARADISE

Terrace Seven - The lustful
Terrace Six - The gluttonous
Terrace Five - The covetous
Terrace Four - The slothful

Terrace Three - The wrathful
Terrace Two - The envious
Terrace One - The proud
Ante Purgatory - The late repentant
Ante Purgatory - The ex-communicate
The seven deadly sins of lust, greed, jealousy, sloth, wrath, envy and pride

The final part, Paradiso / Heaven, consisting of a series of concentric spheres surrounding Earth representing:

Moon - Fortitude
Mercury - Justice
Venus - Love
Sun - Temperance/ Wisdom
Mars - Faith
Jupiter - Hope
Saturn - Prudence
The fixed stars Primum Mobile – Angels Realm
Empyrean – Gods abode

These are the nine levels of angelic hierarchy. This, I believe, then relates to the killer's poem and the sins of the fathers.

One Crow for Malice
Two for Mirth
Three for a Funeral
And Four for a Birth
Five for a Secret
Six for a Thief
Seven for a tale never to tell
Eight for Heaven

Nine for Hell (Dante's final circle)
Ten for the devil wherever he may dwell.

I hope this insight has been helpful; I could be completely wrong.
Sorry for your loss and congratulations on the birth of the twins.
James

Steve sat staring at the letter from James for an age, only stirring when Connor placed a coffee in front of him.

'So, could you make any sense of it, sir?' he enquired of Steve.

'Not really, Connor, but I don't think that we can ever really understand the mind of someone like Matthew Doyle. He seems to have mixed up his religious beliefs with Dante's poem and then took it upon himself to take retribution, on God's behalf, on those that had committed the seven deadly sins.'

'It's all beyond me, sir. I can understand the priests but why Sean?'

Steve looked at Connor, unable to express his grief. He began to feel sick at the thought of what his friend had endured. His mind returned to the list of bodily injuries inflicted on him, which read like a horror novel. James's words in the report played in his head like a bad movie. He stood up abruptly and rushed out of the room, only just making it to the bathroom before throwing up the coffee he had just consumed.

He came back into the room rather sheepishly.

'Sorry, Connor, it's just the thought of what that maniac did to him. I can't get it out of my head; I haven't fully read it yet but I can't seem to face that right now. I am just going to quickly write up my report then I am going to pick up Meg and the babies from the hospital and go home. I am going on paternity leave for a couple of weeks. It will give me time to think where to go from here. I just feel gutted, to be truthful, and I'm not sure that I want to carry on doing this anymore … not without Sean.'

'I understand, sir, but it would be a shame to lose two great detectives all at once. Those boys from Dublin will think that they can come here and take over.'

He gently patted Steve's shoulder and smiled as he walked away.

CHAPTER 32

'The mind is its own place, and in itself can make a Heaven of Hell and a Hell of Heaven.'

Milton (*Paradise Lost*)

Life settled into some kind of routine with Meg and the babies. Steve had told Connor he would use this time to think but he was very tired as he hadn't been sleeping and was having dreams that he couldn't even contemplate telling Meg about; more nightmares than dreams. The vision of Sean hanging in that church was haunting him day and night. He owed it to his friend to keep on living, he knew that he must, but how could he when Sean had been slaughtered like a sacrificial lamb on the altar of his own happiness? He cursed himself daily for being too wrapped up in the wonder of new life to not take notice of his old one and answer that bloody phone … if only he could turn back time, he berated himself constantly.

He was using the excitement of having the new babies as an excuse not to think of anything at all. Every morning he just put one foot in front of the other and tried to carry on as normal. That is if normal even existed in his life … so far it had been anything but normal. Meg found him sat in the chair with baby Sean tucked into the crook of his arm. She had been worried about his behaviour but was more worried about broaching the subject because of his mental state. If anyone had a right to say something to him it was her: she had also been to hell and back and he was yet again shutting her out. Taking a deep breath, she had decided to speak out, so she approached him.

'Sean wouldn't want you to do this to yourself you know that,' she said. 'You did all that you could to save him and he wouldn't want you to sit here wallowing in self-pity. The babies need a father and I need you, and if that sounds harsh, I'm sorry, but it's the truth.'

'You don't understand what I'm feeling, Meg. Something is not right with this case; it's not just my guilt over Sean's death, it's more than that. I can't eat, I can't sleep; I can barely concentrate on anything. What would you know about what I am feeling?' he replied harshly.

'How dare you say that to me, Steve Ryan! I lost my mammy my daddy and my darling brother to a maniac, so yes, I do bloody understand what you are going through! Did you forget that only two years ago I was in the same place that you are now? You sitting here moping, saying poor me is not what I or the babies need right now. So, I suggest if things are not looking right, go do your bloody job and find out what it is that is bugging you about this case. Not that there is a case as the perpetrator is dead or had you forgotten that? Because I need the old Steve back here, in the present, *with* me, not off in a world of his own, not telling me … *yet again* … what is going on in his stupid, selfish, head.'

Meg sobbed before running out of the room.

Steve looked down at the sleeping baby's head. Meg was right – wallowing in self-pity was not helping anyone. He lifted baby Sean from his arms and placed him into the cot alongside his yet to be named sister and followed after her. God, he owed that woman so much for putting up with his selfishness. The biggest apology ever was needed right now and he knew that he had needed that kick up the arse to make him see how lucky he was.

After grovelling profusely and acknowledging how resilient and strong Meg had been over the past couple of years, he promised to put all thoughts of Sean and the case away, and said he would try to concentrate more on her and their babies.

'I don't want you to do that!' Meg cried. 'I would rather you go finish what you have to … go back to bloody work Steve and sort this out! I don't want you half here. I will ask Aunty Sian to help out with the twins' feeds. Just go, leave me in peace. I have two babies to care for and I don't want a needy man too.'

Steve was angry now; he didn't want to hear what Meg was saying to him, although he knew she was right. He slammed his way out of the house, and both babies startled and began to cry at the sound of the banging door.

He marched off up the hill towards his parents' graves that lay at the top, but he found no solace there this time and continued his walk, practically running down the other side. Suddenly he knew where he was going; he ran faster and soon reached the outer wall of the cemetery. It was covered in ivy, moss-filled and crumbling. He vaulted over it, feeling the brambles tearing at his clothing as he pushed forward through the heavy undergrowth towards what was left of the church. He turned suddenly and surveyed the land. There were a few gravestones still upright where they had not been allowed to dig. His heart beat faster as he remembered his last case with Sean. He looked at the piles of weed-covered mounds left behind by the diggers as they had uncovered the pits. He expected to see the figure of the girl staring back at him, the child with red hair that he had seen before, but her ghost had now been laid to rest. It was Sean's that was nagging at his conscience now.

His thoughts turned to the tiny bodies heaped in piles underground. All that had been left were their tiny bones and pieces of rags that had been used to wrap the bodies. It had taken James and his team months of hard work to establish cause of death and DNA for each tiny body. Work that mostly had to be done when things were quiet as it was classed as a cold case with very little budget attached. It was only after Sean had threatened to expose the church to the press that a small amount of money had been found to lay the wee ones to rest. No warm blankets and safe arms for them, he thought, his own darling babies coming to mind, and suddenly he sank to his knees, sobbing. Unfeeling of the stinging nettles and bramble thorns that caught at his clothing and flesh, he held his face in his hands, finally letting go of the grief that he had been holding onto over the past couple of weeks. Sean had been so proud of their work on that case, leaving no stone unturned to find the families and return the small bodies for proper burial. Was that what had brought his name to the attention of Matthew Doyle, he wondered.

Standing up shakily, he made his way to the front of the building where the police seal was still intact on the church door and the tape surrounding the crime scene flapped noisily in the wind. A cawing sound drew his attention away from what he was about to do. He looked up straight into the eye of a huge black bird in a tree opposite him, staring curiously and turning its head from side to side to get a better view of the intruder. Its presence seemed a portent to him to smash the seal from the door and to step through the opening into the large wooden entrance porch. The smell of plant decomposition hit his nostrils first, then underlying the smell of years of decay and neglect was the slight coppery tinge of dried blood. Braving himself to return to the place of Sean's death, he entered slowly at first. What he thought he would find that James and his team had not already discovered he had no idea. Finally seeing it all in broad daylight made it completely real to him. Making his way to the back of the church behind the altar, he could see that the roof had collapsed and sunlight filtered through the overhanging greenery to shed some light into the corners.

He closed his eyes and imagined himself and Sean back here dressed in their choir gowns, pushing and shoving each other in the side to try and reach the tiny wooden recess at the back where Father Benedict hid the communion wine. Sometimes they were able to grab a swig before anyone else noticed or Father Benedict locked the small wooden door covering it. Steve was sure that Father Benedict knew; his black eyes missed nothing and his mammy would often remark on the smell of alcohol clinging to his breath. Steve had sworn then that it must be from his clothing as Father Benedict kept their robes hanging next to the wine bottle. He would point to a small blot of red spreading along the hem of his white chorister's robe like an ink stain.

'Lying is a sin,' she would berate him as he swore that he wasn't lying. She would smile to herself as she left the room.

Opening his eyes, he exclaimed:

'Forgive me, Mammy, for lying to ye. It wasn't meant to fool you, as I could see that ye never were.'

He startled then as a thought struck him. Matthew Doyle had been visiting this place and planning his and Sean's death for a long time. He knew that by the oiled hinges on the door, the sleeping bag and the food store that had been recovered by James and the forensic team. What if he had used this place to hide things? After all, he was as familiar with the place and its layout as Steve himself. Looking around, he began to think he had been wrong as it was completely derelict and anything that might have helped had been buried or squashed under a host of gardaí feet, or tons of rubble and rubbish that had been moved to recover Sean's body. Working his way to the back of the building, he found what he was looking for hidden behind an old rickety table full of woodworm and standing on only three legs. He frantically pulled at the table. It began to creak, then pushing some of the debris away with his foot, it eventually began to move an inch at a time. Excitement caused his heart to race, then, at its peak, disappointment plunged him downwards as he saw the small wooden door that had covered the small recess hanging by one hinge, the opening exposed and definitely empty.

'Well, what exactly did ye think ye would find, Steve Ryan? A holy relic of Saint Paul, or a bloody confession, or even an old bottle of wine?'

He berated himself at his stupidity and kicked at the debris on the floor. A few of the old bibles and hymn books were scattered on there, the pages ripped out to use as fuel for the small fires set by the kids. He was about to turn away in disgust when he spied the corner of a small black book that had been covered by the dust and debris of the others. It looked slightly cleaner than the rest and bending down he picked it up. Brushing the dust from the cover, he turned it over in the palm of his hand; he recognised it immediately. He had one himself, sitting on the bookcase at home in the living room. It had been presented to him by Father Benedict when he had left school to continue his further education at St Peter's High School, aged eleven. Opening the cover, he found what he was looking for … an inscription:

'To Matthew, may God always be by your side as you take his holy path, knowing that your brother will be well looked after by the church.

Father Benedict'

CHAPTER 33

'How sweetly did they float upon the wings of silence through the empty-vaulted night, at every fall, smoothing the Raven down of darkness till it smiled.'

John Milton (*Paradise Lost*)

He stepped out into night that now had fallen. How long he had stood alone listening to the silence and hearing nothing, not even a bird call or insect hum, he couldn't guess. He hadn't picked up his phone; it was still charging in the kitchen so he had no idea of the time or how long he had been away. It felt like hours but it could be just minutes, although the former was more likely looking at the darkness of the night above him. He also knew that Meg would be frantic with worry by now.

He hastily made his way down the long driveway; he wouldn't risk going back through the cemetery in the darkness as he didn't want a broken ankle or, worse still, to fall into the excavations. It would take him longer, but he thought it for the best. His hand grasped onto the small book in his pocket. Luckily, being a good policeman, he always had an evidence bag tucked inside his jacket pocket, a habit that he had picked up in training college that still stood him in good stead today. Every jacket he possessed had one tucked away somewhere. He hoped that James could maybe get some prints from the book. An idea was formulating in his brain and as usual he had gone into detective mode irrelevant of his family's or partner's needs. He needed to remind himself that he was a father now and it was his selfish behaviour that had caused the argument with Meg and he knew it. *Taking the piss* is what Sean would have told him, and he would have been right.

He saw the farmhouse lights in the distance and like a warm hug they drew him home. Whether he would receive a warm hug when he got there was a different matter. He smiled to himself at the thought of his mammy years before, waiting till he had crept into the hall, shoes in hand when he had been late home, and giving him a full-on clatter around the ears as he stepped through the doorway.

Well, if Meg decided to do the same it was what he deserved; he laughed. He felt lighter now after his breakdown in the cemetery and it was as if Sean were guiding him along the right path. He was determined that when he got back, he would make amends with Meg and concentrate on his family for the next week. He also thought that it would be nice to visit Sean's kids just to see how they were doing. Although the eldest had not been speaking to Sean, he knew how upset they would feel about their daddy dying before they could make up. He hoped that wouldn't make the suffering worse for them all.

His head ached as every tumbled thought turned around inside it and he realised that he had had nothing to eat or drink since last night's supper. Suddenly, he felt ravenous and he turned into the short lane leading to the farm from the main road. Glancing up, he noticed the sign hanging above him, now swinging in the wind, creaking gently. He hadn't thought about the name of his parents' farm before but it sort of hit him in the gut all of a sudden. The blackbird on the sign seemed to mock him with the words written underneath it: *Rooks Farm*. He stared blankly at it, then shook himself and shuddered. He hurried up the track as if the Morrigan herself were on his heels. He didn't notice the car with no lights drift slowly past the entrance to the farm then swiftly move up the road, only turning on the headlights once it reached the village end. Or see the figure quietly observing him as he headed home, watching him running up the lane to the farm.

Steve entered the kitchen sheepishly to find Aunty Sian sitting at the table with a cup of tea. He almost stepped back in shock as she could so easily have been his own mammy sitting there.

'Will ye join me in a cup, Steven James?' Sian queried, holding out the brown teapot that his own mammy had kept constantly filled with tea.

The use of his full name was exactly how Mammy would have shown her disapproval, too, the tone not escaping his attention.

'I'm sorry, Sian. I just need to see Meg,' he replied.

Holding her hand in the air to halt any more movement from him, she gestured for him to sit down.

'Meghan and the wee ones are fast asleep and after the day that she has had if ye wake her up, I will hit ye meself.' She began pouring tea into a cup waiting on the table. 'Sugar?' she enquired.

Pulling out a chair, Steve practically collapsed onto it, looking like a boy in trouble.

'Is she OK?'

'Well, no thanks to ye worrying her to death. Your supper's in the oven so I suggest ye eat it and finish yer tea then think of the biggest apology that ye can … I'm stopping over for a few days so I will bid ye goodnight. I'm off to bed … and Steven, don't ever take yer loved ones for granted again, or else one day when you need them, they might not be around.' Sian stood up, placed her cup in the sink and left Steve sitting at the table, stunned.

He listened for any sound of life, of the babies stirring. He heard Sian's steps receding as she entered the spare bedroom then complete silence. Her quiet anger had hit him as if he had been slugged in the guts. The breath left his lungs and he picked up the tea cup, hoping that the warm liquid would soothe him. It hit his stomach and it grumbled gratefully for sustenance of some kind. No cosy comfortable chat at the kitchen table for him tonight as was wont with his mammy before. He could hear Sean's voice clearly in his head:

'Well, ye deserved that for being a total prick!' Sadly, he had to agree. Turning to the stove to find the dinner that had been saved for him, he ate it with relish. Realising just how hungry he was and in between mouthfuls, he mumbled to himself. 'Well, prick or not, I can't grovel on an empty stomach.'

*

The light hit his eyes as the curtains were drawn swiftly back and, blinking in the sunlight, he saw Meg standing over him, her fists clenched, her face full of sadness and despair. He was lying on the sofa, exactly where he had dropped after eating his supper, too much of a coward to go upstairs and face his wife. Sitting bolt upright, he started to apologise, words tumbling out of his mouth, his hands pleading.

'Stop … just bloody stop! Will you listen to yourself saying what you think I want to hear! Well, I don't, Steve, because every word that has come out of your mouth so far has been a lie. Yes, you might be sorry that you upset me and yes, you are sorry that Sean died but all you can think about is yourself and you have forgotten that you are no longer single, that you have responsibilities now. I am sick of it always being about you, Steve Ryan. I have booked a flight home for later today. Uncle John is taking me to the airport and I am going back to stay with Becky, the boys and Romany till my house is free of its tenants.'

She turned on her heel and he sat up from the blast he had just received in time to see Uncle John placing their suitcases in the car and Sian with a baby carrier in each hand, strapping them into the back seat. He watched Meg join them. He looked on in shock … no … no … NO! His brain screamed inside his head, but nothing came out of his mouth until it was too late and then it echoed around the room. He stumbled across the room then watched from the doorway as the back of the car disappeared down the driveway.

CHAPTER 34

'I remained too much inside my head and ended up losing my mind.'

Edgar Allen Poe

A ringing sound woke him; he was unsure if it was inside his head and that he was imagining it but when it became insistent, he tried to open his eyes to follow where the sound was coming from. Pain hit the back of his eyes and spread across his head like wildfire. Closing his eyes again, he felt himself sway; the room was turning even when he wasn't moving. He tried to take a deep breath to steady himself and all he could smell was stale drink and vomit. The ringing continued and he realised it was coming from his phone in his jacket pocket. He held it up and focused long enough to push the answer button. Connor's voice came on. 'Hi Steve, how are you? I have been trying to get you for a few days. Sorry to bother you at home but …'

'Connor, Connor,' Steve managed to croak, his throat raw and dry. 'Wait, I'll call you back; give me half an hour, please.'

Steve cut off the phone and standing up he made his way to the kitchen where he filled a glass with water and downed it in one. Feeling a little sick, he swayed into the hallway and sat on the bottom step of the stairs. He pushed himself up them on his bottom like a child. When he reached the top, he was unable to stand without passing out again. He crawled to the bathroom and flung himself fully clothed into the shower, turning the taps to cold. He screamed as the first stream hit him in the face.

'Ye never could hold yer liquor!' Sean's laughing face swam before him and he reached out to grasp it as it faded before his eyes. After a few moments under the cold water, he managed to divest himself of his clothes and turn the shower to a more temperate warmth and he scrubbed days of filth and grime from his body. Feeling slightly better and able to stand for short periods without passing out, he climbed out of the shower but not before giving himself another blast of cold water. It shocked his body and his brain into movement and he remembered why he had drunk himself into oblivion days ago. In fact, he had no idea how long ago or even what day he was on.

Wrapping himself in a large fluffy towel, he found that even that hurt his skin and muscles. Sensitive still to any form of movement, he cautiously made his way to the bedroom. Grabbing a fleece and some joggers from the wardrobe, he gently pulled them on, wincing as the fleece went over his head. Then, making his way downstairs, he put on the coffee and drank another glass of water. He picked up his phone from the sofa where he had flung it and saw that it was almost out of charge so he headed to the kitchen to plug it in. Several texts popped up, mostly from Connor, but as he scrolled through, he saw that he had had four from Meg over a three-day period, starting the day after she had left. Before opening them, he turned the phone back to his home page and looked at the date and time; it was six days since Meg had gone with the wee ones … six days. He was horrified!

He also knew that he needed to be completely sober and compos mentis before sending any reply to her, so first things first: coffee in gallons was needed and possibly a little toast. He knew that he wasn't anywhere near as robust as Sean, and whilst his friend had always tucked into a full Irish breakfast, Steve had nibbled on toast and still threw up after a weekend of booze, let alone a six-day bender.

After the third cup, he started to feel the caffeine kick in and after pouring the last dregs into his mug, he refilled and put the coffee pot back on. Feeling a little more human, he decided to call Connor whilst the coffee brewed. He held the phone away from his ear as the ringing upset his head again until he heard Connor answer. Speaking rather quietly, he greeted him with a far from cheery hello but not as croaky as before.

'Are you OK now? You sound a little worse for wear. Have you been celebrating?' Connor queried.

'No such luck, Connor. What can I help you with?'

The reply shocked Steve as if he had forgotten why he had lost everything, including his mind, for a week. He had blanked it all from his memory for a few days and now reality smacked him full in the face.

'Well, I'm so sorry to bother you but James asked if I would let you know that Sean's funeral has been arranged for Tuesday next week at St Peter's Church in Dublin. If you want to attend, the service is at noon, and he also wanted to know if you would like to attend the wake, he has organised with some of the lads from the station?'

Steve tried to utter a reply, even a word, but nothing came out.

'I'm so sorry, Steve. I know you are still in shock but I didn't want you to miss the chance to say goodbye to Sean.'

Connor's empathy and caring attitude to everyone was what made him a great candidate to become a brilliant detective one day. Sean had spotted his potential a while back and had nurtured and encouraged him to take his exams. Steve had a choice to make; he could crumble and resort back to the drink and oblivion or he could stand up and face the difficulties that he was experiencing and count his blessings. Connor calling at that moment had been one of them and in that moment a turning point in Steve's life was reached.

'Thank you, Connor. I will attend the funeral but the wake ... err, I think the demon drink and I have just about finished our last waltz for a while.'

Suddenly he remembered the small book that he had found, then dread hit him – had it been in his pocket when he hit the shower? Panicking, he asked Connor to hold while he dashed upstairs to retrieve the book, finding his jacket a soggy mess on the floor of the bathroom. He held it up and reached inside the pocket where he found the book still wrapped in the evidence bag and perfectly dry. Never had he thanked God before for the foresight of evidence bags, but he did now. Racing back downstairs with renewed energy, he grabbed the phone from where he had flung it and gasped out to Connor what he thought he had found. Asking him to set up a search of the records for anything that he could find about a brother of Matthew Doyle, he told him that he would send the book by courier to James and see him at the funeral on Tuesday.

Cutting off the phone, he felt more like himself; he was doing what he knew best. Meg had known him so well that she was able to see what he needed to do before he himself could ... how stupid had he been. She had loved him enough to tell him to go and put things right, even though she needed him the most at that time. It was the most unselfish thing anyone had ever done for him and he had thrown it in her face.

Reaching for another cup of coffee, he sat down at the table and, picking up his phone, he took in a deep breath and scrolled down to where the texts from Meg were, finding that the last one had been yesterday afternoon. Holding the phone tightly, he opened the first text. Reading quickly, he ascertained that they had been unable to board the flight because the babies were not registered, neither had they been added to Meg's passport. He sighed with relief but of course, that was five days ago! Rushing to read the next text it was clear that Meg was staying at Aunty Sian's and Uncle John's but was in the process of making the twins' birth official. This apparently meant that they needed to be officially named and did he have any preferences for their daughter? He hurried onto the next text, just two days ago.

By now he could hear the anger in Meg's words. Why was he not replying to her when she needed an answer today? She would name the baby herself and she still intended leaving Ireland. Why was he behaving like a child? He was a selfish pig! Why didn't he grow up and behave like a man and a father?

Meg!

He realised with horror that he had completely missed a text out and scrolling backwards, he found the one before.

'Hi Steve, I know that we have talked about Sean as a name for our son but we're at odds over a name for our baby girl and I need to officially register the babies to leave the country as I have told you before. I am going to make some suggestions and if I don't hear back from you, I will go ahead and name the wee one myself. I thought that Sean Jonathon Fingal Oscar Ryan was a great name for our boy as it is a nod to not only Sean, but also my darling brother and my father's love of literature. For our darling girl, I thought that Florence Magdalena Bridget Ophelia Ryan was beautiful. I know that you didn't want Magda but I want to honour both of our mammies.

Meg'

He smiled at the names; they were great names for the most beautiful babies in the world. What if Meg didn't want to see him? What if he never saw his babies again? He needed to put things right … *now!*

He hoped that Meg and the babies were still in the village. He grabbed his phone and keys and practically ran to the car. Wrenching open the door, he fell inside and as he started the car, he reflected that he didn't deserve a second chance. He had promised to love and protect his family and he didn't know how to. He was totally inadequate as a husband and a father. Mmm, *husband?* He hadn't thought about marriage but if Meg would agree to be his wife, he would promise her the world and do his best to make her happy.

'You're a total knob if you think that's what she wants, Steve Ryan … you

have a lot to learn about women.' He heard Sean's words as if he were sat next to him in the car. *'Just go and apologise and be bloody honest for once.'*

Turning the key, he heard the engine start and as if on auto pilot he drove the couple of miles to Sian and John's house in the village, hoping against hope that Meg and the babies were still there.

CHAPTER 35

'Death makes Angels of us all and gives us wings where we had shoulders, smooth as ravens' claws.'

Jim Morrison

The rain trickled down his collar and he felt it run down inside his jacket; it felt cold. He at least could feel that, he thought to himself, whereas before he had stood numb inside the church and listened to the many words spoken about his friend, Sean. No, he was more than his friend; he was the brother he'd never had, the play-mate, the comrade in arms, the fellow that he turned to when he needed help or advice… the shoulder that no longer was available for him to cry on. It mattered not; he was constantly talking to him in his head as if he was still here. He watched the soil hit the coffin and could no longer bear the grief of others as they wept for the son, the father, the ex-husband that was no more.

Turning away from the back of the crowd, he had spoken to no one and had crept into the service last minute, leaving as silently as he had arrived. Returning to the path, the crows above him mocked his grief and he swore at them as a small voice caught his ear and he heard his name being called. Turning at the sound of her voice, he saw her: a vision which he was unsure was real or imagined.

'Steve, please wait … please.' He heard the plea in her voice and the hope caught in his throat, unexpectedly and effectively cut off his voice. Mistaking his silence for his reluctance to speak to her after their last angry meeting, she started to turn away.

'Meg … oh Meg, you came?' he managed to gasp out as he

grasped her arm gently and turned her back towards him. He could see the tears and the anguish on her face.

'I'm sorry this isn't the time or the place to talk, Steve … I shouldn't have stopped you leaving,' Meg replied, unaware of Steve's delight that she had and the hope now rising in his chest that was almost stopping him from breathing. He held his breath, unable to speak, just nodding and pulling her towards him. They fell into each other's arms and both began trying to apologise at the same time.

'What happens now?' he asked, holding her face firmly in his hands. 'I love you, Meg, and I can't apologise enough for the times that I let you down when you needed me to be there for you and the babies. I absolutely love the names, by the way!' he said, smiling. 'All perhaps except Fingal … OK, OK, Fingal it is!' he laughed, holding his hands up in the air after seeing the look on Meg's face. 'I promise you that if you give me another chance, I will prove to you I can be the best husband and father for you all.'

'Husband, eh?' Meg smiled back. 'Well, are you asking me to marry you, Steven Ryan, in your usual peculiar way?'

'Oh, I'm definitely asking if you're accepting … Meghan Callahan. I was just unsure if that was what you wanted.' He could see that there was no need for her to reply – the answer showed in her eyes. He could hear Sean cheering them on as he kissed her passionately.

Grasping her arm, they made their way to a small café around the corner where they spent the next few precious hours making plans for a joint future. A figure stepped onto the pathway and watched them leave, totally unaware of anyone or of their surroundings, only each other. They walked down the path, arms around each other and at the gateway they turned left. The figure turned their head as they heard their name being called and an emotional mask slipped over their face and covered their features. The hatred on their face slid away, only to be replaced by the smile on their lips and a twinkle in their eye as they turned to greet the caller.

*

The next few days were taken up with moving the family back into the farmhouse and Steve just settling into the role of being a proper father and partner. Meg and he talked for hours, opening up to each other as never before and laying everything bare, all fears, all anger, all their love for each other. They settled into a comfortable bubble of routine and talked about their plans for when Romany joined them in a few weeks for Christmas break. They named the babies and decided against a church christening, dealing only with the formality of registration. Life was good.

Steve looked out of the window to the hill and his parents' graves; looked at the dew-dropped cobwebs in the grass and wondered how long it would last. Not long, so it seemed, as a phone call broke the reverie of a blissful two weeks.

'Hi Steve. I hope that you are settling into life with the wee family.'

Steve stopped in his tracks at the voice of his boss, Superintendent Simon Reevey, waiting for him to state why he was calling. Steve had prepared the speech that he had been working on to say that he had decided to refuse the offer of Sean's old job. But before he had chance to say anything, the super said, 'Steve, we have another one and I need you back here.'

Steve reeled at this information.

'How? Whaa ... that's impossible, sir! Matthew Doyle is dead!'

Was he going mad ... *How* –? Had they got the wrong person? Doyle had admitted to the killings himself.

'He confessed, sir; I know that he did it.'

Then he remembered the small black book still in the drawer upstairs. Damn it, he had been going to courier it to Connor and he forgot. How could he have forgotten to do his bloody job? The superintendent briefly gave him the details.

'Please, Steve, we need you back here ASAP. The station has been knocked for six: first over Sean's death and now this.'

Stumbling over his words, he said, 'I need to talk to Meg. I'll let you know in an hour. Please give me a little time to take it all in.' Then, cutting off the call he poured the coffee, placed the two mugs on a tray and climbed the stairs, already thinking about the state of his suit and whether he had a clean shirt ironed. Meg knew immediately that something was wrong and she had heard the phone ring from the bedroom. She took a mug from the tray and leant back against the pillows; she wasn't about to make it easy for him as she already knew what he was about to say.

Steve took the other coffee then, after taking a huge gulp, almost burning his mouth in the process, he stuttered out what he had just been told.

'How could that be? It must be a copycat! Matthew Doyle is dead … he killed the priests and Sean; he said he did it … I don't understand!' Meg loudly whispered, trying not to wake the babies, barely containing her anger. Let someone else deal with it, Steve; you're not indispensable, after all.'

'Well, who do you suggest we ask? Sean maybe or what about young Connor – shall I leave him on his own? It takes at least six months to get a replacement for Sean. You know I have to do it … anyway, what if I was wrong about Matthew Doyle all along and he was covering for someone else or if he had a partner? I always wondered how he had the strength to lift the bodies or restrain Sean. There is something that I need to show you. I found it the night that I stormed off after our fight, it was in the old church. I remembered that when we were kids, Sean and I would sneak the communion wine from a little hidden cupboard at the back of the altar, and I found something there.'

He pulled the small book from where he had placed it in the bedside draw, explaining how he had meant to send it on to Connor for analysis but in the middle of everything else he had forgotten. Opening the book to the first page, keeping it sealed inside the plastic bag and handing it to Meg to read, he said, 'Matthew Doyle had a brother that nobody knew about; not even Aidan. I wonder if Aidan's parents knew. I believe that he is the key to everything.'

Meg sighed; she knew that she had lost the argument. Handing the book back to Steve, she said. 'Go get a shower and I will iron you a shirt. I hope your suit is clean.'

Steve smiled down at her – he loved this woman with all of his soul.

CHAPTER 36

'But I couldn't escape who I was or what I'd done – no matter how fast or far I ran. The crows were just a reminder of that. They wanted back in. My past wasn't done with me. Not yet.'

AR Kahler

An hour later, Steve, having made a phone call to work, was climbing into the car when his mobile rang. It was Connor.

'Can I start anything going or get anything ready for you, Steve? I realise that this has been a difficult decision for you to come back in so soon after Sean, but I will be right with you all of the way just as I would have if it were Sean. We are a team.'

Connor's kind and cheerful voice left him feeling rather choked. He thanked him and asked him to ready all of the files from the case, plus to dig out any information on the old case files concerning Matthew Doyle's parents' deaths at the farm and the list of abuse claimants again.

'Thanks, Connor. I also need to know if there was any mention of a sibling? I found something at the church that leads me to think that he had a brother. See you soon and get the coffee ready; it's going to be a late one.'

Hanging up, he turned and saw Meg walking towards him, wrapped in her dressing gown. Leaning in the door she kissed him and said, 'I love you and I understand that you will be late. It's OK. Aunty Sian is coming up later to help with the twins' feeds. So, go, my gallant knight, and save the world.' Laughing, she turned, waved and went back inside. That was what he needed to hear; he couldn't do this without the support of his partners, whether loved ones or professional. He understood that now.

'Well, it took ye long enough,' he heard Sean's chuckle in his ear as he drove off toward the main road.

Why couldn't anything to do with his hometown be cut and dried? It always had to be so complicated; why couldn't he just close the case and mourn his friend?

'You know why, ye eejit, because ye never learnt to walk away from a fight in the playground, always being the hard man … then I would have to rescue ye at the last bloody minute before ye got yer head beat in. Well, this time I can't rescue ye – yer on yer own with this one.'

Steve heard Sean's voice inside his head as if he was talking to him for real and he never found it strange … in a way, it was a comfort to him. As if his friend had never left him. He arrived at the station, parked up and entered the office. Glancing around him, he could see that Connor had already been busy. A board had been laid out and photos of all of the victims plus Matthew Doyle pinned upon it. He flinched as his eyes alighted on Sean's face then a new determination set in; he would find the truth if it meant that his friend could rest and find peace.

Approaching him, Connor stood behind him, then spoke.

'He would want you to find out the truth of it, sir. I can remove his picture from the board if you would like me to … if it's too upsetting?'

'No, leave him up there as a reminder that he wasn't a victim, but a brave man and an even greater detective. This is great work, Connor. How are you doing on the files front?'

'Well, sir, the file that we had here on the murders at the farm show nothing that we didn't know before. There are pictures of the scene and the injuries to both parents; there are even some pictures of Matthew's injuries taken before he was removed to the hospital.

Both parents suffered single gunshot wounds to the head whilst they were in bed and Matthew had been beaten badly. As we know now, he inflicted the fatal wounds on his parents whilst they slept because of the beatings that his father had been dishing out. There is no mention, though, of another child. I double-checked all of the relevant information and found nothing recorded of another child either digitally or in any old paperwork. The box file is on your desk. I retrieved it from evidence. I have tentatively put out any feelers for access to adoption records around the time of the murders and over the next year, plus records of any new entries into the local orphanage but have hit a brick wall.'

'I don't think we will get anything from the church without a warrant. What about the list of names from the abuse allegations file? We found Matthew Doyle on there – any names that might fit? Obviously, we don't have a date of birth for a sibling or even really know if one existed, it's just a hunch at the moment. Also, look at any local hospital or maternity home birth records in the area, say a month before the killings, although to be honest most of the women at the time gave birth at home as everything was so far away; except of course St Theresa's but they only went there if they were single to give the baby up for adoption. We need a paper trail, Connor, then we can follow and find out for sure. Meanwhile, I am popping in to see the super and find out about this new fellow.'

He tapped the latest picture added to the board that morning.

'And I'll ask him for permission for a warrant to access the necessary church records.'

Steve grabbed his mug of coffee thoughtfully left by Connor and headed into the superintendent's office. Tapping the door with the pen still in his hand, he entered after hearing the call to come in.

'Steve, I'm so glad to see you,' the super said as he placed the phone back on its cradle. 'That was the archbishop wanting to know what the hell is going on as he thought that we had captured the killer and before that I had the big boss breathing down my neck, wanting answers to questions that I couldn't give.'

'Well, I'm here now, sir. First of all, what makes you think that this latest priest's death connects to the others?' Steve asked.

'Sit down, Steve, and thanks for coming back in. I can't tell you the pressure I'm under to solve these bloody killings. James can fill you in with the gory details but safe to say there are too many similarities for it not to be the same perpetrator. A feather was found at the scene and a page torn from Dante's *Inferno* on the body.'

The super rubbed his hands over his face and looked at Steve sitting before him.

'A copycat perhaps?' Steve queried.

'See what you make of it and let me know later today. I have a bloody meeting now with the bishop and the commissioner. I've been summoned to explain what is happening.'

'Well, that is good news, sir. Could you put some pressure on the bishop to allow us access to church adoption records? We're trying to follow a lead that Matthew Doyle had a sibling. I really don't think that he did this alone and if this latest killing is the same as those from before, it proves my theory. I was going to ask you for a warrant anyway. Connor informs me that the church is being as obscure as usual.' Steve swigged his coffee; it was cold and he made a face.

'You had better get Connor to make you another one of those,' the super said. 'I think it is going to be a very long day. Can we meet again, at say five?' He turned his watch round to look at the face.

'Yes, sir, see you at five.'

Steve headed out of the room and, calling to Connor to tell him where he was going, he headed to the morgue, hoping James had had time to have finished the post mortem on the latest victim. If that is what it was. Steve had his doubts. Certain facts about the case had been leaked to the press after Sean's death, so this could be a copycat. He would hold judgement till he had seen James and visited the crime scene.

He took a deep breath, shoved two extra strong mints into his mouth, and pushed his way through the plastic curtains that hung in the doorway to the morgue. James was sitting typing in the corner, a body laid on a trolley in the centre of the room, and a bank of fridges hummed quietly in the wall. He was relieved to see that the body was covered with a sheet, but he didn't think he would ever get as strong a stomach as Sean when it came to bodies and gore. He called a greeting to James who turned on his stool and smiled at him.

'Steve, my man, how are you doing? Back so soon from paternity leave? How are the babes?'

'Just doing fine, thanks. I'm back because I hear that you have another dead priest for me to look at. Is it a copycat killing, do you think? Have you finished the autopsy?'

James pointed to the table.

'Just finished it before you arrived and typing up my report as we speak. There is something I want to show you if you can bear to take a look? It's better if you see it for yourself.'

He started to pull back the sheet covering the body laid on the trolley.

'The answer to your question is although this one is slightly different there are forensically too many similarities for it to be a copycat. Here for instance.'

He pointed with his pen to a cut on the left side of the body.

'The wound here was made by the same weapon as seen on all of the other bodies – a long thin blade of some kind with a serrated edge, possibly a kitchen knife. The only discrepancy is that there were a lot more of the same type of wounds inflicted this time, all at different angles. This along with the removal of some of the body parts led me to believe it is the same person, but see this here …' He rolled the body over exposing the neck and pointed at two small burn marks.

'Taser marks,' Steve finished for him.

'Yes. Taser marks again. I also found some on the chest in several places. He really wanted this one to suffer. The only difference as I said before was that there was no rhyme but we do have a corvid feather and a page torn from Dante's *Divine Comedy*. As I explained my theory to you before, I believe that the killer is using Dante's tortures in the circles of Hell to punish the priests for their real or perceived sins.'

'So, Matthew Doyle wasn't working alone. All along it has bugged me after seeing him in the flesh, so to speak … that he was so small in stature to have tackled the priests on his own, especially Sean.' He gulped back his emotion.

'Sean was always a big lad,' James said smiling, 'and if the partner was also a clergy man, he could easily have helped them to gain access to the buildings as well as lift the bodies.'

Steve left the morgue, stunned to think that his theory had been right all along: Matthew Doyle had not been working alone. Why he kept thinking that there was another person involved when nothing had shown that to be the case, he didn't know … all he knew was that if there was someone helping Doyle and who was now continuing on his own, he needed to be caught before anymore priests died. In his hand he grasped the page torn from Dante's book which he hoped might give them some clue.

He headed back to the station to grab Connor and go to the crime scene before his meeting with the super later. He wanted Connor to bring him up to speed on who had reported the murder and who had found the body. Definitely someone else was involved who was from inside the priesthood or closely connected to it. His hunches were never wrong and so far had stood him in good stead.

As they drove to the crime scene, he realised how much he had come to rely on Connor and what an asset to the team he was.

'When are you going to be taking your detective exams, Connor? I will put in a recommendation to the super to have you fast-tracked. You've been invaluable to this case, *and* the last one that we worked on together. Although I wouldn't recommend this bloody job to anybody.' He laughed and Connor joined in.

'Well, I was hoping to go in for them when we finished this case. In fact, I was meant to go for them last week but when this new body landed on our plate, I knew that we weren't finished with this one yet, so I postponed it.'

'I'll still talk to the super later today as I could definitely do with a new DC if I am going to stay on.'

Connor looked sideways at Steve, but his face gave nothing away.

'Yes, I did say *stay on*. I realised after the last couple of weeks that this is my life and when I am away from it, my mind still keeps trying to work things out. I just hope that we never get a serial killer again … what say you?'

Steve turned and smiled at Connor as they approached the turning of the home at Maynooth where the latest murder had taken place.

'By the way, Connor, James didn't introduce me to the body this time. What was the priest's name and was he on our radar at all?'

'It was a Father Thomas Reagan and, yes, he was on the list as one of the accused priests from the abuse file,' Connor replied.

'I thought he might be. Now, I want you to take note of who might be watching us. If you see anyone acting suspiciously, grab them and get their name. Chase them down if you need to. I am sick of these bloody priests giving us the run-around; it's time to get tough,' Steve said as he climbed out of the car and strode purposefully up the drive towards the door.

'Well, there's our first one, Connor; see the two watching us out of the window on the left? If one answers the door, you grab the other one, OK?'

He picked up the large brass knocker and rapped it as hard as he could. He ignored the small electric bell that had been installed on the wall. He wanted them to know that they had arrived; the sound echoed loudly through the hallway inside.

Looking around the murder scene, Steve gained nothing new from it. Father Thomas Reagan's room was plain, almost cell like, and apart from a few books and personal affects it was the same as all of the others. The decoration owed itself to the blood splatter across the wall. *Arterial spray*, he thought, and knew that James would have been thorough in his examination of the crime scene. Moving quickly downstairs he caught a movement out of the corner of his eye. He turned quickly but saw nothing. *Maybe I am imagining bogey men at every corner*, he chuckled to himself but keeping an extra awareness about him as he collected Connor and returned to the car. As he climbed into the driving seat, his phone rang. Glancing briefly at the screen, he saw that it was James but he pressed 'end call'. He asked Connor to take over the driving and climbed into the passenger seat to return the call.

'James, we are at the crime scene now. Quite a large amount of blood spatter which obviously ties in with the number of wounds on the body. Anything I can do to help?'

Listening carefully to James and nodding every now and then, Steve's face became set in an expression of disbelief as the conversation went on. Connor's curiosity was now peaked; perhaps this was the breakthrough that they had been waiting for. He wondered what James had found to send his boss into a paroxysm of disbelief. Cutting off the phone, Steve turned to Connor.

'James reckons that more than one person inflicted the wounds on Father Reagan. After I left, he decided to take a closer look at the body and some of the wounds were impossible to make unless you were stood behind and in front of him at the same time; apparently the angles were all wrong. Some were made with the right hand and some with the left. We were right about it not just being Doyle but now it looks like we have a partner and a third party, or maybe even more people involved. This just gets stranger and stranger. James said that he will take a closer look at the other bodies, too. Unfortunately, he only has the two left unburied that we can study, Father Quinlan and Father O'Grady. We all thought the case was closed with Doyle's death and so James released the other bodies for burial.'

Connor's face now held the same look of disbelief as his boss and they returned to the station in silence.

CHAPTER 37

'If men had wings and bore black feathers, very few of them would be clever enough to be crows.'

Henry Ward Beecher

Steve lay it all out before the superintendent that afternoon. His reaction was just as Steve had expected.

'So, what you are saying is that two or possibly more people killed Father Reagan and could have been involved in the other murders?' The disbelief in the superintendent's voice matched Steve's when he too first heard the news, but now that it had sunk in, it made perfect sense.

'That is exactly what I am saying, sir. James is taking another look at the two bodies still left in the morgue – the others had been released for burial.'

'Well. no reason not to. We thought we had the bugger, didn't we? What do we do now, Steve? I just got permission from the bishop to access church records so we need to tread very carefully here. We can't go arresting priests willy-nilly, now, or I am telling you the church will shut up shop and close us down. Let me think on it. Get on home and we can meet in the morning briefing. We need to keep this quiet … no leaks … tell Connor.'

Dismissed, Steve turned.

'One more thing, sir. I want to try to establish the name of Matthew Doyle's sibling if I can, or even prove his existence. The only people that can tell me that are his uncle and aunt. I'm going to call in and speak to them on my way home. We will get to the bottom of this no matter who is offended, sir, I promise you that. Sean at least deserves that much and so does his family.'

There was a track that ran along the back of the farm that joined onto Aidan's family farm, but in the winter it became impassable so the main road it was. Dreading what he might find out, he realised that it was time to bring things out in the open. For years this community had held on to a whole host of secrets – well, no more! No matter whose feelings he hurt, he would get to the bottom of this case. It had taken his best friend's life and he was determined that no one else would die who had any kind of connection to Bally-Bay, including himself. He wasn't so naïve to think that Aidan's family had been covering for a killer and knew all along *who* it was. However, whatever they did know he needed to find out. As these thoughts went through his mind, he turned the car into the farm yard. He had played hide and seek in that barn many a time as a child. Now, he was here as a policeman, not a friend. It was late so he hoped to catch them all still eating in the kitchen. The cows would have been milked hours ago. He marched up to the back door and rapped firmly. Soon he heard feet and cursing as boots were pushed to one side and the door swung inwards.

'Steve! Come away in. I thought I heard a car. Mammy has just made a pot of tea.'

Thanking Aidan, Steve followed him through into the kitchen where the warmth hit him immediately as the range threw out the heat. Smells of dinner hit his nose and his stomach grumbled; he hadn't had time to eat all day.

'Mr and Mrs Doyle,' he said and nodded his head in greeting. Aidan's mammy poured him a cup of tea and without asking placed a piece of cake in front of him. He nodded his thanks and wondered if they would feel their hospitality abused in a moment when he asked his questions.

'So, what brings you here, Steve? I had hoped that the case was closed now that Matthew is dead? His funeral is next week. None of us want to attend but we are the only family that he had,' Aidan's father said as he reached for his mug of tea.

'Well, that's just the thing. Are you really the only family Matthew had? I believe we have since discovered that there was another child. Can ye shed any light on what happened to them?' Steve stared into their faces but only Aidan had a puzzled look; his mammy and daddy couldn't meet his eye.

'That can't be right, Steve. No one has ever mentioned another child. In fact, no one ever mentioned Matthew after he left. I don't remember there being another bairn ... Mammy? Daddy?' Aidan turned directly to his parents for an explanation.'

Under her breath, Mrs Doyle whispered quietly, almost too quietly to hear her words.

'Yes, there was. We had you, a young one, and I couldn't cope with another wee one. Father Benedict arranged for him to be adopted. He went to the orphanage and Matthew to the seminary.'

Aidan looked shocked and stared at his parents in disbelief.

'So, all this time you kept quiet? You lied to the police and ye lied to me? Why would ye do that?'

Steve took control of the conversation.

'Please, I'm not here to blame anyone I'm just trying to find out facts. So, there was definitely another child ... a boy?' he asked.

Mr Doyle, quiet up to that moment, suddenly and vehemently spat his words across the room.

'Tainted, they were, all of them. Tainted blood. No matter what Father Benedict told us, we knew ... Oh we knew alright. Matthew killed his parents that night, and no way were we taking on an diabhul's children. I was right – they were born evil and that's all I got to say on the matter.'

He stormed past his wife, and Steve could hear him asking God to protect them all from an diabhul and swearing as he slammed the door behind him.

'Please don't judge us too harshly, Steve. We kept this all from Aidan to protect him and we were all frightened of Father Benedict … he told us to forget that they ever existed and he helped to get the farm signed over to Ned. He was always frightened that Matthew or the baby, when they grew up, would come back and take the farm from him. We did it for Aidan; it's his inheritance we were protecting. Then we heard that the baby had joined the priesthood like his brother so it didn't matter anymore.'

Aidan's mammy looked at him pleadingly and Aidan rose to leave with a look of utter disgust on his face.

Steve stood too.

'I'm so sorry to bring this all out and upset you all although I wish you had told me this earlier as it would have explained an awful lot. What was the baby's name, do you know?' Steve asked as he patted her hand.

'Well, he hadn't even been christened at the time; he was only a couple of days old when it happened, but they were going to call him Michael. If he was adopted, he could have been called anything but we never knew, and never asked.'

Steve could see the exhaustion in her face as she spoke, from the toll of keeping secrets. He had seen it in the faces of others before, especially his own mammy, and the sadness of her loss nearly overwhelmed him again. He left quickly; there was no sign of Aidan or his father. They would have to sort their own problems out he decided. He had what he needed and the sooner he traced Matthew Doyle's brother the better.

Driving along the road, he mused to himself about the man that was Matthew Doyle's brother – was he a part of this or just an innocent? Maybe he had been adopted and never even knew about his birth family. Or maybe he had been Matthew's partner in crime, helping him to take revenge on his abusers. He would have been at least ten years younger than Matthew when their parents died, and eight years younger than himself. He knew from before how obstructive the church could be about adoptive records and they very rarely gave any information out about their own. He thought that yet again he had found himself in the same situation, seeking the truth from people that had held secrets for many years, many of them dead now too.

He needed to go home. He was exhausted and what he needed most of all was to hold Meg and his wee ones in his arms. No … not his wee ones, he thought: Sean and Florence … his son and daughter. He was so proud of the names Meg had chosen for their children. Time to start being a husband and father. He smiled to himself as he turned into the farmyard. The welcoming sign of lights and the smell of cooking greeting him as he opened the door, as did the wailing of two babies. He laughed.

'Honey, I'm home!' he called as Meg thrust a baby into each of his arms at the same time that she kissed him. 'I'm going for a bath,' she called half-way out of the door. 'Your son and daughter need feeding, the bottles are warming on the side. Bye!'

Steve looked at the two squalling babies in his arms and realised how lucky he was.

CHAPTER 38

'Never a good sign, he thought, when the crows showed up.'

Justin Cronin

Steve arrived bright and early for the morning briefing. As he entered the station, he was pulled to one side by the sergeant on the front desk.

'Just a head-up, sir. The vultures have arrived from Dublin to pick over the bones.'

'What! Just when we'd pretty much solved the case, ye mean?' Steve joked back, but his face fell. The last thing he needed was some jumped-up detective from the smoke thinking he was superior to them and taking over the case. He wondered if the superintendent had had a say in it, or if he had even called them in himself. What was the point then of doing his job? If his superiors had such little faith in him to find the answers, how the hell was he supposed to? This case was a difficult enough one from the start, which is why Sean had asked him for help. The bodies piled up too quickly to get any kind of a handle on it and they certainly hadn't been given any breaks. Sean had given his all to it, even his own life, so he wasn't going to let anyone take over. He needed to do this for Sean.

Pushing open the double doors before entering his office, he was prepared to do battle with whoever it was waiting for him. Standing before him with superintendent Reevey, holding a mug of coffee in his hand, was DS Josh Hall. He remembered the lad from the last case at Bally-Bay. He'd spent most of his time in the pub chatting up the barmaid if he remembered rightly. *'Useless, snot-nosed little tosser.'* He heard Sean's voice clear as a bell and, trying not to smile, he stepped forward, hand extended.

'Josh, isn't it? I remember you from the last case. To what do we owe this pleasure?' He turned an enquiring eye to the super.

'DS Hall has been assigned to help us out. Obviously we have been pretty busy on this case, and losing Sean … well, anyway, as Josh has worked with you before, the fellows in Dublin thought that he might be of some use to you. Well, I will leave you to settle in, DS Hall, and perhaps you could join me for a quick update before the briefing, Steve. Josh, perhaps you could make Detective Ryan a cup of coffee whilst we have a quick word?'

If looks could kill! Josh was sending death arrows towards him … great start to the day, Steve thought as he followed the super into his office. Once seated with the door closed, Reevey gave Steve a smile.

'Sorry about this. I had to agree to something or they were going to take the case completely away from us. I'm sure that you can keep him busy making coffee? According to Sean, he was a bit of a useless tosser.'

Steve chuckled but quickly settled down to business. After relaying the information gained from Aidan Doyle's parents confirming that Matthew Doyle did indeed have a brother, he stood up to leave the room.

'We will be concentrating on finding the brother from adoption records and I am also going to take another look at the list of complainants in the accusations of abuse file while I await any news from James, sir.' The super nodded in agreement and Steve dismissed himself.

'Oh, one more thing, sir. About Connor – I would like to recommend him to be fast-tracked into the detective training programme. He has proved himself to be a worthy detective already … his skills in information finding are legendary. I also would like to state here and now that I won't tolerate any bullying or pulling of rank from DS Hall.'

'Thank you, Steve, I heartily agree, and I will make a few calls about Connor this afternoon although I warn you, we might lose him to the big boys as that young man will definitely go far. As for DS Hall, I wouldn't expect any of my staff to tolerate that kind of behaviour, either. Any such goings on and he will find himself back in the smoke with a size eleven up his arse. Now, go catch me a priest killer and for God's sake bring me something positive!'

Leaving the room, Steve let out a heavy sigh; his face said it all. Connor looked at the emotions flitting over his boss's face.

'Coffee! That will do the trick.'

That made Steve smile.

'Josh Hall should have made us some by now. Come on, let's get cracking. I'll explain on the way.'

Connor looked puzzled until Steve explained. Opening the door, he was greeted by the smug face of Josh Hall sitting at his desk and leaning back in his chair as if he owned the place, holding a mug of coffee.

'Oh good! Coffee is ready? Get me and Connor a cup, will ye, Josh?' Then turning to Connor with a wink, he continued. 'You remember DS Hall from the Bally-Bay case, don't ye? He's going to be working with us.'

Josh Hall stared at Steve in horror – asking him to make coffee for a lower rank was taking the piss.

'Well, chop, chop, we haven't got all day, come on or you will miss the briefing.'

Steve headed to the front of the room where the boards were located and chuckled under his breath. Connor sat in the chair vacated by Josh Hall and couldn't resist a huge grin.

Waiting for their coffee to arrive, Steve displayed a solemn expression and started the briefing.

'This morning I would like to go over everything we have. It shouldn't take long as we don't have a lot. The super has assured me, Connor, that the bishop has allowed you to access information so I would like you to concentrate if you will on finding Matthew Doyle's sibling. I am going to look over all of the files we have and I am hoping to make contact with the abuse victims on the list. Something is telling me that the answer lies there.' He wearily rested his hands on the desk in front of him.

'What about me, what shall I do? I can interview all of the suspects for you, try and get an angle on them.' Josh asked.

'Well, actually that sounds like a pretty good idea except he is in the morgue, which is exactly where you are headed. I want you to sit in on the re-examination of the two dead priests. James is doing that this morning and I want you to wait around for him to give you the file on his findings. I need that ASAP.'

'Dead priests! Yuck …' Josh shuddered.

'Do you have a problem with priests, son? Because if ye do, ye are definitely on the wrong feckin' case in the wrong feckin' country.' Steve's accent grew broader the angrier he got and for Connor it was a warning to get out sharpish and make more coffee.

Josh Hall, being the moron that he was, then tried to say he could be better placed doing something else and that Connor should go to the morgue. Connor sat back in his chair, waiting; he watched as Steve's face grew redder. He could see the undercurrent of emotion that he was holding back. He had never seen him this angry, not since he found Sean … in fact, it reminded him of his old boss Sean more than it did Steve.

'Are you questioning my skills as lead detective, DS Hall?' he asked quietly.

'Err, no, sir, it's just that I am more superi–'

'Get your arse down to the morgue now before I report you for insubordination and refusal to carry out orders. Is that clear enough?'

Even Connor felt sorry for him … just a little … but he ducked his head down as if nothing had happened. Opening up the file he had made with adoption agency contacts, he hoped that he wouldn't have any problems finding what he needed now that the bishop had intervened. He picked up the phone and dialled the first number on the list.

Steve's colour soon returned to normal. He knew that Hall would be reporting back to Dublin so he really needed to find a way to work with him. He had already managed to rub him up the wrong way and Steve wanted to keep his temper in check where he was concerned … even if the man *was* an eejit. Rubbing his hands over his face, he took a deep breath then picked up the first case file on Father Murphy and re-read everything in it, jotting down notes as he went. He then went on to closely read the autopsy reports on each of the murdered priests and noted any wounds similar in size or shape that occurred in all of them. His notepaper soon filled and it added to the sheets of paper and files now strewn across his desk in a chaotic mess. After two hours of intense reading and thought, he lifted his head. Looking around him at the disordered paper pile, he realised that he was no further on than when he started that morning. He ran his fingers through his hair for the umpteenth time. He was beginning to look as dishevelled as his desk. Perhaps Connor was having more luck. He stood up and moved to the kitchen area and the coffee machine; time for a break. Returning with two cups, he slid one towards Connor, who was just finishing up a call.

'How goes it? Any news yet?'

Connor nodded in the negative, his hair flopped across his face as he gestured. He looked as forlorn as Steve.

'Let's just drink our coffee and let our brains rest a minute; I don't know about you but I can't think straight anymore,' Steve said as he sipped from his cup. 'It might be that we need to face the possibility that we will never find Matthew Doyle's brother if he was adopted, although Aidan's mammy told me that he later became a priest so they didn't need to worry about the farm being taken from them anymore. Quite convenient sending kids into the priesthood and taking away their rights to inherit; classed as "worldly goods", I suppose, and they give up everything to be a priest.'

'I hadn't thought of that really. It has quite a knock-on effect for the family members … they're the ones who gain, I suppose,' Connor reflected.

Just then, Josh Hall returned carrying cakes.

'Sorry about this morning, boss. I brought cakes as an apology.'

'Oh, thanks!' Steve dived into the bag and took a cake for him and passed one to Connor. 'We could do with a bit of sugar, couldn't we?'

He wouldn't acknowledge the gesture as he didn't want Josh to get off that easy but he gave him a smile – maybe he was useful for something after all.

CHAPTER 39

'The raven spread out its glossy wings and departed like hope.'
Cecilia Dart-Thornton

Tasking Josh with making appointments to speak to as many of the abuse claimants as possible, Steve shoved the file towards him.

'All of the original paperwork is in there and a list of priests and names of the accusers. Every one of them attended St Patrick's Seminary at some point in time when the alleged abuse took place. The range in years is quite wide, so see if you can wheedle out the ones of an appropriate age first, please. Oh, and although we know it will be, can you double-check that our latest victim, Father Thomas Reagan, is on the list? I want to be one hundred percent sure that he is.'

Turning his back in dismissal, he looked at the other member of his workforce.

'Connor, I want you to continue your dance-around with the church records office. I'm going to do some more reading, though little good it's doing me.'

Steve retreated to his office, the findings sent by James clasped in his hand after his re-examination of all of the bodies that he still had access to. Before settling in to reading, he decided to tidy up his desk, putting the paperwork back in the relevant files. He sat with only the notes that he himself had made earlier in front of him, plus James's report. He looked at his watch; it was getting late. Maybe he should leave this until the morning; they could all do with an early night. A fresh mind gave a fresh perspective, he thought. Popping his head out of the door, he called out: 'Give it half an hour, lads, then head on home. We will meet bright and early, say 7:30am, for the morning briefing.'

He sat back down at his desk and started playing with the corner of the file. He knew that he never took his own advice but he wasn't single anymore and he had Meg and the children to think of. So many colleagues over the years had bemoaned missing out on the important milestones in their children's lives. He was determined not to with the twins; he had missed so much already when they had been apart for a couple of weeks and he was sure that baby Sean had given him a proper smile the other morning.

He forced the urge to open the file down into his gut and then tucked it underneath the notes that he had made earlier. Out of sight and all that, he mumbled to himself, then swigging down the cold dregs of his coffee and hearing calls of goodnight coming through the open door, he retrieved his jacket from the back of the chair. Swinging it over his shoulder, he hastened to the door and switched off the lights on his way out.

Meg was pleased to see him home nice and early for once and the twins settled down easily, so they had a quiet evening. That is until the phone rang at 11pm just as Steve had climbed into bed. It was Josh Hall.

'Sorry to disturb you, sir, but we nearly had another one, but this time the priest managed to fight them off and call for help. I'll give you the details when I see you.'

He looked around helplessly as Meg mouthed at him, 'Go!' He told Josh he would be there as soon as and to call forensics as they might pick up DNA if there had been contact. Pulling the clothes on that he had just abandoned on the chair, he blew Meg a kiss as he tiptoed out the door and down the stairs. Luckily, he had only had one glass of wine at dinner so he knew that he wouldn't be over the limit.

Entering the outskirts of Dublin, Steve heard his mobile ring.

'DCI Ryan speaking. What have you got for me, Josh?'

'Sir, Father Devlin, that's the priest that was attacked tonight, took a turn for the worse, and has been rushed to St Mary's Hospital with shock and a possible heart attack. The forensic team have arrived at the seminary and are looking at the scene. Shall I wait with them or meet you at the hospital?' Josh enquired.

'I'll meet you there, stay put,' replied Steve. 'I'll call at the hospital on the way.'

Josh would rather be at home in his warm bed. He shivered in the cold air; he had forgotten his overcoat in the rush and he had gone outside to make the call to Steve, away from listening ears. It seemed to him that every priest in Ireland had gathered in the corridor outside the room where Father Devlin had been found. He had sent them back to their rooms without a single thought, though some still lingered in the corridors. They scuttled away like beetles as he approached, their hushed whisperings following behind him down the corridor. He resented being told to stay put – what exactly could he do here? Except count priests. He looked out of the window; it would be light soon. The sky was turning deep orange. He could hear the crows in the trees down the drive, cawing and squabbling in their nests high up in the branches. He shivered; it ran down his back and a thought hit him! Maybe one of the priests was the killer? He hastened towards the room with light spilling out of the doorway, leaving the dark corridor far behind him, glad to find the forensic team inside busy and some human company.

Steve entered the hospital building accompanied by a garda and soon established that Father Devlin had been rushed to theatre to stem a bleed from a wound inflicted by the perpetrator. This had led to a heart attack, caused by the blood loss.

After talking to the garda who had accompanied him into the

hospital, Steve ascertained that Father Devlin had given no clue as to his attacker and had not spoken at all after his initial cries for help. Leaving the garda on duty with orders to call him immediately Father Devlin was out of theatre and able to speak, Steve ran back to the car and proceeded to the crime scene to talk to Josh. He hoped that he had made a note of who had found the body and anyone else on the scene but he didn't hold his breath. Calling Connor on the way, he asked him to meet them at the station in an hour. He was calling the briefing an hour earlier than intended. Things were heating up and accelerating at a speed that left him in no doubt that the killer had only failed this time because of Father Devlin's own strength to fight back.

Reaching the seminary at daylight, the forensic team were packing up the van. Steve stopped briefly to talk to James.

'Well, thank God you don't have another body to take with you this time. I thought that ye needed a bit of a break.' Steve smiled at the CSI and James smiled back at him.

'It makes a change. I thought for a minute you were going to carry on where Sean had left off … Seriously, we have taken prints and samples for DNA analysis but with the amount of people that trucked through that room before we arrived, I won't hold my breath of catching anyone. That new DS is a bit of a numpty; he didn't seal the room until we arrived and he left the building to have a cigarette and make phone calls. Anyone could have been in and out with no one knowing and removed or planted evidence. To be honest, it was just a waste of time us coming.'

'Thanks, James. I'm sorry, he is on loan from the smoke, and he needs to buck his bloody ideas up or he will be sent back quicker than he came.'

'Yes, I remember him from the Bally-Bay case, bit of a knob according to Sean, which is correct from what I have seen so far.'

Steve waved goodbye, his face a mêlée of emotion, absolute fury being the most dominant one. Turning towards the building, anger seemed to pulse off of him in waves.

'Feckin' eejit!' he mumbled as he went to find DS Josh Hall.

Driving back to the station after venting his fury at Hall, he began to feel the anger seep away, leaving him with an empty feeling. He did not like the person he had become, shouting and ordering Hall to stay where he was for at least another bloody hour or until he had gathered the names of each and every person that had set a big toe in that feckin' room. But somehow Josh pushed his button … the man was a liability and he had probably destroyed the only bloody clues that they might have had with his useless behaviour.

An hour later, he had calmed enough to greet Connor with some semblance of himself. After explaining where they stood now, he pointed out how imperative it was that they found out *who* Matthew Doyle's brother was.

'So, keep on calling the people concerned. Threaten them with a visit from a couple of guards, cop cars and blue lights, the works. That should loosen some tongues. I am going to look at the file from James and await a call from the hospital. When DS Hall arrives, tell him to get on to making those appointments immediately. We will start interviewing priests as soon as possible even if we have to haul them in and put them in a cell for a couple of hours. I *will* have some answers by the end of the day.'

Connor nodded in agreement; he had never seen Steve quite so angry. That bloody idiot Josh could have lost them the case. If he didn't know better, he would swear that it was sabotage, just to make them look like eejits from the pale in front of the big boys. He made two mugs of coffee, sent out for a couple of bacon sandwiches and hoped that if he fed Steve with both, he would settle back into less of a bear with a sore head and more like his old boss.

Steve slammed the brown file onto his desk, made a deep sigh then got himself under control. It would do no good to continue to feel angry; he needed a clear head and determination if he was going to see this through to the end. He hadn't given up hope quite yet although, after reading the first few lines of James's report, he might.

Reading the words over out loud to himself somehow made it seem more real and his shoulders dropped in despair.

'I have re-looked at the two bodies of Father O'Grady and Father Fitzgerald. Both were still in the morgue and had not been removed yet for burial. Each body shows clear marks from the same type of weapon being used, a long thin serrated edged blade, but there were so many wounds that I can't comprehensively say which had caused the fatal blow. The wounds were mostly defensive on these two bodies and I would say that because of the depth, pressure and consistency they were made by only one person. There were also less of them than on the latest body. This concurred with my earlier conclusions on each of the previous nine bodies, including that of Detective Chief Inspector Sean O'Dowd.

The wounds inflicted on the latest body, that of Father Thomas Reagan, the most recent of the priests killed, appear to have been made in all directions, plus there were many more than on the previous bodies but I would say that they were made by a similar weapon to the earlier killings: a long thin serrated-edged blade. Equal pressure had been applied on the majority of wounds and all of them made with a slashing or hacking motion, rather than a thrusting action. All wounds could have been applied by the left or the right hands as point of entry differed in direction but I would definitely say that at least one of the perpetrators was left-handed. DNA was found at the scene and on the body but it did not match any from the other crime scenes, and came from more than one source. My conclusion, therefore, is that more than one person could be responsible for Father Reagan's death and the attack on Father Devlin but with the samples taken having been compromised by the lack of security at the scene and showing that they were inconclusive, it would be difficult to prove.'

Just then, Josh Hall knocked, popped his head round the door and laid a list of appointment times and names on his desk before retreating. Seeing that the first one was for two hours time, Steve lifted his jacket and opened the door. He was in need of sustenance before meeting them all.

'Connor, you're with me, Josh take over where Connor left off and let me know as soon as you hear from the hospital.'

Without even a glance, he left the station and Connor followed on behind, racing to catch him up. Before Steve reached the car, his phone rang. He answered it quickly when he saw that it was Josh. He flung it back in his pocket and swore.

'Father Devlin is dead! Just before he died, the garda on duty allowed a priest to take in some clothing, and to offer comfort and prayers. Have I got a station full of bloody eejits for Jesus, Mary and Joseph's sake!'

Connor couldn't quite believe what he was hearing either but was reluctant to stop Steve in full flow.

'What now, sir?' he asked tentatively.

'I tell ye what now, Connor, we bring in all six of those priests on that piece of paper, we put them in interview rooms and let the feckers sweat till someone is ready to talk to me. I'm fed up with this shit-show.'

CHAPTER 40

'There is a bird who by his coat, and by the hoarseness of his note, might be supposed a crow.'

William Cowper

A few hours later, a calmness overcame Steve. He was where he belonged, being a detective. He could do *that* OK. All of the named priests on the list were now sitting either in reception or interview rooms dotted around the station, including Father Michael from the homeless shelter. He would start with him. Steve had been a little surprised to see his name on the list, and it poked the itch that he had been feeling on this case. Then rising from his seat, he headed for the door.

'Josh, Connor, I want you to take two each, establish where they were on the night of the attack and ask if they knew Matthew Doyle; if so how and why? I also want to know if they are right- or left-handed. I want dates of birth and to know if they were adopted … take note, please, of their reactions to the questions and ask them to give DNA samples for elimination purposes … Let's shake the tree and see what falls out.'

The priest's head turned as he entered the room and after giving Steve an appraising look, he folded his hands in his lap. Steve sat down in the chair opposite and could see by his demeanour that he would glean nothing from him. Instead, he laid his file on the desk and sat back in his chair. Father Michael gave nothing away in his body language.

'How old are you, Father?'

Puzzled, the priest replied, 'I will be forty next month.'

'Well, you're the right age.'

'For what, Detective Ryan?'

Ignoring the question, Steve sat forward.

'Why did you decide to become a priest, Father? Was it so that you could find your brother?'

Sitting back in his chair, he waited for his reply; would he deny any knowledge of the existence of a sibling? He could wait … he had plenty of time.

Looking a little flustered, the priest sputtered out a reply.

'Err, like my colleagues I found that I had a calling to be a priest.'

Denial, then, Steve thought, but pushed on.

'How well did you know Matthew Doyle, Father?'

'I don't really understand, Detective. I thought that you wanted to discuss the allegations that myself and other students at St Patrick's made years ago about the abuse that we all suffered and witnessed at the hands of some of the Jesuit fathers that taught us. It was swept under the carpet at the time and I was hopeful that in these more enlightened times it would be re-opened. So, I don't really understand your line of questioning.'

So, he is playing that old chestnut, Steve thought. Accuse the police of wrong doing just to distract from the real reason he is sitting in a garda station. The only way to get under his skin was to get him on the back- foot.

'As for re-opening the case against the Jesuit fathers – the perpetrators of the alleged abuse are all dead. So, we would have no one to prosecute, Father Reagan and Father Devlin being the last two of the ten accused priests. The others, as you know, all eight of them, and my colleague DCI Sean O'Dowd, were killed by Matthew Doyle.

So, we now are investigating the deaths of Father Reagan and Father Devlin.'

'You don't seem particularly surprised by me informing you of Father Devlin's death, which as far as I know, is not common knowledge yet. Also, I don't think that you have replied to my question, Father, so I will repeat it for you in case that you didn't hear. *How well did you know Matthew Doyle?* Was he an old acquaintance? You weren't in the seminary together as he was ten years older than you, so tell me, Father, how well *did* you know Matthew Doyle?'

'Well, I actually think that is two questions, Detective, but so that we can bring this … whatever this is to an end, I will say just this. Matthew Doyle was a very sick person. The deterioration in his mental health had been happening over a number of years. Long before he acted in the way that he did, killing all those people was an appalling act of someone who, if they had been helped earlier, would not have suffered so.'

'That is a very interesting answer, Father, although we could say that you never really answered my questions, whether there was one or two of them. It seems to me that you have a lot of sympathy for Matthew Doyle, especially as according to your earlier statement you hardly knew him and yet you reported him missing, I believe? So, I will ask yet again, what if any, was your relationship to Matthew Doyle?'

'I already answered that question when I reported him missing. I didn't know him at all really, he was just on my radar as someone who needed some help and he had been struggling … even more so since leaving the priesthood … with his day-to-day functions. We gave him a meal at the shelter and a bed now and then.'

'So, if you didn't know him very well, why did you report him missing? Did you often report a homeless person missing if you hadn't seen them for a while? Is it church policy?'

'No, usually they drifted and turned up at another of our homeless stations so no, it's not policy.'

'Then what was different about Matthew Doyle? Was it because he had turned up looking for you, Michael? Was it personal?'

Father Michael just continued to stare into his clasped hands but Steve could see that the knuckles had whitened.

'Where were you last Thursday evening, Father, the third of December?' Steve continued the pressure. Father Michael looked up suddenly and almost smiled but caught himself before his features gave him away. He pulled his face into an empathic, almost simpering look.

'Oh, that's the night that poor Father Devlin was attacked. What an absolutely dreadful thing to happen and in our seminary too. It should have been a place of safety. Don't you think, Detective? He was not the first one of our elderly residents to be attacked there, either, may Father Reagan rest in peace.' He made the sign of the cross. 'On the night in question, I and two of my colleagues were discussing and planning the forthcoming Christmas nativity in the small chapel annexe. We arrived back to absolute mayhem and found out that Father Devlin had been attacked in his room. The nativity is always performed at the seminary by the local school children and we throw a little party for them afterwards. I can give you my colleagues' names if you like.'

He looked at Steve almost with a smirk on his face.

'No need, Father Michael. I suspect that they are two of the other priests that we have in the custody suite at the moment. Good alibi, by the way. So tell me, Father, did the three of you carry out the attack or was it your turn to provide the alibis?'

Not expecting any kind of reply, he continued pressuring, but he may as well have been told, '*No comment.*' as was his suspects' usual response, but he wasn't giving up that easily.

'By the way, Father, one more question for you: were you adopted?'

'What has any of this got to do with me? The answer to your question is, yes, I was adopted as a baby and I had the most wonderful parents. You are not making yourself very clear, Detective.'

Steve could see that he had ruffled a few feathers and didn't want to ease back now.

'Well let me make it very clear, Father, shall I? So far, we have a lot of dead priests that we know Matthew Doyle was responsible for killing. But I also lost a dear friend and colleague and I am getting pretty sick of being stonewalled by the church at every turn. Now answer my bloody question.'

Steve stood and slammed his hands onto the table in front of the priest, who didn't even flinch.

'What was your relationship with Matthew Doyle?'

'I have answered all of your questions, Detective, and if there is nothing else, I am going to leave. I feel your attitude to me and the church is questionable and if you continue to harass me and my colleagues, I will be putting in a complaint.'

With that, Father Michael Donnelly stood to leave the room as coolly as he had entered it.

Frustration burned in Steve like a fire. He knew that Father Michael was Matthew Doyle's brother and if he wouldn't admit it, he would have to do it another way.

'By the way, Father, would you be happy to give us a DNA sample to help us eliminate you from our enquiries? I shall be asking everyone at the seminary to do so.'

'Why of course, Detective, anything to help.'

'Please wait here until I can arrange it. I won't be two minutes.'

He could sit and stew for a while; he hadn't quite finished with him yet.

CHAPTER 41

'The law is a gun, which if it misses a pigeon always kills a crow, if it does not strike the guilty.'

Edward Bulwer-Lytton, 1ˢᵗ Baron Lytton

After arranging for a team to come and take DNA from all six of the priests and working their way through the list, he could rule out any that were not the right age to be Matthew Doyle's brother. Most of the others were either younger or slightly older, but being young and strong physically couldn't be ruled out over the deaths of Father Reagan and now Father Devlin. One thing he was pleased about was that out of all of the priests only one had a birthday that coincided with being ten years younger than Matthew Doyle and had been adopted: Michael Donnelly. He didn't need to be told that he had found Matthew Doyle's brother, his gut did that for him.

After consulting with Connor and Josh, he asked them to go through their findings with particular emphasis on reactions to being asked certain questions.

'Nothing came up as untoward until …' Josh said, '… one of the priests that I interviewed … a Father Peter Bernard,' he said, flipping his notebook open and reading from it, 'corroborated Father Michael's story about the meeting for the school nativity, giving them both an alibi as well as Father Joseph Connelly who apparently was with them.' He read on. 'Though there was some discrepancy about where the meeting had occurred. He said *in the small chapel* but Father Michael told you different,' he nodded at Steve.

'Yes, that it took place *in the annexe next to the chapel*,' said Steve.

'Which could just have been an error as both buildings are in close proximity to each other,' Josh continued. 'He also was a bit twitchy about the attack on Father Reagan but he showed real shock when I told him that Father Devlin had died too. He is right-handed and not adopted. As is Father Connelly who gave out even less but confirmed that he was with Father Bernard and Father Michael at the nativity meeting *in the small chapel.*'

Connor flipped his notebook open and read out the names of two other priests, Father Dermot Wheaton and Father Sean O'Leary.

'Nothing to be gained from these two, I'm afraid. According to this, they were in the kitchen together preparing hot drinks for later and clearing the dinner things. Apparently, they take it in turns on a rota to cook and clear away. Both are right-handed and neither are adopted. One was quite a bit older and one a lot younger than Father Michael. One did react with a smile, though, when I told them that Father Devlin had died.'

'Well done, lads, good work both of you. It seems that Josh's two may be covering for Father Michael. He could have easily slipped out and attacked Father Devlin and popped back when it went wrong. That just leaves us with one priest,' he said, turning over a piece of paper on the desk. 'A Father Alex Byrne. I wonder if he is our missing piece of the puzzle? Maybe *he* attacked Father Devlin. Josh, can you interview him please, same as before? And Connor, I would like you to go and tell the others that they can leave as soon as they have had a sample taken. I will deal with Father Michael Donnelly myself.'

On re-entering the room where Father Michael was still waiting, Steve found one of James's forensic team taking a DNA sample from him.

'Thank-you for co-operating, Father. I'm sure we can rule you out and have you on your way soon. I just have a couple more questions for you.'

As the person finished taking the sample, Steve handed him a piece of paper with instructions to James to please see if this sample was a match to Matthew and Aidan Doyle and to let him know ASAP.

'I don't understand why you have yet more questions, Detective! I believe that I have answered them all and co-operated with you fully.'

'Oh, just a silly thing really and then you can go. Can you tell me, Father, are you right-handed?'

'I don't understand your questioning but actually I am left-handed, Detective. Now may I leave?'

'Nearly there – just one more. What is the sixth commandment, Father?'

'I think that you and I both know that it is *Thou shalt not kill*. Can we both say that we have kept it, Detective?'

'That's it for now, Father, thank you for your time.'

Giving nothing away, Steve watched as Father Michael left the room. What a slippery customer, he thought. He nearly had me at that last answer but don't worry, Father, we haven't finished our little game of questions and answers yet, he mumbled to himself.

Looking down at the priests from his office window as they left the building, Steve stood watching them cross the carpark. Outside, night was approaching; he looked at his watch – only 4pm and already getting dark. He hated the nights drawing in early in winter time. Spying the last black robed figure climbing into the back of a car, he thought how similar they all looked to a group of crows, their robes flapping in the wind like wings.

'A murder of crows. I believe that's what it's called?' he said of the collective noun for a gathering of crows. 'That sums them up pretty well,' he said out loud.

Connor came up to stand beside him.

'I think I can agree with you there, sir, definitely a couple of murderers in amongst that bunch, I would bet anything on that.'

'The problem we have now is proving it, Connor. Let's see what James turns up with the DNA results tomorrow. We may not have seen the last of our crows. I am pretty tired, I don't know about you two, time to head on home, I think. Get a good night's sleep and see you in the morning.'

Steve hadn't seen Meg and the babies since late yesterday evening and he was exhausted. Driving home, he was struggling to concentrate on the road and was pleased to see the lights of the farmhouse in the distance.

Meg handed the babies over to him but soon found him asleep on the sofa, one in each arm. She left him to it; he needed to catch up. She couldn't wait for Romany to arrive next week for some company if nothing else. She had been too occupied with the twins since they had arrived in Ireland and going out was a logistical nightmare with two babies. She couldn't wait to be able to get some Christmas shopping and actually go into the city and do some normal things. Having Romany with her would be fun.

Steve woke early next morning, still on the sofa. A blanket had been thrown over him and a cushion tucked under his head. He would need to start making it up to Meg soon. What a time to get into a complicated case! *No wonder the majority of policemen are divorced*, he thought.

'Still need to get married first,' he heard Sean's voice in his head. 'Yeah, yeah!' he replied.

He showered, crept into the bedroom and grabbed clean clothes. Then he realised that he was starving. Meg joined him in the kitchen fifteen minutes later where he was cooking breakfast.

'Mmm, something smells good.'

'Coffee and eggs, madam, if you would like to be seated.'

247

Steve pulled out a chair at the table and placed two plates and two steaming mugs of coffee on it.

'Tuck in,' he said, kissing Meg's neck. 'I'm sorry about last night, a mhuirnín. I'm not exactly proving to you that I am good husband material, am I? I will soon have this case wrapped up and I promise then I will be all yours.'

'And the children, Steve. I don't want them to grow up never seeing their father.'

'I promise, love.'

'Don't make promises that you can't keep, Steve,' Meg sighed and tucked into her eggs before they got cold. This was a treat and the babies were quiet for once.

Steve following her lead and tucked in too. He hadn't realised just how hungry he was and his stomach growled loudly as the first mouthful went down. They both started to laugh and it lightened the mood, but Steve was well aware that he was treading a very fine line.

*

A good night's sleep had bolstered the team and finding a coffee waiting on his desk alongside a file from forensics, he was in a much better mood. He must remember to buy James a pint. The man had been an absolute star, working day and night to get Steve his answers and he knew that he was lucky that James had prioritised Michael Donnelly's swab. He knew from experience that most labs would take at least 48 hours to get back to them, and sometimes in the city it took weeks for results to become available, no matter the need for haste. Lifting the folder, he called Josh and Connor into the room.

'Well, are you ready to find out for sure that Father Michael Donnelly is Matthew Doyle's baby brother, who was adopted? Then we can put this to bed and arrest him for the deaths of Father Reagan and Father Devlin. I know that he has been covering up the crimes that Doyle committed and possibly was helping him to carry them out. When Matthew died, Donnelly carried on his work, I believe, killing priests until the last one in that folder died.'

'Well, if they did it, they succeeded, sir.'

Connor nodded in agreement.

Opening the folder, Steve started to read from the report out loud. It contained only one sentence.

'The DNA sample taken yesterday from Father Michael Donnelly was **not** *a familial match for Matthew Doyle.'*

Steve slumped in his chair.

'How the fuck could I have been so wrong?'

CHAPTER 42

'Angels and crows passed each other, one leaving, the other coming.'

Jerry Spinelli

Steve was unsure whether everything that had taken place over the past few months had ever been a reality. He was glad to see the super headed his way.

'Give us a moment, please … Connor, Josh,' the super said.

The two men obeyed the super and left him and Steve together. Closing the door behind him, Josh followed Connor into the next room and flopped onto a chair, putting his feet up on the desk. He swivelled back and forth. He couldn't wait to gossip to Connor.

'I bet he feels a right numpty, probably going to get a bollocking from the big boss now. He was convinced that Father Michael did it. I told him that was rubbish! Why would a priest do that to another priest anyway? He's probably for the high jump now after hauling all those priests in yesterday. Anyway, I don't care. I can leave this shithole and get back to some decent work, important work in the city, instead of this shite.'

Connor glared at him. He was about to give him a lecture when he heard raised voices coming from Steve's office.

'What do you mean, I had no right to haul them in? I had every right! They were suspects in an ongoing murder investigation, for fucks sake!'

'I know this is hard for you to take in, Steve, but you are no longer in England. The Church has a lot of power here. Seeing as the evidence was compromised to the point that the prosecution service has no real evidence or would be unable to prove who the perpetrator was, the decision has been made and the case has been closed. I'm sorry. I know it's not what you wanted to hear, but that is my final word; just drop it. You have a pile of other cases on your desk so just ease yourself along with an easy burglary or break-in for a few days then have some time off with the family for Christmas.'

Turning on his heel, Superintendent Simon Reevey left the room.

'Patronising prick … a feckin' burglary! By Christ, those black-robed bastards have got away with murder, so they have!' Steve steamed.

Connor headed for the kitchen. His boss was in dire need of coffee – and so was he – before he landed a punch on Josh's nose. He understood how his boss felt; it was a slap in the face to be told to abandon the case at this point. If they had just a little more time, he was convinced that his boss would have found something to convict them all and prove what he had said, that they had all killed the two priests and covered for each other. How Father Michael had not turned out to be Matthew Doyle's brother he would never understand. He had been as sure as Steve that they had the right man. In his quiet moments, he would continue looking through the adoption files; he would find their man for Steve.

Steve's fury stayed with him all day. He sent Josh packing back to Dublin and set Connor on the task of packing away all of the paperwork and returning everything back to evidence, whilst he took himself off to look at a burglary crime scene that had come in that morning. Meeting a CSI at the scene, he interviewed the homeowner and returned to the station just as Connor had made coffee.

'I swear that you have the second sight, Connor. You know exactly when I need coffee,' Steve said as he tried to make light of his terrible mood; after all, it wasn't Connor's fault.

It was now late afternoon and sitting down, Steve realised that he hadn't eaten since breakfast with Meg that morning.

'You hungry, Connor?' he asked.

'Well, yes, sir, I am. Why?'

'Come on then, forget the coffee. I will buy ye a pint and get ye something to eat. My treat, to say thanks for not killing Josh or letting me do it either.' They laughed together and picking up their jackets, they turned out the lights on their way out.

'Feckin' burglary my arse,' Steve said.

'Yep, more and more like Sean every day,' Connor laughed.

After they were seated in a quiet corner of the pub, Steve ordered them both a huge steak. He picked up his pint and sipped it thoughtfully.

'Ye know what I am going to say, Connor. *Thanks*. I couldn't have made it through these past months without yer support and dedication to the job. Well, after today, fuck the job.' He raised his glass.

Connor looked at him thoughtfully.

'That sounds pretty ominous, Steve. Please don't do anything rash. I know it isn't the outcome that we wanted, but I would just like to say that I agree with you, sir … I mean, Steve. The priests definitely did it! I just think that we are going to have to accept that we can never prove it and know that we did our best. No one can fault the hard work and long hours that went into the investigation; maybe we can take some satisfaction from that at least.'

Steve looked up as a raucous bunch of office workers having their Christmas party started singing loudly.

'Maybe this wasn't such a good idea after all! I forgot all of the numpties would be out celebrating this time of year. Have you got plans for Christmas, Connor?'

Keeping the conversation light for the rest of the evening, they finished their meal and parted company. Steve looked at his watch; it was still early. Perhaps he could pick up something for Meg's Christmas present while he was in town so he headed for the shopping mall. His breath came out in a misty vapour; he shivered and pulled his jacket in tighter around him

The figure stepped out from behind the side wall of the pub and followed him. Even though he had been told to back off, they needed to be sure that this detective had got the message loud and clear. Perhaps a little scare would do the trick.

Steve, totally relaxed after his meal, headed back to the car after he had bought a gorgeous scarf for Meg and her favourite perfume. Pleased with himself, he didn't take much notice of the figure following behind. It was always busy at Christmas time. Loud laughter and traditional Irish music spilled out into the night as someone opened the pub door. Smiling to himself, he fumbled in his pocket for his car key and turned just in time to feel a sting to his chest and a dark figure bending over him.

'Leave it alone now, Detective. Go back to yer wee family and leave it be.'

Steve's knees buckled as another shock hit him in the chest. He wanted to shout out, *'Don't you dare threaten my family!'* but the figure had disappeared as quickly as he came. Two girls in short sparkly dresses laughed at him as they passed by.

'Too much Christmas spirit, love?' they called and their laughter carried with them as they passed into the distance.

Getting up slowly from the wet ground on unsteady legs, he managed to unlock the car door and climb in. He knew he'd been tasered. He suddenly remembered his packages and opening the door again, he looked out and saw the scarf sprawled across the carpark the beautiful colours of the silk reflected in the puddle it was now lying in. The perfume hadn't fared much better. As he approached the bag that it had been in, the overpowering sweet smell of flowers and citrus hit his nostrils. The chink of glass as he retrieved the bag confirmed that it was smashed. After throwing the lot into the wheely bin that was leaning against the far wall of the carpark, he staggered back to his car then drove home.

Meg could see straight away that something was wrong. Steve looked deathly pale and his hands were clammy. He briefly explained what had happened in the carpark less than an hour ago.

'Are you sure it wasn't just a mugging?' she asked.

'I don't want to frighten you, my darling, but I need you to be vigilant. I will see about maybe getting some protection for you all and first thing in the morning I will have some alarms installed in the house.'

Holding on tight to Steve, Meg lifted the jacket from his still shaking shoulders and sat him down. He rubbed his chest and lifting his shirt he examined the dark marks left behind by the taser.

'I don't think muggers use tasers.' He felt sore and bruised, but otherwise unhurt.

'I would be happier if you went to A&E,' Meg said as she touched his chest.

'Really, I'm fine I just need a rest; but first we need to chat.'

'Let's get you settled and I'll make a cup of tea with lots of sugar for the shock … then we will talk.' Meg bustled off into the kitchen, leaving Steve on the sofa.

'Yeah, you had a bit of a shock … twice, in fact.' Steve chuckled as he heard Sean's voice.

'I don't think I can put my family at risk anymore, Sean. I'm sorry man!'

'I don't want ye to … do like the man says and just let it go; it won't help me now and I'm sure that the killings will stop as the priests are all dead now. Let it go.'

Sean's voice tailed off as if he had left him for good and Steve felt bereft, the held back grief surfacing.

'What, no goodbye for your old friend?' Steve began to weep softly, tears streaming down his face as Meg returned, mugs in hand. Putting them down quickly, she came to his side. Then, holding each other till the tears subsided, Steve wept out his sorrow at not getting those responsible for the death of his friend.

'Ah, but you did love. Matthew Doyle killed Sean and almost killed you, too. I know that murder is wrong and that it breaks the sixth commandment but those priests deserved to die. And if this is the only way that those boys can get any justice, then actually I don't blame them.'

'I know you are right, love. I should have seen that it would end like this in the first place, but you know me, I like to dig till I get to the bottom whatever the consequences, but not if it puts my family in danger … Sean is right, I need to let this one go.'

Meg looked at Steve strangely … how could Sean have told him to let it go? Oh well, she wasn't going to ask, he could have been killed tonight and she loved and needed him, and so did the children.

'Just do it then, love, for once listen to what is the right thing to do. There is no shame in doing the right thing.'

They held each other tightly until the squalls of the babies interrupted them …

'Some little people are hungry and they know that Daddy is home and he gives the best cuddles.'

EPILOGUE

'My guide and I went into a hidden tunnel … where we came forth and once more saw the stars.'

Dante Alhigeri (*The Divine Comedy*)

The excitement of Christmas had given Steve a new purpose in life. For the first time, he would experience it as a father. Romany had arrived for the holidays and the house smelled of wonderful things. A tree sparkled in the corner of the living room, lit with a rainbow of fairy lights. How Meg had pulled it off with everything that had happened was a miracle to him. He couldn't remember the last time that he had experienced this feeling … not since he had been a child himself. He even found a few of his old childhood ornaments hanging from the tree. Sian and John and Meg's cousins were all joining them for Christmas lunch after church. Meg had tried to explain that anything religious at this time would not be appropriate for Steve and that they had no intention of bringing the children up as Catholic, to the dismay of Aunt Sian.

Meg had got to grips with the gigantic Aga in the kitchen and was pleased that Christmas dinner was well on its way to being ready. Steve had helped as much as he could and she had seen him visibly relax once Romany had joined them. He seemed to hold them all a little tighter. Things were good and they all felt a little festive. For the first time in a couple of weeks, Steve had managed not to see a sinister black-robed figure around every corner. He had even managed to replace the presents for Meg that had been destroyed the night of his attack.

Work had been quiet apart from the few pickpockets and drunks, the usual yuletide offences coming through the station. Connor had left to sit his exams and Steve was pleased to have a little time off to just be a partner and father.

*

As people sang and celebrated throughout the country, priests' words echoed around the church walls as they had done for hundreds of years. In a small chapel, more voices joined the joyous day's celebrations.

'Oh God who created human nature, we pray that we may share in the divinity of Christ who himself shared our humanity.' The words tumbled from Father Michael's mouth and he watched as his fellow priests echoed them back, the congregation long gone home to celebrate in their own way the birth of the Christ child. They turned to each other, seated in a circle, hands clasped together as if in prayer. Michael spoke first.

'Forgive me, Father, for I have sinned, and broken the sixth commandment. I am responsible for the deaths of two of my holy brothers and covered up the cardinal sin of the murder of eight more.'

The words *and I, and I, and I, and I, and I, and I* echoed around the circle till each and every one of the priests had said his confession.

'We here today are bound by the rules of the confessional. I confess with my brothers never to tell a living soul. Lord, we await your judgement when the time comes ...'

The sound of *amen* from several voices echoed around the stone walls of the church.

*

Steve looked around the room laughter and joy emanated from every corner ... this was family ... *I'm so happy*. His thoughts were interrupted by his phone ringing. He had promised Meg no work over Christmas but it was Connor.

'Hi, Connor, Merry Christmas to ye. Are you ringing to tell me that ye passed the detective exams? Am I to call you DC O'Brian now?'

'Actually, I have been fast-tracked, thanks to you! I am now DS O'Brian but that's not why I called … I wanted you to know that I have found Matthew Doyle's brother …'

~

My ode to Poe, my writing inspiration ever since I read *The Raven* at age eleven and my influence for this book:

IN THE HALLS OF THE RAVEN KING

In the halls of the raven king
A dozen blackbirds sweetly sing,
A thirteenth sits at judgement's side,
Your fate, and others to decide.
An eye as black as darkest jet,
He oversees it all … and lets
His gaze, most circumspect,
Pass over every face.
Until at last on yours does rest.

In the court of the raven king
Eleven maidens dance a ring.
Around and round their dresses fall,
As if in trance, a ghostly ball.
Mesmerised, we watch them twirl,
As if in flight, their wings unfurl.
And passing by the rush, a whispered sound,
They're feet arisen from the ground.

In the heart of the raven king,
Blackness reigns, no light within.
Darkness falls as though its night,
No day, no breach, to let in light.
Ten magpies turn and turn about,
Squawk and squabble, converse and shout.
Sparkling silver souls they bring,
To lay at the feet of the raven king.

In the tower of the raven king
Nine rooks, a rabble, are rioting.
Each one tied with faery thorn,
Around their legs, now scratched and torn.
Twisted up around so fierce,
Their beating heart a thorn does pierce.
And underneath each fiery flood,
A bowl to catch each drop of blood.

On the walls of the raven king,
Eight figures hang, by neck and limb.
Their mouths held open, in a scream,
As though a nightmare ... or a dream.
So all may feed their suffering.
Upon the walls of the raven king.
A mask of death, a twisted face,
Acceptance of their fate ... misplaced.

On the floor of the raven king,
Once you enter through the door
You'll find them prostrate on the floor
Seven carpets lay in line,
Weaved with silken thread and gold so fine.
Soft as cloud and tough as skin.
Patched with flesh and hair so thin.
A hundred breaths are woven in.

In the hall of the raven king
Six birds in cages softly call,
'Do come in, and welcome all.'
They're siren song ... will lure you in.
'Step forward, those now, without sin,
Come inside' ... your steps will fall,
And echo, muffled, off the walls.
Silently a breath, will call.

Five towers rise from the raven's loft
An eyrie ... high upon a croft,
A lonely outpost, for those now lost.
A nest of bones, a path of kings,
The raven rests upon his throne,
Whilst down below, a maiden sings.
A song as mournful as a sigh,
As he sails, way up high.

Four trees do stand out bleak and bare,
Nary a leaf ... a skeleton there
Of blackened bone, they
Line the path of twist and turns,
As tortured souls do blaze and burn.
They're life of sin, to now atone.
Payment due from them alone.
As silently he watches, from his lofty throne.

Three jackdaw jesters, all enthral,
Tricksters three within the hall.
Pain, suffering and greed.
Their names a blight,
Their call a need.
On all our sin they drop and feed.
Curiosity will draw you in,
To hear their laughter ... stop and heed.

Two times around the circle walk,
Go forwards then turn back.
For this path, can only lead.
To all that you do lack.
The king does watch his subject fall,
To get back up, to try again,
Encouragement he calls.
The circle never ending – insanity for all.

One raven king to rule us all,
Never lonely in his hall.
Whilst looking in that gaping maw,
Ever wary … raven's claw,
His burning eye upon him saw.
To Poe
He doth quoth nevermore …
Whilst weeping for his Eleanor.

What a sorry path our king does pave.
Never so un-valiant knaves,
Together an unkindness made.
Come enter now,
Come, one and all.
Into the king of the raven's hall.

© Jayne Stennett 12-04 2019

ACKNOWLEDGMENTS & AUTHORS NOTES

Thank you to the wonderful poets whose inspiration I have found invaluable in the writing of this book.

Edgar Allen Poe

Dante Alighieri

Doris Potter

John Milton

Plus, the various sources of quotes and research, especially this article from *The Irish Times* 24-02-2001 with reference to an earlier article written in 1931.

SIN-EATING

I recently came across mention of a strange custom which exists still today. The sin-eater was a person, often a former priest, who for a trifling payment or remuneration, given in the form of a meal, took upon him the sins of a deceased person. It was usual for nearly every village to have a professional sin-eater. As soon as a death occurred, this official was notified, and repairing straight to the house of the deceased he was given at the door a coin and a meal (often bread and ale). By eating the meal, he took upon him the sin of the departed; he pawned his own soul for them to go to Heaven.

Sometimes he was expected to eat the food off the corpse, or in the presence of the body. After consuming his meal, he would pronounce the soul departed for which his sins he would bear. Then he was driven from the house with abuse, sticks and missiles being hurled at him. It is supposed to be a survival of the expiatory use of the word "scapegoat" mentioned in the 16th chapter of the book of Leviticus in *The Old Testament*. To be made a scapegoat was to take the guilt of others or the blame for something. On the death of the sin-eater, his soul would enter Hell. The practice of sin-eating was done by women or men … usually poverty-driven, it was widely practised throughout the world and was still practised well into the 20th century in England and Ireland – and is possibly still practised today.

Although the character who took on the role of the sin-eater in my book partook of the flesh of the dead as a penance, the real sin-eaters, as in documented evidence from many cultures, only ate the food provided, sometimes from the body but not the actual body itself.

I sincerely hope that you have enjoyed the last book in the trilogy and if you wish to read the other two books:

The Girl (book one)

The Detective – The Primrose Path (book two)

Both books are available via the links on Amazon as an e-book, paperback and hardcover.

You can also find me on my Facebook page @Jayne Stennett Author, and on Instagram too. Follow me for updates on new books and poems.

Printed in Great Britain
by Amazon

27138383R00155